Master Class

BC

Harriet was quite carried away by Mr. Andrews' prowess as an archer. His arrow had barely penetrated the bull's-eye when she threw her arms around him to kiss his cheek in congratulation. But he turned his head, and her lips met his.

When at last they disengaged, she blurted with a face as pink as a petunia from Peru, "I did not mean that. I intended a mere kiss on the cheek, as I might kiss my uncle, you see." But her voice faded as a wicked gleam danced in his eyes.

"However, I am not your uncle," he said.

"No," she agreed.

"We could try again, just to see if what we experienced before could be repeated," he suggested.

"Mr. Andrews, you are a scamp," Harriet declared.

"No, a solid citizen," he countered. "You can tell by touching, you see."

And as he placed her hand to his heart and she felt the solidity of his chest, so reassuring, so very masculine, Harriet remembered that this gentleman was a well-known master of a sport far different than archery as well.

Harriet's Beau

Emily Hendrickson

A SIGNET BOOK

SIGNET
Published by the Penguin Group
Penguin Books USA Inc., 375 Hudson Street,
New York, New York 10014, U.S.A.
Penguin Books Ltd, 27 Wrights Lane,
London W8 5TZ, England
Penguin Books Australia Ltd, Ringwood,
Victoria, Australia
Penguin Books Canada Ltd, 10 Alcorn Avenue,
Toronto, Ontario, Canada M4V 3B2
Penguin Books (N.Z.) Ltd, 182–190 Wairau Road,
Auckland 10, New Zealand

Penguin Books Ltd, Registered Offices:
Harmondsworth, Middlesex, England

First published by Signet, an imprint of Dutton Signet,
a division of Penguin Books USA Inc.

First Printing, April, 1997
10 9 8 7 6 5 4 3 2 1

Chapter One

Ferdy Andrews slanted a look across the park, feeling contented with the world and quite at peace with himself. London in the Season—with plenty of money and friends, a pretty woman on one's arm, and an abundance of things to do—was a good place to be. Sun filtered through the trees in the quiet of the early morning haze. Hyde Park appeared to be nearly empty save for down near the Serpentine. Two bright carroty heads caught his eye and he slowed his horse to a walk. A redhead of sorts himself, he tended to take note of others of similar coloring.

What on earth were those youngsters about? For they had to be sprigs, and doubtless were up to no good at this hour of the day when most respectable folk were either in bed or at their breakfast table. He urged his horse across the green, studying the unlikely pair with a shrewd eye as he neared. The female might have bright hair, but on closer inspection, she possessed a fetching figure.

"I can too beat you from here to the gate, Harry," the miss declared in ringing tones. "And I am not afraid of being found out. Why, there is not a soul in the park at this hour!"

Affixing a steely gaze on the slender figure garbed in pine green, her hat perched precariously to one side, and her limerick-gloved hands clenching the reins firmly, Ferdy relished the young lady's reaction when he spoke from his vantage point directly behind her. "I very much fear you have it wrong, lass. Not only am *I* here, but I suspect that before you reach that gate, there will be others here as well. Just what do you think might be accomplished by such a stupid thing—other than to ruin a reputation that shows signs of being uncertain at best?"

Whirling about, she gave a startled cry, and Ferdy found a pair of brilliant green eyes glaring at him from a freckled face framed by flyaway carrot-hued hair that looked quite as impossible to tame as she herself no doubt was.

"And who sought your opinion, may I ask?" she demanded in a clear voice that might sound sweet when it wasn't furious. She maintained admirable control over her mare, quickly calming the equally startled animal.

"*You* obviously didn't. However, I have five sisters and know a fair bit about your sex. I also know that while you might not care about your reputation at this moment, you might be sorry for such a harebrained escapade later when the damage has been done. There's little to be mended in such an occasion, you know." He hoped his admittedly intimidating size would have an effect on the lass; clearly she was not one to take advice willingly.

She had the grace to blush—a painfully pink color that clashed dreadfully with her hair—and murmured a reluctant reply. "I expect you have the right of it." Turning to look at her companion, she added, "But you know I could win the race, Harry. I would at home—where I wish I was this instant, I can tell you."

"No race?" Ferdy prompted, watching the pair with an amused gaze.

"No race," she replied, turning back to face Ferdy, then adding reluctantly, "but I must thank you for your interference. Oh, not for my sake, you understand. But I would not wish to bring disgrace to my family. I am a sad enough trial to them already." And with those words she seemed to shrivel. That was the only way Ferdy could describe her response. It sat ill with her pert face and otherwise excellent carriage. For a girl who must have considerable backbone, she had been whipped into submission, and although he knew it might be necessary, he realized he rather hated to see such spirit defeated.

"Good day, sir." With that she slowly moved away from him, talking quietly to the young chap at her side. The lad glanced back at Ferdy, but made no effort to make himself known.

Ferdy hadn't asked her name. It wouldn't have been proper.

It would be simple enough to learn, however. There couldn't be many carrot-haired lasses making a come-out this Season. One of his sisters—Diana, most likely—would know. It would be interesting to see how this lass made it through the hazards of a London Season. As he rode to his bachelor establishment, a neat apartment at the Albany, he thought he'd keep an eye on the girl. Ought to be interesting.

It was highly extraordinary that Ferdinand Andrews, Esquire—known as Ferdy to one and all—would display even the slightest interest in a proper young lady. He usually surrounded himself with opera dancers, not gently bred girls. He instantly perceived that this carroty lass might be gently bred, but hardly the sort to simper and sigh—a behavior he detested and from which he always fled.

Taking himself off to his rooms, he then forgot about the redheaded chit in the park for the time being, having more pressing matters to hand.

The following morning found Ferdy in the park at an early hour when he could reflect on his past evening's entertainment and plan his day in the peaceful and pleasant environs of greenery. Across the park by the Serpentine, he caught sight of a familiar flash of red and pine green and quickened his horse's pace, curious as to what the lass might be up to this day. He'd not called on his sister so the girl was still unknown to him. She had, however, lingered in the back of his memory.

Over by the lake, Harriet sighed. Water lapped serenely against the pebbled shore of the Serpentine, birds twittered gaily in the leafy boughs of the trees, and the distant sounds of the city drifted to her ears, but they didn't help a great deal to bring peace and serenity to a troubled heart. She bent over to gaze at her reflection in the muddy water. Even there she could not fail to see her defects.

Drawing away, she considered her prospects—which were not good. Pacing back and forth along the shore, she deliberated on her siblings. With Coralie well betrothed and Victoria as good as engaged, that left only her brother unwed—besides Harriet. But George didn't count. Mother didn't fuss near as much at him to find a spouse. But then, George was so perfect that when the time was appropriate he was bound to produce a proper bride without prompting.

Her mother spoke of nothing else but the necessity of marriage in regard to Harriet. Had it not been so serious, it would have been hilarious. Imagine, expecting a girl like Harriet to find a husband among the *ton*.

It would be perfectly splendid when Coralie married Lord Perth. Visions of her gorgeous titian hair peeping out from beneath her wisp of a veil, flattering Coralie's dark green eyes and white skin—without a freckle in sight—were enough to give Harriet a fit of the dismals. And Victoria would undoubtedly be just as beautiful, her shimmering strawberry blond hair wrapped about her head like a crown, her eyes the color of fine emeralds, with skin like pure cream to boot. They were the magnificent Mayne sisters. They couldn't be blamed for pretending she didn't exist.

Even her tiresome brother, George, had dark red, almost mahogany, hair that was quite dashing when paired with blue-green eyes and lightly tanned skin. It didn't matter that he possessed a few freckles. Whoever cared about a man's skin?

Harriet's assets were few. Her slim body was nicely curved. She sang pleasantly, danced gracefully, and could manage a tolerable hand when writing a letter. But on the other hand, she was too tall, couldn't embroider worth a farthing, nor could she play the pianoforte or harp. But the worst of it all . . . and here she bent over to gaze at that sad reflection again, sighing. The worst of it . . .

Ferdy Andrews approached with care, fearful of what the lass might do. What in the world was that chit doing at the Serpentine all by herself? Bad enough she was alone, but she appeared to be bending over as though contemplating jumping into the cold, dirty water. Now Ferdy, having five sisters, knew they often had odd starts which they regretted later. If this creature thought she was going to put an end to her existence, she was going to have to reckon with Ferdy. He'd not stand for such a thing. Whatever bothered her could be fixed.

In moments, his horse had covered the ground that separated them. For a large man, he moved rapidly. Sliding quickly from his mount, he marched along the shore to confront the young lass in the pine-green habit that fitted her superbly. Behind her, her mare gave Ferdy a wary look.

"Whatever it is, it can't be that bad," he began.

"That is what you think," she replied with a sniff, turning away from him, not looking surprised in the least that he had popped up again out of seemingly nowhere.

"Suppose you tell me and let me decide?" Ferdy said in his most avuncular manner, reaching out to gently, ever so gently, draw her away from the lure of the Serpentine. "Now, commence."

Harriet allowed the gentleman to walk her away from the water into the soft dappled green beneath the trees. "I doubt you would understand, sir."

"Try me," he coaxed.

"I am in London," she said, plunging into a stark recital of her woes, "for a Season, but I know I will not take, and my mama and my sisters harp at me day and night. Now I ask you as a gentleman, am I not right to insist I be allowed to become an old maid, retiring to a cottage by the sea in peace and quiet?"

Ferdy studied the lass, determined to see what it was about her that would put a fellow off—aside from a few freckles and a pert nose. The carrot hair he discounted, having come from a family of redheads. She looked perfectly fine to him.

She pulled the little hat from her head, revealing a mass of springy curls. He took a step back to further assess her qualities. Here was truly an original.

"You see! Even you are repelled." Turning away from him she said in a muffled voice that he suspected masked tears, "I am hopeless."

"I cannot see why."

Harriet slowly turned to stare at him. "But look at me! I have hair—a great amount of it—the color of carrots, eyes that are seaweed green—so I am told—and worst of all, I have freckles! There is nothing to be done—I have tried every potion known to woman. Who will have such a one as I? You really ought to have allowed me to race yesterday. Perhaps if I ruined my reputation, they would have let me go home again."

Ferdy gazed down at the slim maiden and shook his head. "You need help."

"A miracle is more like it," she muttered by way of reply.

"Your family believes they have nothing more to do than put a white dress on you, drag you to Almack's, and you will find a husband?"

When Harriet glanced at him, she had to smile at his friendly and sympathetic grin. At least, he seemed understanding of her dilemma. He'd said he had sisters. Harriet wondered if they had followed that pattern and said so to him. "Did your sisters do that?"

"The first one did, but she was such a comely lass that she was snapped up in a trice. The others were more like you—not that you are not comely, mind you. But they also have red hair and freckles, and I'd be the first to admit that white is not their best color. You at least wear green and 'tis most becoming on you," he concluded with a bow.

Had Ferdy's friends heard this charming compliment, they would have stared, for he usually became silent in the presence of ladies—young or old—too wary by half. Ferdy knew he had nothing to fear from this lass, however. She didn't even want a Season, much less a husband, and she certainly didn't cast a lure in his direction.

"My habit belonged to Victoria, the one garment of hers I can wear." At his questioning look, she added, "Victoria is slender and pretty with her strawberry blonde hair and perfect skin. Alas, she is shorter. I am the tallest in the family, even taller than George, my brother."

"How does George feel about being outshone in height?"

"I've never asked," she said in surprise. "He does tease me about being a beanpole at times," she mused, wrinkling her nose at the memory.

"Unkind, but not unusual in a brother, I fancy," Ferdy said, concealing a smile behind a swiftly raised hand.

"How did your sisters manage a Season? Did they all marry? Happily? I vow I had rather remain on the shelf than wed a dreadful old man." Harriet gave Ferdy a wide-eyed look that brought forth a chuckle.

"Not all old men are dreadful, you know. Merely the ones

your mother wants you to marry, I suppose. For instance, do
you consider me old?" It took Ferdy down considerably more
than a notch when she studied him for a time before replying.
If nothing else, this lass was not about to flatter a chap.

"No, I doubt you are more than in your late twenties. Am I
correct? George is eight-and-twenty and you look about his
age."

"George being—other than your brother?" Ferdy had to
know who this family might be.

"He is George Mayne," she stammered, blushing wildly
again. "My sisters are Victoria and Coralie, soon to be Lady
Perth. Sir Edward Mayne is my father. And I," she hesitated a
moment, then continued, "am Harriet Anne Mayne, the black
sheep of the perfect family." She said this as though daring
Ferdy to disagree.

"Ferdinand Andrews, Esquire at your service, Miss Harriet
Mayne." Ferdy was truly put in his place when he realized his
name meant nothing to the lass. She merely gave him a wistful
smile, then turned to gaze across the Serpentine. Obviously
she had not yet been coached on which gentleman was
wealthy and considered a good catch.

"You took a risk again today—no Harry and not a groom in
sight. What am I going to do with such a girl, I ask you?" he
said in mock scolding, although he meant the business about
the lack of a groom.

"My cousin Harry was sent back to school yesterday. I
won't see him until holidays—which Mama says is all to the
good. Mama thinks Harry tends to lead me astray," Harriet
said with a sidelong glance at Ferdy.

"I have no doubt she is in the right there. It strikes me that
you are a lass given to trouble like some are to good works and
others to flirting."

"Well, I would not mind going back to school. Only I'd be
the eldest girl there. I'd not like being so alone. 'Tis bad
enough at home. Do you have any notion of what it is like to
live in a perfect family, where no one ever puts a foot wrong
and they are all as beautiful as can be? 'Tis very lowering, I
can tell you." She cast him a baleful look, then resumed poking at the pebbles with the toe of her boot.

"As I said before, I believe you need help."

"How lovely. Just like that? I need help and a kind fairy will come to my rescue? My freckles will disappear and my hair turn a beautiful dark mahogany like George's or luscious strawberry blond like Victoria's? Indeed! And I suppose I will magically be able to play a harp or converse with those intimidating gentlemen my mama wants me to charm? Pooh bah!"

"Goodness, but you do have the temper to match your hair." Ferdy leaned against an oak, his amusement with this young woman increasing by the minute.

"Of course. I've had nineteen years to practice, after all."

"I have an idea. Why do I not talk to my sister—Diana might be the best one, for she is always up on the latest—and see what she suggests? Would you be willing to come with me to meet her some afternoon?"

"Perhaps it might be best were she to issue an invitation for me to call on her?" Harriet suggested hesitantly. "I'd not have Mama acquiring notions about you. From that splendid mount and your fine clothes, I would gather you are not at *point non plus.*"

Ferdy thought of his excellent bank account, his investments and properties, and shook his head. "No, you could say I am well to grass and not be wrong."

Harriet gave him an arrested look, then quickly turned to her mare. "I do know a groom is proper but Ben was ill this morning, and I refused to give up a little time of my own." She flashed Ferdy a look of appeal, a plea for understanding.

"Since I've seen no one else around, you are most likely safe enough. Here, allow me to assist." It was a mere nothing for him to sweep Harriet up in his firm clasp to settle her in the saddle.

"My, you certainly are strong," she observed, wide-eyed, while arranging her skirt, then fiddling with her reins. "And you are rather large, too. Do you find that an asset?"

Ferdy bit back the urge to laugh at this impossible lass, and with a straight face replied, "Indeed, I do. Probably as handy as your being tall enough to see over the heads of most of those insipid girls at the balls you attend."

Harriet chuckled—a charming little sound—and agreed.

"Not all of them are insipid, you know," she confided. "Their mothers make them that way, thinking that the gentlemen prefer a girl without two thoughts to rub together. With no looks to speak of, I expect it best to cultivate my brains. Who knows, perhaps I may find myself a scholar who does not mind red hair!"

Ferdy succumbed to the urge that had been building within and let out a hearty laugh. "What an impudent lass you are. True to your hair." While walking along at her side he looked around the deserted park. A figure could be seen in the distance but no one had observed them conversing together as of yet.

"I had best go home," she said. Then she shyly added, "Thank you again for your kind advice and offer of help. What a pity you are not my uncle, for you would be my favorite, I believe." With that, she blushed that dreadful shade of pink and was away before he could stop her impetuous dash.

Her uncle? Good grief! Ferdy thought over his words and actions and decided it was as well she considered him in that light. It would never do for that budding temptress to develop a *tendresse* for him. That she would be a temptress, he had no doubt. All she needed was to tame that hair, learn how to dress properly, obtain an introduction to the right people, and she would be fired off before you could sneeze. There was something about her eyes—the sparkling green depths intrigued a fellow.

Ferdy watched Miss Harriet disappear from the park, then rode with a thoughtful mien to where he stabled his mount. He'd have a hearty breakfast, then present himself at Diana's house as early as he dared. She was most unfashionable, rising well before noon and spending considerable time with her children. Most of the young mothers he'd met seemed to think that all that was required of motherhood was to produce the babes.

It was about two hours later—Ferdy did not believe in rushing through a meal—that Diana's housekeeper opened the door to usher him inside. One thing about being large and amiable, you were most always welcome, at least within the family.

"My sister up and about, Mrs. Poole?"

"Breakfast room. Master Timothy wants his porridge with his mum," the white-haired woman explained.

Ferdy nodded, then quietly marched down the hall to the small breakfast room at the rear of the house, which overlooked a minuscule garden. He paused, absorbing the pleasant scene. His sister sat at the table coaxing her four-year-old to consume his porridge, sunlight blessing her snowy cap and the auburn curls that peeped from beneath.

Diana had heard him enter and turned to greet her only brother. "Ferdy, what brings you here at this hour? Timothy, greet your Uncle Ferdy."

"Good morning." Ferdy accepted the salutation from Timothy and pulled up a chair. He absently took a bit of plum cake that Mrs. Poole had hastily brought and began to nibble while he collected his thoughts.

"This looks serious," Diana began, tucking a stray curl beneath the pretty lace cap. "Dare I ask what it is?"

"Well, you see . . . I met a young lady in the park and she needs help. I wonder if you would be willing to lend an expert hand?"

He fiddled with a cup, which Diana took to mean a request for tea. Leaning over to pour, his sister gave him a piercing look. "Why?"

"Could you see the lass, you'd know. She has a wild mass of carroty hair, freckles enough to hide her face, says she neither paints, embroiders, nor plays an instrument, nor talks—although she seemed to have no trouble chatting with me," he added in reflection.

"But then you are the most gentle giant of a man who wouldn't harm a soul and it is obvious. That is why all the children adore you," Diana said with a smile, shooing a reluctant Master Timothy off to his nurse.

"She is a taking lass, or would be if not so conscious of that carroty hair. Says she's tried everything possible to cure her freckles. Nothing worked. They were worse than Clair's."

"Goodness!" a horrified Diana exclaimed, recalling her dearest sister, who had serious freckles, as even those who adored her must admit.

"Will you help her?" Ferdy inquired, trying to sound diffident.

Diana gave him a startled look, then studied her hands a moment before nodding. "Of course, I will. Poor dear, she must be utterly miserable. Now how shall we accomplish this good and kind deed?" She gave her brother an impish look that quickly changed when she saw he was most serious, highly unusual for her normally lighthearted sibling.

"She suggested you invite her to call. I cannot think where you are suppose to have met. I shall leave that up to your inventive mind. Be prepared to offer advice on cutting that mop of hair, perhaps tinting it slightly—as you do yours, and see what you can do about her clothes. She claims the only decent thing she owns is a riding habit she acquired from her sister."

"And the sister is?"

"Victoria Mayne."

"Good heavens! Your young lady is sister to that glorious creature? Which means she is also sister to the heavenly Coralie and dashing George. How utterly depressing for her. I can see why her plight touched your generous heart." Diana rose from her chair to give her big brother a swift hug. "I shall write a note immediately. I fancy I have credit enough so her mother will permit the girl to accept an invitation to tea."

"The wealthy and dashing Mrs. Damon Oliver? Acceptable? Why else do you think I came to you?" Ferdy asked with a grin. Then he added, "Besides, you have a heart far larger than mine, you know. I know none better."

"Except for Emma and Clair and Annis and Bella," she said with an answering look, listing her other sisters who were also known for their caring and warm hearts. "We have all overcome the affliction of red hair and have learned how to make the best of it. I assure you, this girl will be no problem at all."

At that blithe statement, Ferdy laughed. "I hope so," he said, giving his sister a sheepish look. "Harriet is not some meek little dab of a girl. She is taller than you are and a trifle outspoken—at least to me."

"Perhaps she trusts you."

"That is rather a mixed compliment for a gentleman of my years, my dear Diana."

"Yes, I know," she said kindly, strolling at his side until they reached the morning room where her writing desk was located. "Be off with you. I shall write Lady Mayne a polite note requesting the presence of herself and her youngest daughter for tea." At his sound of protest, she said, "You did not think I could ask the girl and not her mother this first call?"

He threw up his hands and shrugged. "Do what you must. Shall I attend this affair?"

"Perhaps you should. You are nicely intimidating and surely Lady Mayne knows your standing even if her daughter does not." Diana giggled at his look of affront.

Since Ferdy had omitted that bit of information, he bestowed a calculating look on Diana. "How did you know that?"

"Simple, actually. You did not run a mile from the chit after meeting her."

Somewhat puzzled at this rejoinder, Ferdy made his farewell and left the house to begin his rounds of the day.

Diana dashed off a note to Emma, her only sister in London at the moment; then composed a beautifully worded invitation to Lady Mayne, one she was certain would be eagerly accepted.

It was. Within a remarkably short time, a reply written in a fine hand on exquisite vellum arrived accepting Mrs. Oliver's kind invitation to tea.

Three afternoons later, Lady Mayne and Harriet entered the tastefully furnished home belonging to the very social Olivers. They were greeted by the charming Mrs. Oliver and her beautiful sister Emma, Lady Wynnstay.

Diana noted that Lady Mayne had the titian hair and stunning beauty possessed by Coralie. What a trial it must be for such a belle to be burdened with Harriet.

After the usual sort of social conversation one encounters at tea, Diana gave Harriet—who had sat as silent as a sphinx all the while and appeared as miserable as possible—an assessing look. She turned to the mother.

"Lady Mayne, Harriet reminds me so much of myself when I was her age."

For the first time Harriet perked up, giving Diana an astounded stare. "I do not believe it. I mean, you are so lovely," she stammered.

"Well, it took the ministrations of some truly exceptional women to achieve the transformation, I assure you. First I acquired my abigail, who is a wizard with dressing hair like ours. Then I went to see Madame Clotilde. She helped select colors and styles so I might appear to best advantage."

At this moment, Ferdy entered the room, apologizing for his tardiness with great polish. "My man of business kept me longer than I expected, Diana."

Lady Mayne sat in confounded silence at his entry. Apparently, she had not connected the delicately beautiful Emma and the graceful Diana with their brother, a giant of a man and one as wealthy as could stare, if all was to be believed.

Harriet ignored the sought-after Mr. Andrews, Esquire, and concentrated on Diana. "Do you, that is, would you, or could you help me? Advise me, perhaps?" At her side Lady Mayne sputtered words that had more of an admonishing sound than anything else.

Diana exchanged a look with her sister, who nodded ever so slightly in return. "Why, yes, I believe I should enjoy that. With a daughter of my own, it would give me practice—for Anne has hair as red as yours."

Apparently heartened to know there was another so afflicted, Harriet beamed a smile on her benefactress. Her beautiful eyes lit with anticipation as she said, "Mama, I do believe you have a chance of ridding the family of me after all." At which remark, the good lady looked as though she might dearly love to faint.

Diana ignored the mother, smiling at Harriet, instead. "We shall find you a proper beau, make no mistake. And I dare say he will be enchanted with the new Harriet."

"The new Harriet," Harriet echoed, looking dazed and quite starry-eyed. "Oh, my."

Chapter Two

Once Lady Mayne accepted the notion of Harriet receiving guidance from the stylish Mrs. Oliver, it was a mere step to Harriet being swept under Diana's wing. It didn't hurt that Lady Wynnstay had chimed in with her enthusiastic encouragement for the proposition. When that was accompanied by a suggestion that she introduce Harriet to a number of her select friends, Lady Mayne had been completely won over—and most likely relieved that her impossible daughter had become another's problem.

Lady Mayne later explained to Harriet that Mr. Andrews was enormously wealthy and his company courted everywhere. However, that he was heir to a barony mattered little to Harriet at this point. She saw him mainly as her friend and confidant.

When next she saw him in the park early the following morning, Harriet told Ferdy, "I do hope that your sister Diana knows what she is doing in sweeping me up as she has." *Sweeping* was the only word Harriet could think of when describing matters to Mr. Andrews, Esquire.

"At least you have your groom along with you this morning," Ferdy said with approval, looking back at the chap with a minatory eye. "And you may trust Diana to do what is best. When does she intend to commence her efforts on your behalf?"

"I am to present myself this morning. I would not be surprised were this to be my last free time for some days." Harriet sighed. Then—lest Mr. Andrews mistake her feelings—she added, "Please know that I am most grateful to you. It is encouraging to think I not only might find myself presentable but a husband as well. That *would* please Mama."

Ferdy nodded in silence, knowing only too well that it was most important for a young lady to make a suitable marriage. Her only other recourse was to be a governess or a companion—and those were not much in demand these days, there usually being sufficient poor relations to make hiring a companion unnecessary.

"Why don't I ride along with you? I could keep you company at my sister's—that is, after you have changed and are prepared to go to Diana's," Ferdy amended when he realized that Miss Mayne would scarcely be wanting to present herself in her riding habit.

Bestowing a smile on the man at her side, Harriet nodded. "That would be welcome." She turned her mare and headed back toward the Maynes' house. It was but a short walk from the park, and in a brief time, Ferdy found himself entrusting his steed to the groom. This good man took the horses along to the mews, promising to take care of Ferdy's mount until he chose to return.

While Mr. Andrews enjoyed a glass of her papa's finest claret in the peace of the drawing room, Harriet dashed up to her room to change. It scarcely mattered what she wore, for she was to be totally remade. She felt as though she were to be reborn, for Mrs. Oliver had declared that her hair would be utterly altered, her wardrobe as well. It was all rather exciting—if somewhat daunting.

Ferdy found it took fortitude to exchange the peace of the Mayne household for his sister's often chaotic residence. He only hoped that the younger children would be kept with Nurse. When they arrived to relative quiet, he discovered that the children had been banished for the morning. Nonetheless, he felt so sorry for the lot of them that he deposited Harriet Mayne with Diana and took himself off to the nursery to offer himself as substitute horse or whatever pleased the little beggars.

"He pretends to be repelled by the infants, you know," Diana confided to Harriet as she drew her along to the morning room located at the rear of the large town house. "Truth to tell, he dotes on them and they on him. A more indulgent uncle would be hard to find. Pity he has no children of his own. Every Season I pray he will find a young lady to catch his fancy. Perhaps thìs year . . ."

They entered the morning room to find Lady Wynnstay and an austere-looking woman awaiting them. Harriet's instant guess as to the identity of the second woman proved right.

"Talbot, this is the young lady you are to work your magic on today." To Harriet, Diana added, "Do not be alarmed at what she decrees, for she was responsible for turning me from a carrot-topped hoyden into what I am today."

Suitably impressed, Harriet approached the tall, prim woman, whose gray hair was impeccably dressed and tucked beneath a starched white cap. Gray eyes assessed Harriet in a way that made her feel as though she not only wore no clothes, but that Talbot could see to the very core of her being.

"Hmm," the woman said at last. "First we wash the hair, put a bit of tint on it, then the scissors."

Feeling quite as though her ship was about to sink, Harriet submitted to the ministrations. Her head was scrubbed, then some nasty-smelling solution was worked into her curls, to be followed later by a rinse and cream, this with the pleasant scent of lemons.

She wasn't permitted to observe her hair cutting in a looking glass, which was probably just as well. At one point she heard Mr. Andrews' voice in the hallway. Mrs. Oliver, who had insisted that Harriet call her Diana, scurried to prevent him from entering the workroom, as she called it.

"Not until the transformation is complete are you to see our protégée," she said with an affectionate laugh.

Transformation. What would be the result? Harriet knew enough about coloring hair to be aware that sometimes matters went wrong. She'd heard of girls having hair a bright chartreuse after experimenting with hair dye. She prayed that Talbot would not allow this to happen.

She need not have worried. The experienced abigail calmly snipped and combed, studied and snipped some more, until Harriet wondered if there would be anything left.

Lady Wynnstay had left the room to spend some time in the nursery. When she returned, Talbot was combing out Harriet's hair for what had to be the twentieth time. Harriet had submitted in silence to the toweling and combing and snipping, believing that this woman might truly work a miracle.

The abigail drew back to await a verdict from the very fashionable Lady Wynnstay.

"Splendid!" she cried when she caught sight of Harriet.

Her enthusiasm gave Harriet hope.

"Diana, come, see," she called to her sister who had gone to the kitchen to attend to a minor crisis.

"Excellent, indeed," Diana pronounced when she caught sight of her protégée. "The hair is most acceptable, I believe. Now what about her skin? Other than a dusting of your special powder, is there anything to be done with those freckles?"

Talbot studied Harriet again, moving around her, taking Harriet's face in her cool grip to turn it this way and that. "No," she said at last, "we will have to use the powder, keep her out of the sun, and hope for the best."

Still not permitted to view herself in a looking glass, Harriet was drawn along to the front of the house. Talbot hustled her into a cloak. Then the four women left the house, entering a fine landau that had drawn up before the Oliver residence.

"You truly must not worry, my dear," Lady Wynnstay said with a sympathetic touch of her soft hand. "Diana decided it would be fun to keep your new looks a surprise. All will be revealed in good time."

Harriet gave her an apprehensive smile, but said nothing. Time would tell, indeed.

The carriage drew to a halt before the discreet establishment belonging to the famed Madame Clotilde. Harriet had passed it any number of times, but her mother had not deemed her worthy of a Clotilde gown. Only her sisters had merited the mantua-maker's skill.

It was with mixed emotions that Harriet entered the shop now. Uppermost in her mind was curiosity as to what the famous Madame Clotilde would say to Harriet's appearance. She was known to be blunt in her assessments. Could she assist in creating an acceptable Harriet Mayne, fit to be presented in Almack's assembly rooms?

"Madame, I am pleased you are willing to work with us on

our transformation. What do you think so far?" Diana said, quite as though she had been the one to color and snip.

Tossing an understanding glance at the abigail, the mantua-maker studied Harriet. She turned her head this way and that, nodding and making little penciled notes on a pad she carried.

"She cannot have white, even though she makes her come-out," the madame stated flatly. "Ivory silk, cream muslin of the finest quality, palest peach taffeta, perhaps a delicate willow green for a pelisse. Her come-out ball gown will be in cream faille, I believe. No ruffles or flounces. Simple lines and quality fabric will become her most."

Diana nodded, then conferred in soft tones with the lady while Lady Wynnstay urged Harriet to look over a selection of fabrics on display, pointing out the charms of each.

"Come along, one and all," Diana said at last. "Madame has a gown that she feels would be suitable to complete this first day of Harriet's transformation."

The five made their way to a tiny room in the rear of the establishment, where Harriet was given no quarter. She was stripped to her stays and redressed in a delicate shift of finest batiste, followed by a pretty dress of cream-and-willow-green striped lutestring. The high neck was touched by blond lace with tiny buttons for trim. Cording accented the high waist and long sleeves. Talbot did up the back, then stepped aside for the others to see.

"Now you may look at the new Harriet," Diana Oliver said with obvious satisfaction. "I believe we shall celebrate with an ice at Gunter's."

Harriet stared at the creature in the looking glass, wondering if that interesting young woman could actually be herself. Not beautiful, not even pretty in the accepted mode, she was rather striking in a singular way. Her hair, now a soft red-gold, curled about her head in ringlets something like a cherubim. The face powder softened and diminished her freckles. The dress enhanced the soft coloring of her hair and skin, giving her a gentle radiance instead of the bright glow it usually reflected. It remained to see what a gentleman might think.

"She will be an original, you shall see," Madame promised, nodding her improbably red head most emphatically while she placed a small but appealing hat on Harriet's curls. "She must think of something unique as an accessory. And she must acquire a particularly uncommon pastime of note, something in which she excels."

"I know she will," Diana bubbled with delight.

"You sing, *non?*" the mantua-maker said.

"I sing passably and I can dance fairly well. But I do not play an instrument nor can I do needlework."

"I shall create gowns for singing and dancing," Madame pronounced. "You will be a quiet rage, one I believe will do very nicely."

"All I ask is—" Harriet began only to be silenced by Lady Wynnstay.

"She will also capture the heart of a most discerning gentleman." Lady Wynnstay did not say where this man would be found.

"But of course," Madame agreed, quite as though that was naturally assumed.

Harriet wished she felt as confident about her future. She had heard family murmurs of marrying her off to the most repellent of elderly gentlemen did she not take this Season, and *that* little worry continued to nag at the back of her mind.

The ladies, including the redoubtable Talbot, whisked themselves to Gunter's for pineapple ices.

It was there that Mr. Andrews happened upon them, recognizing the Oliver landau from a distance.

"Ladies," he said gallantly as he rode up to the carriage, looking a trifle apprehensive. "And how did you make out with Miss Mayne?"

"See for yourself," Diana said with pert grace.

He had glanced at the occupants of the carriage when he rode up. Now he examined the one he had not at first recognized.

Harriet thought she just might expire while awaiting his reaction. Precisely why she felt his opinion so important, she could not have said, but it was. She stilled her hands in her lap with difficulty. Forcing her gaze to meet his, she smiled, the gamin grin she'd worn when he had first offered his help. "Here I am, as you see," she said without much originality. As the one who had first thought she had possibilities, it was important he agree she had turned out well.

"Talbot," he turned unerringly to the one whose magic had worked so well, "you are to be congratulated. You saw her possibilities and brought out the charm within. I believe she just might take." His pronouncement was met with a sigh of relief from Harriet and a round of cries from his sisters.

"What do you mean, *might* take. She will be a veritable belle," Diana insisted.

"We shall do all we can to help make her the rage," Lady Wynnstay said in her cultured, soft voice.

"Then Society had best prepare itself to be stormed," he said quietly. That he did not look quite as pleased as he might at this notion was noticed by Diana who, for once, failed to tease him about it.

The ices consumed, the women left the shade of the trees in Berkeley Square to return to the Oliver residence.

"Tomorrow you must attend Madame Clotilde for measurements and all that entails," Diana said to Harriet when they exited the open carriage.

Harriet thanked them all profusely, Talbot especially for her tender concern. She promised to present herself at Madame Clotilde's establishment on the morrow at ten of the clock, then turned to leave.

Mr. Andrews had ridden by the carriage and now spoke. "I shall see you safely home, Miss Mayne."

At this bit of concern, his sisters exchanged looks, but said not a word, other than farewell for the moment.

Harriet was handed back into the landau by an insistent Mr. Andrews, who ignored her murmured pleas to walk to her nearby home. She settled back to gaze at him over the side of the carriage.

"It will not distress these chaps one whit, for I believe they must circle the block to return to the mews. How do you feel?" He studied her new looks and finery, making Harriet feel most uncomfortable.

"Madame Clotilde says I must be an original and find a unique accessory. What do you think about a dog? Perhaps one to match my hair? I know that it is not terribly original, but I have always wanted a dog and this would be a wonderful excuse. Mama could not deny the dictum of Madame Clotilde, could she?"

Ferdy gazed down at the winsome face with her pixy grin and sighed, feeling as though a fire was about to explode and there was nothing he might do to prevent its spread. "Well," he said, stalling.

"I know Mr. Byng has his poodle, but he is a man. I know of no woman who has a dog that matches her hair, if you see what I mean. What do you think? Please say you agree."

"Why," Ferdy said with forced gallantry, "I believe it might work, at that. Allow me to search around, for a red-gold dog might not be as easy to find as, for instance, a cat." He felt sorry for the girl who had always wanted a dog and not been allowed to have one. Why, everyone he knew had owned a dog or cat, in addition to a pony, then a horse. It was downright un-English to forbid such.

"But you cannot have a cat on a leash," she pointed out with perfect logic. "And they are not always very agreeable to being taken in a carriage."

Ferdy nodded, thinking that it might be a good thing were more items kept on a leash, namely the minds of certain young women. He suspected that if he did not help her find a suitable dog, she would be off hunting on her own, and that was to be avoided at all costs. Gentlemen ought to take care of such matters, and if her father were half the man he should be, he'd have seen to it.

He assisted her from the carriage when it came to a stop before the Mayne town house, from where he strolled back to the Oliver residence, deep in thought.

Once he found his sister, he demanded, "Have you any notion where this might lead?"

"What now?" Diana queried, knowing young ladies fairly well.

"She wants a dog to match her hair! Where can we find one that odd color—other than an Irish setter, which I hardly think is an appropriate animal to have in a drawing room, much less a carriage." Ferdy ran his fingers through his hair in frustration. This was not what he had envisioned when he asked his sisters to help Harriet.

"How should I know?" Diana said with a grin.

"I suppose this means I am off to find a kennel?"

"You want success, do you not?" Diana said reasonably.

"I believe I shall have a look-in on Poodle Byng. He may be of assistance," Ferdy mused, searching his memory for snippets of conversation dealing with dogs and the purchase thereof.

"Do that," Diana said softly and with a complaisance that ought to have made Ferdy suspicious had his mind been functioning in that direction.

"I shall report when success is achieved. Suggest to Talbot that it is not beyond possibility that she may be called upon to color a dog to match its mistress."

"She won't turn a hair, if you are worried about a tantrum. Talbot is superior."

The following morning found Harriet being used as a human pincushion, with swaths of fabric draped over her tall, slender form by the great Madame Clotilde. The muttering and *tsk-tsks* were ignored by Harriet. The pins were a different matter. But worst of all was the boredom. Harriet quickly realized that she was simply not cut out to be a diamond of the first, second, or for that matter third water if standing for hours during fittings was the requirement. But, the lure of improvement spurred her. She would tolerate most anything to become more stylish. A pity her mother wasn't there to witness her transformation.

At last, her shift and stays freed of stray pins, her clothing restored to her, she was allowed to leave the fitting room—which had assumed the aspect of a torture chamber rather than a place of delight.

"Here is a list of bonnets and hats which I feel will accent your new gowns very well," Madame said. "And do not forget the gloves you require, nor the slippers. Have you thought of a unique accessory yet?" She placed her hand on the front door, effectively penning Harriet inside until she had accepted the lists. Of course, lists were valuable. How many girls had a wardrobe of head coverings and accessories selected for them by the great mantua-maker? Harriet was simply rebellious by nature and disliked being told what she must do or wear.

"Well, I had thought of a dog, perhaps. One the color of my hair?"

The mantua-maker stared at Harriet a moment, then opened the door for her, not saying a word. Meekly accepting the list, Harriet fled the salon, hurrying along Bond Street with her maid hardpressed to keep up with her.

"Thinking to race on Bond Street, Miss Mayne?" The familiar voice reached Harriet through her fury and she came to an abrupt stop, and her thankful maid as well.

"I fear," Harriet reported to Mr. Andrews, "that I am not cut out to be a model of the *dernier cri*. In fact, I have my doubts about parading in the latest of fashions."

"But," he said suavely, "you want to find an acceptable husband."

"True," Harriet admitted. "I suppose it is a necessity. However, I give leave to tell you that I do not fancy becoming a human repository for pins anytime soon."

"And you must return on the morrow?"

"Next week. I need to do something quite different for a time—to soothe my sensibilities, you know. Perhaps the pond and a few ducks?" She grinned at Ferdy, her eyes sparkling and the sun glinting in her red-gold curls. He decided he had best think of something for her to do, for she looked quite capable of haring off to the park again, doing heaven knew what.

"I have made inquiries regarding a dog. You would not require a puppy?"

"No, for I suspect they are a great deal of trouble to train not to leave puddles, and Mama has little patience with animals as it is. Best it be a proper dog."

"You are certain this is what you want?" Ferdy asked, trying to keep the pessimism from his voice and failing.

"Can you think of anything better that would be unique? I have looked about me and I cannot imagine anything else. Everyone has parasols, and a carriage would not do. I will not have a little page to follow me; besides, that is hardly *unique*."

Miss Mayne paused at the corner as though expecting her carriage to arrive. "I will say one thing, if there is anything more boring than standing on a pedestal for hours to be fitted for a series of garments I cannot fathom what it might be. I long for a pastime, something active that would not put me to the blush, if you take my meaning?"

"I shall endeavor to give it my utmost consideration, Miss Mayne," Ferdy said with a sinking heart. Amusing a bored beauty was one thing; to entertain a girl as lively and prone to trouble as Harriet Mayne was quite another. "I do have a thought. We might schedule an outing in the park with my nephews and nieces and this enormous sailing boat I own. They find that jolly fun and you might enjoy it as well." He gave her a hopeful look. You never knew what a young lady might like. That was why he preferred opera dancers. You always knew how to please them.

"Why not? It does sound like rare fun. I have never sailed a toy boat before. Is it difficult? Do all gentlemen possess toy boats, or are you uncommon?"

"I am most uncommon, Miss Mayne. Most uncommon. But then," he added reflectively, "so are you."

"Really? Not just because of my hair?" At his nod, she looked pleased for a moment, then said, "That does not solve my dilemma of finding a favorite pursuit that will pass inspection with the *ton*."

"I shall make it a point to give it thought—while I am searching kennels for your dog."

"Mr. Andrews, you are truly a gem," Harriet cried, then reached up to plant a delicate kiss on his cheek, blushing furiously as she did. Well, he had behaved like an uncle, she reasoned, and she always kissed her uncles on the cheek. Only she suspected this wasn't quite the same thing.

Ferdy looked astounded, then pleased as punch, then frowned. He glanced about them. "Best confine that to indoors, Miss Mayne, if you must."

But he hadn't scolded her and Harriet entered the Mayne house with a lighter heart.

"Good heavens, is that you, Harriet?" Victoria cried in surprise. "I vow, I'd not have known you elsewhere. It is an improvement, although I doubt it will earn you much in the way of a husband." That frank opinion was given before she sailed from the house, trailed by her superior maid.

Downcast for a moment before cheering herself up with the reminder that Madame Clotilde wouldn't help anyone who didn't show promise, Harriet went to her room. Here she remained for the evening, having a tray sent to her, not wanting to listen to a debate over her looks. If Victoria had made a cutting remark, what would the rest of her family think?

She found out the next morning when she went down to an early breakfast before going for her ride in the park.

"Good heavens, girl!" Lady Mayne sneered. "I cannot see what you hope to gain. You'll not change your face."

"What ho?" Her brother chortled. "I say, I've heard of trying to make a silk purse out of a sow's ear and this proves it cannot be done. Why bother, dear girl? Accept your fate and marry that chap that Father's picked out for you. Save time and money."

"So that you might have more to gamble with?" That was unfair because George never gambled to excess. He never did anything to excess except, perhaps, tease Harriet.

He didn't deign to answer. Harriet watched him march from the room, feeling she might have tinged his hide with a barb, but it was unlikely to have much effect. Her family had rejected her for so many years it was doubtful they would change overnight.

Peace and tranquillity reigned in the park however. Harriet—followed by her groom and wearing the pine-green habit with a fall of cream batiste at her neck—cantered along the path, her thoughts much occupied with the coming Season. She wasn't desperate yet, but George's warning about her father's choice was quite enough to frighten her. She must become sought after. She had to find that unique touch, something a bit different, but within acceptability to set her apart from the rest of the girls making their come-out.

If only Mr. Andrews might find a suitable dog. What could

she name the animal? Something amusing, ear-catching. Prinney? No, that was disrespectful. Cupid? Suggestive, but it might work. She'd try the name on Mr. Andrews when next she saw him.

Across the park Ferdy strode along the path, the dog trotting at his heels. The poodle was a tan color that Talbot had tinted with a mixture to match Harriet's hair.

At last he espied Miss Harriet, as he ought to think of her. He marched forward with determination. She caught sight of him and rode over to greet him. Then, seeing the poodle squirming on a leash, she slid from her mare at once.

"What a cunning little dog. Does it have a name?"

"Not yet. Here," he handed over the leash, forgetting for the moment that she had been riding.

"Does it match?" she asked hesitantly, gathering the poodle up, then holding the little dog close to her face.

Ferdy nodded. "Thank goodness Talbot was able to work her wonders. I hope you are pleased."

"My manners and wits have gone begging! Thank you ever so much," she cried. Ignoring the possibility of their being seen, she again reached to give him a butterfly kiss on his cheek, then turned her attention to the dog. "I must think of a name."

"Ahem. I dislike reminding you . . ." Ferdy gave up. She would do as she pleased and he quite liked those gentle salutes on his cheek, even if the kiss was one of the avuncular sort.

"Cupid."

"I beg your pardon?" Ferdy sputtered, thinking he must have missed something along the way.

"Its name is to be Cupid. That is certainly different from Rover and Spot, is it not?"

"Certainly." Ferdy could not help laughing. Cupid, of all things. Yet it would be silly enough to be remembered: Miss Harriet and her dog, Cupid.

"Thank you again, Mr. Andrews. Will you walk me home? I find it difficult trying to carry Cupid while riding."

And so those of Society who were out and about that morning were treated to the sight of that determined bachelor, Mr. Ferdy Andrews, Esquire, and a pretty young lady garbed in pine green, who had lovely red-gold curls accompanied by a dog whose color exactly matched those curls. It was a notable sight, one that was described over a number of tea tables and wineglasses later in the day.

Chapter Three

Harriet entered her father's book-lined library with a few trepidations. Rarely was she summoned into his presence. "You wished to see me, Papa?"

He lowered the newspaper to stare at her over the top of it with his customary frown. "Your mother says your hair has been colored. I see she did not exaggerate. This was done in the interest of attracting a husband?"

"Bluntly put, you might say that." Harriet felt a brush against her skirts and realized that Cupid must have escaped from her room to follow. What her father might say to a dog in the household, much less one that had its fur dyed, she couldn't imagine.

The silence lengthened as he studied her. "What is causing that twitching of your dress, Harriet?"

She was saved from a reply by having Cupid push his way past her to sit gazing at her father, head cocked to one side, tongue lolling in best canine fashion.

"Good grief," Sir Edward exclaimed softly. "I gather there is a good reason for this dog?"

"Mr. Andrews gave him to me. Madame Clotilde said I must have a unique accessory, something different from the usual matching parasol, particular color gowns, or fancy carriage. Mr. Andrews agreed that a poodle the color of my hair would be just the thing." Harriet gauged her father's reactions by his frown. It seemed to lessen and she breathed easier.

"Very well. See to it that you do nothing to disgrace the family name and do not allow that animal to disturb anyone. Is that clear?" He shook out his paper and prepared to return to his reading.

Harriet murmured her agreement and escaped to the quiet and safety of her room. "At least he didn't ask your name," she consoled the dog. "But you must be on your best behavior—which means I had better take you for a long walk." With this in mind she donned a walking dress and put on one of her new little hats that showed off her red-gold curls to advantage before pulling on her gloves. Affixing the leash to the pup, she slipped from the house with her maid trailing behind her.

Cupid was far too eager to trail behind. Rather, he strained at his leash, half dragging Harriet to the park, with innumerable investigative pauses along the way.

She saw Mr. Andrews shortly after entering the park. Catching sight of her with Cupid at her side, he rode to join her with gratifying promptness.

"You make a charming pair," he pronounced when close enough for speech. "The dog is, ah, behaving himself?"

"So far," she said, hoping this good behavior would continue. "He is a quiet animal, thank heavens. My father would not be best pleased were Cupid to wake the house over the slightest thing."

"Cupid," Mr. Andrews muttered as though in disbelief.

"Actually, it may be a most appropriate name if the dog is helpful in finding me a husband." Harriet patted Cupid on the head, urging the dog to sit—which he did nicely.

"For pity's sake, I trust you do not say things like that to anyone else?" Mr. Andrews exclaimed.

"I am not quite that green, sir," Harriet said with umbrage at the gentleman who was so nattily dressed and exuded an air of such confidence she found it catching.

"No, of course you aren't," he replied in that soothing way he had when dealing with the children.

"Sirrah, I will not be treated like a child," she began.

"Speaking of children, I plan to take the older ones for a treat in the park this afternoon," he interjected. "Plan to bring along my boat for them to sail. Would you and, er, Cupid like to join us?"

Harriet, rather bored with the fitting of gowns and the restrictive life found in London, promptly agreed. "That sounds lovely. What time?"

"We shall come for you about two of the clock if that is agreeable." Although it might seem like a question, it sounded more like a statement.

Harriet was so pleased to have something interesting to look forward to that she would not quibble with him over the manner of invitation. After all, he did not *have* to ask her along. She admitted a curiosity about his young relatives.

"Cupid and I shall await you—and the children—with pleasure." She turned, then paused, looking at him over her shoulder. "How many and how old?"

"Emma has Edward who is eight, Harry who is six, and Jane, who is five. I may bring along Diana's brood as well. Her three are William, five, Timothy, four, and Anne, who is three." He gave her a look that dared her to back out of the acceptance.

"Six! Well, with Cupid and a boat, it ought not be dull," Harriet said with more enthusiasm than she had shown at the prospect of selecting gowns and bonnets.

Ferdy watched the redoubtable Miss Harriet Mayne march along the path with the poodle trotting at her side. A most obedient animal, from all to be seen. Even the maid seemed not to be frightened of the dog. Cupid! Poor dog.

Ferdy wheeled about and left the park to head for Emma's house. There he announced his intention to escort the three eldest Wynnstay offspring to the park.

"Are you sure, Ferdy?" Emma asked with well-concealed surprise.

"We manage quite well, you know. And Miss Harriet and her dog will be there. I trust we will do marvelously well." His sister agreed instantly, leaving Ferdy to tackle Diana next. He needn't have worried. She didn't bother to query him regarding his motives.

"Delightful. I'll send a picnic along with Nanny, for you will remember how hungry we always were when we went to the Serpentine. Sailing the boat? The children will be in alt, to be sure. All that plus a dog? Providential!"

So, at thirty minutes past one Ferdy gathered Emma's brood, then proceeded to Diana's to collect her three. By the time he reached the Mayne house, it was almost two.

He needn't have worried about Harriet. Wearing a pretty

willow green muslin gown trimmed with blond lace and a pert straw hat bedecked with daisies, she sallied forth in obvious good spirits. She enthusiastically greeted the group, with Cupid trotting at her side, quite as though she went on outings with six children, a dog, and a very large gentleman plus an enormous boat protruding from the rear of the landau every day of the week.

They rolled into the park and settled in a pleasant spot not far from the wind-ruffled Serpentine. The nanny—loaded down with rugs, a basket of food, cushions, and sundry other items deemed necessary for an outing of this magnitude—soon settled beneath a tree to observe.

Edward proved to be a leader, instantly demanding that his uncle launch the magnificent sailing craft while he and his younger brother deployed themselves on the far side so as to return the boat to Uncle Ferdy. Timothy and William stayed close to their uncle.

"Uncle Ferdy, Uncle Ferdy," Jane insisted, "me, too."

Seeing that a war of sorts might begin, Harriet calmly took Jane by the hand to where Anne had plunked herself off to one side, looking on with wide-eyed apprehension.

"Let us allow the boys to sail for a bit while we play catch with Cupid and a ball." Jane seemed dubious while Anne took a cautious look at Cupid, neatly trimmed so that he appeared to be wearing a pretty ruff about his neck.

"Will he bite?" she demanded to know, hiding her hands behind her back while awaiting the answer.

"I doubt he will, unless teased too much," Harriet said, hoping this was the case.

A ball was produced and the two girls were persuaded to toss it back and forth, scampering across the green grass in the welcome shade provided by dancing leaves overhead. Occasionally Cupid grabbed the ball and had to be convinced to return it to the girls, who were not pleased to share their toy when their brothers had commandeered the boat. When Jane conceived the notion to run with Cupid, Anne followed. Soon a game of tag developed, with the dog dashing madly about to the delight of the girls. Harriet watched with amusement and not a little relief.

"Active little beggars, are they not?" Mr. Andrews commented from over her shoulder upon joining her, seeing that the boat was safely on the far side of the pond.

"I can well see why Uncle Ferdy is a favorite. I doubt that Nanny would allow such spirited goings-on if in charge." A glance at the starched, disapproving figure in gray poplin confirmed that view.

"No," he agreed. "We always had a time convincing our nanny that we would not come to harm if we did something a bit strenuous. You grew up in the country?"

She nodded. "My sisters preferred to be indoors. I was the hoyden, I fear. I climbed trees, fished in the stream, rode my pony pell-mell over the fields, and picked berries in midsummer, smearing red juice from top to toes. At least it couldn't be seen in my hair," she said, exchanging an amused look with Mr. Andrews. "I believe I was universally considered a horror by Nanny, our governess, and all the maids—especially the one who had to mend my dresses."

"Diana and Annis as well. Emma, Bella, and Clair were the more proper of the clutch of Andrews children. However, yours sounds like an idyllic childhood." There was a question in his words that she surprised herself by answering.

"Not so, actually. My mother frowned on what was reported to her; my father would birch me, causing me to behave even more outrageously in the days to follow. Only my growing up helped. I acquired a bit of common sense and knowledge that a young lady had to be more circumspect if she wished to attain some independence."

"You wish independence? How odd for someone wanting to find a husband." Ferdy tossed the wayward ball to the girls.

"True," she admitted reluctantly, then added, "but you will confess that only within the confines of marriage can a woman know a measure of freedom."

Ferdy frowned, thinking that Miss Harriet had to be the oddest creature around, to consider a confining marriage as offering freedom. His noncommittal, "I see," gave no indication of his thoughts, however. The girl at his side stirred, glancing up at him with reproving eyes.

"You do put me to the blush, Mr. Andrews. I find myself

saying the most monstrously wicked things to you. Do you have this effect on all females?" She picked up the errant ball, tossing it to Jane, who promptly threw it to Anne. That game resumed, Cupid avidly watched with hope that he might snatch the ball and run off with it.

Ferdy laughed, recalling that most of his feminine company consisted of opera dancers who were outspoken to a fault. They only stopped short of offending. Apparently Miss Harriet Mayne did not have this compunction.

"You had best tend your boat, else it may sink." Miss Harriet declared suddenly, a gust of wind threatening the magnificent craft. Across the way, the boys argued over who was to take control of the next round.

Alarmed that his beautiful and expensive boat might become the object of a battle, Ferdy hurried to settle a dispute between Edward and William. Harry and Timothy stood by, assuming the role of peacemakers along with their uncle.

Harriet sank down on one of the cushions and began to set out the picnic that had been sent by Diana. She paused, glancing at the boys and girls running happily about. How different from her childhood, where she had been so alone. Perhaps when her sisters had children she might plan activities like this for them. But that would be some years away. Although, were Harriet to marry promptly, she might begin her own little clutch of players.

The notion that a gentleman on the order of Mr. Andrews would make an admirable father flitted through her head only to be immediately dismissed. She had heard about those opera dancers. But how many men could be found who tolerated children with such amiability?

The girls finally had a chance to sail the boat, while the boys offered their advice and words of wisdom. Then they ran and roughed about with Cupid before settling down to an eagerly consumed picnic.

"Pity we cannot do something like this every day," Harriet murmured to Mr. Andrews over a delicious plum tart. "But even the best of things pall if done too often."

"What you need is a pastime to occupy your spare hours. I shall apply my mind to the matter."

Nothing more was said on that score. Amid much hilarity, they all played ball, including Cupid. Then, tired and becoming cross, the children were bundled into the landau and returned to their respective homes.

There were a considerable number of fashionable people in the park who chanced to notice the pretty girl with the red-gold curls who seemed in such charity with the wealthy Mr. Andrews and his young relatives. It was a sight never viewed before so therefore all the more cause for gossip. Who was she and what were her prospects?

Unaware of her plunge into the gossip world of the *ton*, Harriet agreed to see Mr. Andrews on the morrow to discuss the matter of a pastime in which she might excel.

"Poor man," she confided to Cupid later, "little does he know how daunting his task is."

And so it proved. When she attempted to demonstrate her talent with watercolors, she splattered paint over her gown and the paper, ruining both. Since her perspective was utterly dreadful, the painting was not deemed a loss, and her gown, being an old one, was consigned to the dust bin.

Before he could inquire, she demonstrated her lack of ability on the pianoforte and harp, although he admired the songs she sang while mangling the instrumental music.

"Needlework?" Ferdy asked with more optimism than he felt. Surely she must have been overly modest about her gifts in this line.

Harriet brought forth her last attempt at canvas work, a cushion for her bedroom chair.

"I see," Ferdy said, his expectation sinking as swiftly as lead in a pond. "Well, I must give this more thought," he concluded, feeling sorry for the little redhead. She looked so dejected that he felt an urge to comfort her and solve all her problems. He would, too. Somehow.

The following morning he met Harriet by the gate to the park, as arranged the previous day, then walked his horse alongside hers. Her groom properly rode behind them at a discreet distance.

"Good to see you remembered to bring that chap," Ferdy commented.

"I am capable of learning, I should hope," she said, but without her usual snap.

Worried at her lack of spirit, a thing which he much admired in Miss Harriet Mayne, Ferdy hated to confess that he had yet to think of a proper pastime for her.

Then he noticed her eyeing a dashing fellow in the uniform of a Hussar. Captain Benwell, as Ferdy knew, was nothing more than a half-pay officer and acknowledged fortune hunter—as those fellows usually were.

"Can you introduce me, Mr. Andrews?" she murmured as the fellow cantered showily to where Ferdy and Miss Harriet rode properly along the path. She straightened her spine and glanced down at her pine-green habit, wishing she owned something more jaunty and modish.

"Not the thing, you know," Ferdy muttered back, then did the polite, seeing no way out of it.

"Captain Benwell, how nicely you ride," Harriet said, admiration ringing in her voice.

Captain Benwell, who had catalogued every heiress in town, knew to a penny what Harriet was due in dowry. The fellow smoothed his side-whiskers and smiled at Miss Harriet Mayne with that devilish leer that seemed to captivate women. He fawned over her until Ferdy wanted to hit the chap on the jaw and knock him clear to next Tuesday.

"Time to get on, Miss Mayne," Ferdy at last inserted, tired of being amiable and ignored.

Benwell took the hint, noting the fierce look on the very large gentleman whom he had no desire to cross. He left, begging a dance with Miss Mayne at the first ball they would both attend. Finally, he rode off in a flurry of prancing hoofs and showy manners.

"You were rather rude to that nice man," Harriet admonished while she and Mr. Andrews rode to the far end of the park. The cool green around them seemed to temper his obvious annoyance with the captain.

"As I began to say earlier, the chap is nothing more than a

half-pay officer and most likely on the hunt for a fortune," Ferdy declared more bluntly than was his wont.

"Dear me, what a pity. For if he were not, he would be a possibility, wouldn't he?"

Ferdy struggled with his conscience, then decided to tell her the truth. "Did he not require a fortune—for he likes to gamble—I doubt you would see him other than as a flirt. Somehow I believe that Benwell is not the sort to marry unless forced."

"I see," she replied in such a subdued manner that Ferdy became alarmed.

"It has nothing to do with you, you know. It is just how that chap is—and a good many others as well."

"You mean they also prefer their opera dancers?" She cast him a sidelong glance of speculation.

Ferdy wondered if it was possible for him to blush. Just as he had spoken bluntly to Miss Mayne, she now spoke to him. When the shoe went to the other foot, it was less than comfortable.

"Some chaps prefer the unmarried state," he finally mumbled.

"As do I—at least for the moment." She commented on the lush greenery about them, then moved on to kind remarks about his young relatives.

Ferdy relaxed, assured that this young woman showed not the least interest in snaring him for a husband. Then a twinge of pique crept in, for he knew he was considered a prime article on the potential husband lists. It rather galled him to think that this pert miss found him wanting in some manner.

They were about to return to the Mayne residence when Harriet returned to the topic that had occupied them before the appearance of the dashing captain—whom Harriet still considered interesting, no matter that Mr. Andrews had disparaged him rather shamefully.

"Did you think of any possibility for my pastime? 'Tis a pity I cannot ride all the day," she murmured as an afterthought.

Ferdy glanced about him, searching his memory, dredging up all the likely pastimes he could recall. "Archery," he at last offered. This was followed by a brief time of silence while his companion gave his suggestion respectful consideration.

"There is an archery society not far from where we live in Surrey—the Royal Surrey Archers," she said at last. "And wasn't the Marchioness of Salisbury a keen bowman? I should think that might make the sport quite acceptable to my family. One can never underestimate the value of peerage endorsement, you know," she concluded, half laughing.

"Ever tried it? Archery, that is," Ferdy asked, admiring her for not rejecting his suggestion out of hand.

"No. But that does not mean I might not wish to make a stab at it. At least it would be out of doors."

"As to that, there are some who set up clouts in a barn during inclement weather to practice when they please," he said, referring to the white pieces of fabric on frames used as targets for archers.

"That would make it nice," Miss Harriet said with an infectious giggle quite unlike the simpering sort offered by the milk-and-water brigade of misses making come-outs.

"A little decorum, please," Ferdy replied with mock severity. He had to admit that perky Miss Harriet Mayne was far from the norm, which made assisting her a good deal more pleasant. That he had no comparison, other than the young lady he had assisted his friend Val, Lord Latham, to capture, escaped him. But Phoebe Thorpe had been quiet and collected and he'd never had a personal interest in her.

"Do you plan to take the children out again? I think you are a wonderful uncle to be so kind to them."

She seemed in such great charity with him that Ferdy, who had thought nothing of the sort, said, "I had thought to take them fishing." Even after the words left his mouth, he figured that he could always claim he forgot the excursion if queried later about it.

"Oh, smashing!" she exclaimed.

"Indeed?" Ferdy's heart sank without a bubble.

"I adore fishing," she said as they rode up before the Mayne house. "May I come along? Will you go early in the morning? That is usually the best time. I do not have my pole with me; could I borrow one from you, please? Oh, you must be the most devoted of uncles in all of London—the most adored as well."

With that spate of words Ferdy could scarcely beg off from the fishing expedition. Gamely he said, "I do not see why you cannot join us. I warn you, you may be required to bait a few hooks." If that didn't put her off the idea he was well and truly hooked as well.

"Pooh bah," she said with a chuckle. "As though a dab of worm would hurt a soul. I shall be ready early and waiting for you. And this time I shall have Cook prepare a picnic for the hungry fishermen, if you are agreeable."

Ferdy gazed into those magnificent green eyes looking at him with such admiration and hope that he could merely nod. "We shall collect you early on the morrow, say eight of the clock?" Any chance that this would be too early was dashed in an instant when a radiant smile lit her face.

"Fine." She dismounted with the help of her groom, then paused on the front steps of the house. "I look forward to this far more than the hours spent with Madame Clotilde, I assure you."

Immediately going to Emma's house, Ferdy sauntered into the morning room where he explained his mission to his quiet sister. Amazingly, Emma did not query his motives, but merely suggested the fishing poles be hunted out and repaired if necessary.

After this success, he went to Diana's where he found dubious agreement. "Are you certain you want *all three* of the children?" she demanded to know. "You know how Anne is with worms."

"Miss Harriet does not appear squeamish regarding the things, so Anne may learn a lesson from it all," Ferdy said, thinking that his idea might prove to be an excellent one.

"Harriet is going with you?" Diana said, as though that explained something puzzling. "I see."

"I doubt you do. Harriet, that is, Miss Harriet, is in need of a pastime and seems most fond of fishing. It is the least I could do for her. She was such a good sport about the afternoon spent sailing the boat."

"Yes, I heard all about the poodle who plays ball. Well, I shall find some poles. Shall I send a picnic with Nanny?"

"Miss Harriet insists upon bringing a repast this time."

"Lovely," Diana purred.

Thus it was that early the following morning—so early that Ferdy had of necessity neglected his current opera dancer so he might be fresh and alert—he collected the children and proceeded to the Mayne house, wondering if the audacious Harriet would truly be about at this ungodly hour. She was.

The door opened promptly. Cupid trotted at her side followed by a footman and maid bearing enormous baskets. These were placed with Nanny in the carriage that followed the one containing the six children, Ferdy, Harriet, and Cupid.

"I noticed you looked askance at having Cupid along, but he has promised to be very quiet and good and not bark at the fish we shall catch," Harriet assured him.

Ferdy said nothing on that score, having little faith in conversations Harriet might have with Cupid.

The weather held greater promise than Ferdy's hope for the outing. If he could manage to scrape through the day without someone falling into the river, a hook being entangled in a root—or something equally devious such as the nanny having mild hysterics when one of the children dropped a fish in her lap, he would be much surprised.

Harriet looked about her with approval. They had traveled north until reaching a tranquil river that wound around a level, grassy area perfect for a picnic. There were spreading oaks for Nanny to lean against that promised cool shade later on. It took but moments for the groom, the driver, and Nanny to place the assortment of baskets, cushions and rugs, and the paraphernalia necessary for a comfortable day of fishing under a shady tree close to the water's edge.

Jane and Anne tugged at Harriet to play with them. Harriet produced a ball, then suggested they play a silent game with Cupid. "You must see if you can communicate with the dog without saying a word," Harriet insisted. "Fishing is of necessity a silent sport, for talking will frighten the fish."

Anne pouted and sought Nanny. Jane requested a fishing

pole and declared she would catch the first fish. Cupid sought solace at Anne's side, inviting her tentative pats.

Once hooks were baited, they all settled down on the banks of the pretty river, expectations varying with the age of the fishermen. Harriet was simply happy to be in the country again with congenial company. The children were darlings and Mr. Andrews the most indulgent of uncles.

Mr. Andrews was the first to land a trout of modest size. Edward followed, looking most superior when his fish was found to be of a size with his uncle's. Harry, Timothy, and Jane caught small fish, but thought it grand. Harriet waited. She had the patience of a true fisherman, nursing her line in the water, expertly casting it to land in calm pools where the canny fish hid.

Then everything happened at once, as is often the case when children are along. Harriet's pole dipped madly. As she coped with landing a sizable trout, Anne's curiosity took her close to the river where she tumbled into the placid flow with high-pitched screams.

Nanny dashed madly to the water's edge, while Ferdy wisely removed his coat on his run up the river, intent upon pulling his niece from a watery grave.

Cupid raced after Anne, plunging into the water and grasping her dress with sharp teeth that refused to let go in spite of her thrashing about. He persisted until he tugged her to shore where Nanny and Ferdy were able to pull her to safety.

Harriet dropped her fish on the ground, ignoring its excellent size. She grabbed up a soft blanket, hurrying after the others. As Anne stood trembling, dripping and miserable, Harriet swiftly wrapped her in the blanket, then handed her to Nanny with a gentle look. "Best see she changes her clothing lest she take a chill. We shall try to find a restorative."

William hugged Cupid, praising him extravagantly. "What a splendid dog, Miss Mayne. I wish we had a dog like him. Champion, that's what he is."

"He saved Miss Anne and that's no mistake," Nanny cried with a kindly look at the animal she had previously barely tolerated.

"Back to the fish," Ferdy said with relief when all had died down and they returned to admire Harriet's splendid catch.

Harriet wondered if excursions with Mr. Andrews were always fraught with excitement. If that were the case, archery might well be an enticing diversion.

Chapter Four

The promised lesson in archery was postponed when Harriet began to receive the lovely clothes from Madame Clotilde. She'd had to accept castoffs from her sisters all these years, so it was exciting to actually have gowns fitted to her form. She held no animosity over the castoffs. After all, she would be the first to admit that she had scarcely paid for dressing—at least before acquiring her new hair color and its becoming style.

Crossing to the looking glass, she studied the effect of a pale lime green walking dress against her fair skin and the soft golden-red of her hair—now curling in ringlets about her face. Acceptable. Actually, *most* acceptable. Handing the pretty gown to Betsy, her new maid, she caught up a delicate apricot carriage dress that had cream lace trim and piping, and looked to see how it affected her appearance. Madame was right. These delicate colors suited her far more than the dramatic hues her sisters wore.

Choosing a morning dress of palest periwinkle blue that she would have sworn would look dreadful with her hair, she was pleased to see it had quite the opposite effect. She quickly dressed and went down to see if her mother noticed the change.

"Mother, the clothes from Madame Clotilde are truly lovely. I must thank you and Papa for such generosity."

"Prettily said, indeed," Lady Mayne replied while casting a considering look at her youngest child. "You are improved, I must admit. Perhaps, just perhaps, you might find a husband on your own after all. You do remember that your father has limited patience? It behooves you to encourage a gentleman to ask for your hand before the end of the Season. Else your father will have no choice but to affiance you to Lord Pomeroy."

Harriet had not hitherto been aware of the identity of the man her father intended for her husband. It was a distinct shock to discover that he had selected Lord Pomeroy—who must be ninety if a day. The certitude that she would most likely be widowed soon into her marriage made no difference. The man—according to all she'd heard and observed—did not believe in bathing and considered changing his garments a waste of time. She supposed at his age time meant a great deal, as he likely had little left of it. However, it was disheartening to know her father was willing to toss her to just anyone without regard for her sensibilities.

But then, Papa believed that females were not as gifted with the understanding and intelligence given to the human male. Although, from what she had seen while in London, there were a goodly number of rattle-pated men about. Goodness, there was that man who walked his turtle—studded with green gems and on a green leash—in the park. And there was Lord Petersham, with his silly collection of snuff boxes and his affected airs, not to mention his ever-present apricot tart. And the mincing dandies and devil-may-care Corinthians who paraded in the park looked to be a bit buffle-headed, to be sure.

Well, the chance of a *preux chevallier* coming to her rescue like a knight of old was a trifle absurd. Never mind that Mr. Andrews had assisted her in the matter of her hair and dress, by way of his sisters. That scarcely counted. And besides, she'd never be able to compete with the opera dancers and wasn't certain if she wanted to. Compete, that is. And, come to think on it, he did not much resemble a knight in shining armor. She doubted if they made armor that large.

But . . . he made a nice friend.

She left her mother studying the menu for an upcoming dinner she was planning and wandered along the hall to the front room from which she might observe the passersby. Thus it was that she spotted Mr. Andrews approaching while he was still some distance from the house.

Rushing to her room, she didn't bother to ring for Betsy, but found her new teal-blue pelisse on her own. After slipping it on, she clapped a dainty hat bedecked with teal-blue feathers and cream ribbons atop her head. Hastily buttoning the pelisse, she pulled on her cream silk gloves and picked up a clever parasol that Madame had instructed her to purchase. It was hinged, in cream silk with a folding wooden handle, and it had a dear little knot of silk fringe at the very tip.

Cupid stood at the ready, eagerly waiting to go with her for their morning walk. Clasping on his leash, she descended the stairs just as the housekeeper opened the door to Mr. Andrews.

"Why, what a surprise," she said with a grin. "Cupid and I were preparing for our morning walk. Would you care to join us?" Behind her, Betsy now hovered, her simple brown dress and shawl blending into the shadows.

"I am fortunate to catch you before you left." Ferdy studied the little minx who smiled at him with such impish glee. As he'd come expressly to escort her, he could scarcely twit her about her prompt appearance. And she *was* a treat for the eyes this morning in her new finery that enhanced her vibrant charm.

"Good. I wished to discuss a matter with you and I'd not want to be so forward as to send you a message." She marched down the last of the steps and presented Cupid. "He is a remarkably clever dog." She turned to the animal and said sweetly, "Sit and offer your paw."

Cupid obediently sat and held out a dainty paw for Ferdy to shake.

Ferdy did as indicated, then escorted Harriet and her pet from the house. Betsy trailed behind, not about to allow her new mistress a chance to be the slightest bit improper.

They strolled along toward the park in quiet amiability. Deciding he had best find out what the matter might be that Harriet wished to discuss, he said, "Well, I await your question." The flush that covered her fine peach-tinted skin almost obliterated her freckles.

"It is so difficult to talk about." She sighed, then appeared to plunge to the heart of the problem. "Mama informed me this morning that if I do not find myself a husband before the end of the Season that Papa will affiance me to Lord Pomeroy."

"That old bird? Why, he's ninety if he's a day." Then Ferdy reconsidered, "However, even though he's as repellent as a jailbird, he's no doddering ancient. He claims his activity keeps him going—that and not bathing. Insists that cleansing the skin allows dangerous diseases to enter the body. Old chap will probably live to be a hundred and fifty—providing anyone can come close enough to see if he's still alive."

"I think he is disgusting—if you will pardon my frankness. Thus it seems most imperative I find a husband." She was about to ask her new friend if a half-pay officer was really so terrible when he inserted a suggestion.

"I shall call on Emma. She has the greatest good sense of all our family. I feel certain she can think of something to help you."

"That does sound lovely. I am sorry that my sisters and brother care so little about my future. Papa has arranged husbands for my sisters, so I suppose they assume he will do as well for me."

What Ferdy thought of such an uncaring family was not spoken aloud, but he tightened his clasp on the slender elbow entrusted to his care and guided Harriet into the park with the air of a gentleman handling a fine china shepherdess.

Their walk was uneventful, if you considered they were ogled by only four matrons and two gentlemen who chanced their way. Captain Benwell cantered his showy way along Rotten Row, causing Harriet to wonder what he did with his time. It must be dreary to have been so active and now have nothing but time on your hands.

When Ferdy returned the pert Miss Harriet to her home, after duly admiring the wonderful tricks Cupid had learned, he went to Emma's. When she was appraised of the fate that awaited Harriet Mayne should she not find herself a husband, Emma was horrified.

"Can you imagine a young and innocent girl handed over to that smelly old lecher? It is outrageous! I'm thankful our parents treated us with more consideration. We must do something. Have you any ideas?" she asked her dearest and only brother.

"I hoped you might think of something," Ferdy confessed. "Invite her to one of your afternoon gatherings to meet some other women. Too, she might enjoy one of your musical evenings—she sings like an angel."

Emma brightened considerably. "Does she, now. Hmm. I shall invite her to participate at the next one, which is next Thursday. Does she go to Almack's, do you know?"

"She hasn't mentioned it. I forgot to ask." Ferdy still was not accustomed to dealing with a young lady who might aspire to such heights. Opera dancers never bothered; they knew better.

"Would you bring her here for an afternoon? She is probably too shy to come by herself," Emma said with a downward glance at the embroidery in her lap.

"Hand me the invitation and I'll carry it over to her now. I forgot to inquire when I can give her archery lessons."

"*You* are teaching her?" Emma asked with unconcealed surprise tinging her voice. "You never teach women. You wouldn't even teach me!"

"Well, that Madame Clotilde insisted that Harriet has to do something different. She doesn't embroider or play an instrument, and no one with any brains would let her drive a carriage. Archery, it is."

"You have a low opinion of her driving skills. Or is it that she is a trifle daring? Certainly *you* might teach her," Emma said tartly.

"She isn't the most docile female. I only hope that she can hit a target." His mien was gloomy at the prospect of a woman using a bow and arrow. Never mind that archery continued to grow in popularity with the fair sex. Ferdy held the belief that they took advantage of the sport to use their wiles on the gentlemen attending.

"I believe she will be able to hit her target with far more skill than you would credit," Emma said while rising to cross the room to her little desk. Here she sat down to dash off a pretty note to Harriet, inviting her to visit the following afternoon.

Once Ferdy had gone, Emma also wrote notes to Diana, Lady Sefton, and Lady Jersey, deciding to skip Mrs. Drummond-Burrell, even though they were friends. She doubted if Clementina Drummond-Burrell had a very well-developed sense of humor.

Ferdy presented himself at the Mayne house not long after visiting his sister. Harriet, accompanied by a well-mannered

Cupid, briskly entered the drawing room, followed by her shadow, Betsy.

"How pleasant to see you so soon. You have rescued me from my singing lesson with Signor Carvallo."

"Singing lesson! I ought not have disturbed you," Ferdy said, taking a furtive step toward the door.

"We were almost finished. I must now practice what I have learned this day. But, I natter on. What did you wish to see me about, pray tell?"

Ferdy hadn't seen Harriet in her new ensemble of pretty pale periwinkle blue with its tiny rows of tucks and feminine embroidery circling the hem and sleeves. He frowned at her, for it seemed to him that his hoyden was turning into a fine lady, and he wasn't certain he liked it.

Cupid growled, backing Ferdy to a chair, whereupon he promptly sat. Cupid elected to curl up on Ferdy's boots while Harriet giggled, her gamin grin once again in place.

Reassured that his little redhead was not so very changed after all, Ferdy delved into a pocket to extract the note from Emma.

Taking pity on him, Harriet walked to where he was kept prisoner by Cupid and accepted the message. It was short and it took but seconds to scan the contents, then look back to Mr. Andrews. "I shall be delighted to visit. Shall I send my reply with you—or with a footman?"

"Oh, I could drop it off on my way to the club," Ferdy said with a sigh of relief. How obliging Harriet was to fall in with his sister's plans so nicely.

They chatted a bit. Cupid demonstrated his tricks again. And Harriet decided that perhaps they had best wait until the weather looked better before attempting archery.

"If you do well, you may want to do as the other women and wear a forest green dress and a hat decked with feathers. Seems all the crack," he mused. "Although why you'd want to wear a hat while at archery is more than I can see."

"I may not be up to snuff—as you would say—but I do know a young lady is supposed to keep her head properly covered," Harriet said with a laugh. "Come, admit it, would you not be shocked were I to appear sans hat?"

Ferdy tilted his head, admiring the pretty curls that adorned his young friend. He shook his head. "Not I. I like your curls—as well as the new color. You will not forget the special rinse, will you? Diana begged me remind you not to forget," he said earnestly.

"Lemon plus an infusion of mullein flowers. I shan't forget, for it does make a difference."

He soon left the Mayne house, dropping off her acceptance on the way to his club and wondering how the following afternoon would go. He doubted there would be a problem as Emma got along fine with Harriet. It was as well he knew nothing of the plans afoot.

Diana arrived early in the afternoon, seeking out her sister at once. "I gather Harriet accepted. Does her father actually intend to betroth her to Pomeroy? I could not credit such a horrific tale. And what did our dear brother say to that?"

"He seemed to think it our duty to save her from such a fate. I agree. Do you not as well?" Emma gave her sister a mischievous smile, then assumed the mien appropriate for a young matron who was an intimate friend of Clementina Drummond-Burrell.

When Harriet arrived, she was aghast to discover that the awesome ladies from Almack's were present. Sure she would fall over her own feet, she whispered to Diana, "Had I known Lady Jersey and Lady Sefton were to be here, I'd have had a cold."

"Nonsense," Diana said briskly. "Come and meet them. I assure you that they do not bite."

Emma introduced Harriet to the older ladies, then prettily begged Harriet to sing a tune for them.

Having just practiced a romantic Italian ballad, Harriet acquiesced with none of the usual girlish flutterings. Emma—who played splendidly—inquired the name of the tune, then admired the lovely voice as it poured forth in artless simplicity and in perfect pitch, while Emma played a soft accompaniment. Rather than let Harriet take her seat, Emma began the introduction to a lively English air.

Later, after the others had left, Harriet admonished her hostess. "It was a good thing that I knew that song or you'd have looked a bit silly."

"I trusted you'd not fail me," Emma said complacently.

"You would have deserved it," Harriet replied, but with a smile.

"One thing I like about Harriet," Diana observed at large, "is that she doesn't toady to people." She turned to face Harriet to add, "You were simply yourself with those ladies. I would not be surprised were you to receive vouchers to Almack's—even if your mother did not seek them. Did your sisters attend?" She exchanged glances with Emma.

"For one Season, only. Victoria and Coralie both came out the same year—which created a spectacular effect when they entered a room—their magnificent hair, you know. After that, it was considered an unnecessary expense as both became betrothed."

"Not many people view it like that. And no attempt was made on your behalf?" Emma asked, looking bemused.

"Well, you saw what I used to look like," Harriet said with her practical head well in place. She discounted the promise of a voucher, for she well knew how difficult they were to obtain and how few were given out.

"But now you are as pretty as can be. Even those freckles are adorable," Diana said with an unladylike bounce. "I predict you will be declared an original—just as Madame Clotilde intended. And Cupid is doing well?"

"I was not sure if I ought to bring him along. Not all ladies appreciate dogs, you know. But he does splendidly."

"How considerate of you," Emma said. "However, in the future, I believe you ought to have him with you wherever you go, at least in the daytime."

"I agree," Diana said. "And it ought to please Ferdy, since he was the one who bought the dog for you."

"You must know that I would do anything to please your brother. I cannot thank him enough for all he has done for me. Is it not unusual for a gentleman to concern himself about a young miss like me? I mean, I have heard tales about opera dancers engaging much of a man's time, not to mention races, carriages, Fives' Court, and such. Gentlemen have much to occupy their time," she concluded wistfully.

"Never you mind about that," Diana said quickly. "Ferdy has a heart of gold and something in your plight touched it. I can't tell you how delighted I am that you are to learn how to shoot with a bow and arrow. I have this feeling that you will excel."

"I hope so. As soon as the weather improves—and I receive delivery of that forest green dress I ordered—I shall begin lessons."

"Good," Diana and Emma said in unison.

It was agreed that Harriet would keep the sisters posted on her progress and come to tea the following week.

Somehow it did not unduly surprise Harriet that she should encounter Captain Benwell when she walked Cupid the next day. She astutely gathered that the captain had reasoned that after escorting Harriet the day before, Mr. Andrews was not likely to dance attendance so soon.

"Ah, fair maiden," he said, ignoring the growls emanating from Cupid, who it seemed had taken an instant dislike to the captain, "how fortunate I am to find you in the park this morning."

"Dogs require walking and I enjoy the fresh air as well." She glanced behind her to note that her maid was but a pace behind her and looked as if she would gladly hit the captain over the head were he to become too familiar.

"May I stroll along with you, dear Miss Mayne?" he begged in what Harriet considered to be an unctuous manner. However, she decided she was being a trifle touchy.

"We would be pleased to have the escort of a gallant captain. Tell me, do you find life in London to be tedious?" she inquired when they continued on the path toward the Serpentine.

"Tedious?" he said, clearly astounded that anyone could think London dull. "Hardly, Miss Mayne."

"I suppose, like all the other men, you are busy with Gentleman Jackson's boxing saloon and Lord's cricket field. Do you drive as well?" She twirled her new silk parasol and retained a firm hold on Cupid's leash. The dog's dislike for the captain had not lessened and she hoped Cupid would not take to biting. He'd been so well-behaved thus far. Perhaps the captain's polished Hessians would not be to Cupid's liking. She prayed that might be the case.

The captain, who didn't have the money to lavish on a fancy team much less a curricle, said, "I content myself with admiring them, and I ride in the park with the fashionable lot."

She guessed he was right, for the park late in the afternoon was the place to be in all of London. Certainly Mr. Andrews frequented the park and looked quite at home among the polished members of the *ton*.

Captain Benwell proceeded to pour the butter boat over her head to a point that she wondered if she might slide in the grease. Since it was a totally novel experience for her to wallow in compliments, she merely smiled and kept silent. But she couldn't help but contrast the outrageous flattery from Captain Benwell with the sincere remarks on her improved appearance offered by Mr. Andrews.

They reached the Serpentine, where a number of ducks paddled noisily about, entrancing Cupid to the point that he refused to budge. Patiently, Harriet waited for this fascination to end. It didn't.

"Wonder if he would make a bird dog?" the captain said in a jocular manner.

"Heavens, I hope not," Harriet declared fervently. Visions of being pulled along the paths while Cupid chased a robin flashed before her.

It was then that Mr. Andrews rode up to join them, earning a hostile look from the captain.

"Beautiful day. Weather is improving by leaps and bounds. I daresay that by next week you will find the temperature sufficient to spend the required time at the archery grounds."

"Archery grounds?" the captain inquired, looking displeased.

"Indeed," Ferdy said smugly, knowing that the captain neither had the money required to be a member of the exclusive archery club to which Ferdy belonged nor the ability deemed necessary to be a first-class bowman.

"Enjoy that sort of thing do you?" the captain asked in a disparaging manner.

Cupid, having finally tired of the ducks that had managed to distance themselves from him, pulled in the direction of a grove of trees. Harriet deemed it wise to move.

"Gentlemen, please excuse me. Cupid wants to walk."

"Cupid?" the captain said with a scornful laugh.

"Clever name, isn't it?" Ferdy said blandly.

"No one names a dog Cupid," came the snapped reply.

"What a pity no one thought to tell Miss Mayne that. Good day, Captain Benwell. Another time, perhaps?" Ferdy dismounted and stood facing the captain, fully aware of his intimidating height and girth. Every so often it came in handy. Today it was an instance that gave him great pleasure.

With the captain fading into the distance, Ferdy caught up to Harriet. "Not good *ton,* to walk with that chap. Ought to be more careful."

"He has been all that is courteous and it is rather dull to walk in the park all by myself." She discounted her maid, who was as mute as a fish.

Ferdy had no rejoinder to that complaint for he guessed she was right. Rather he elected a different tack. "Emma said you charmed the ladies yesterday. May send you vouchers, you know. You dance?"

"It was excessively kind of Emma and Diana to go to so much trouble on my behalf. It is more than my family has done, let me tell you." Then, feeling disloyal, she added, "But then, who was to know I might improve?"

"And dancing?" he prompted.

"I adore dancing," she admitted. "It is my chief accomplishment."

"Heard you warble like a bird, my dear girl." He gave her a facetious look, pretending amazement.

"There are birds and there are birds," she pointed out. "Not all are pleasing to the ear."

"Emma said you are very good and she should know. She is the musical one in the family."

"She is most kind. How surprised she would have been had I cackled like a hen!" Harriet said with a laugh.

At that moment Cupid took it into his head to dash after a stray duck. Harriet had but a light grasp on his leash. He tugged free in an instant and was off, to her dismay.

Ferdy leaped on his horse and dashed madly after the dog, causing that animal to run all the faster. Harriet, on the other hand, walked quickly to the end of the Serpentine, where she guessed the duck might seek refuge. Thus it was that Cupid nearly ran into her while the duck escaped, quacking all the while.

"Good thinking, Harriet, that is, Miss Mayne," Ferdy said, while dismounting. "Dash it all, we are old friends, are we not? And you know my sisters and my nieces and nephews, right? Well, why can't we be on a first-name basis, I'd like to know." He scratched his head in an endearing manner, causing Harriet to grin back at him.

"Well, I cannot tell you, for I do not know all the ins and outs. There is most likely a reason. However, if I do not tell and you don't say anything, who is to know what is said when we are not in company?" she reasoned.

"I told them you have a sound head on your shoulders," Ferdy said.

"Fine. Does that mean I may call you Ferdy as Emma and Diana do? I should like that." Cupid tugged on the leash, dragging Harriet along the Serpentine, while he kept a sharp eye on the elusive duck.

Ferdy related a number of amusing stories that had Harriet chuckling in the manner he enjoyed. This might have continued for a long time had not one of Ferdy's friends happened along and demanded an introduction to the fair charmer at his side.

Taking umbrage at the casual attitude of his friend, the Honorable Justin Armitage, Ferdy made the introduction with all the stiffness of a dowager.

"Miss Mayne, I am indeed pleased to meet you at last. Ferdy has mentioned you, but kept you to himself. I can see why. Old boy, it isn't fair."

Harriet glanced from the large gentleman at her side to the handsome and polished man-about-town, who looked like a page from a book on dandies. She smiled and sidled a trifle closer to Ferdy. "It is accomplished without difficulty. I am dreadfully sorry, but I fear I must head for home. Charming to make your acquaintance, sir." She curtsied in her engaging way, then turned to Ferdy. "May I beg your company home? I must discuss a matter with you—something to do with Cupid."

Harriet missed the flash of amazement that crossed the eligible Mr. Armitage's face at her mention of Cupid for, of course, he had no idea Cupid was a dog. Accustomed to the stupid name bestowed on the poodle, Ferdy gave the matter nary a thought and instantly agreed. The sooner he drew Harriet away from that dasher Armitage, the better.

Once alone with Ferdy, Harriet rashly confided, "I just wished to be rid of your friend. I am sorry, Ferdy. I am certain he's very nice, but I prefer someone less overwhelming."

Ferdy beamed a smile of approval on his little friend. "Quite so. You need a man of distinction, with understanding and tact."

"And not a dandy," she added with her usual forthright speech. "I truly do not care for dandies."

"Is there something concerning Cupid that you wish to discuss?"

"Only to wonder if I might bring him along when I take lessons in archery. He is so fond of the fresh air and watching birds and all that," she said with a vague wave of her hand.

Ferdy agreed Cupid might come, ignoring any misgivings he might have. He parted with Harriet, to saunter along deep in thought to his club. This effort to help the redhead was taking an unexpected turn. He didn't care for the chaps attracted to his charming little friend with the gamin smile. They were not the sort to appreciate her unusual qualities. And this worried him a great deal. So deep in thought was he that he passed one of his cronies and never noticed.

The omission was duly noted, however, and much discussed.

Chapter Five

"**Y**ou may acquire a voucher for Almack's, but it still will not make you stand out," Coralie said without obvious malice. "Your hair may now be passable, but you still have freckles. Harriet, you may as well resign yourself to the marriage Papa has decided is best for you. Look at me—I am most pleased with Lord Perth. Do you know who Papa has in mind for you?" she asked, concluding her summary of her sister's chances in the race for marriage.

"Lord Pomeroy." Harriet watched Coralie's face carefully, determined to see if her sister was as heartless as she had long suspected.

"Oh, my," Coralie said, shifting her gaze and uneasily moving on her chair. "Well, he is reputed to be fabulously wealthy and you can always hold your nose when you need to be near him."

"I could not believe you to be so callous," Harriet said without heat. "I would never condemn one of my own to such a life as he offers. How would you like to face a future with that man?"

"That is scarcely the point, is it? I have Lord Perth and Papa cannot take him from me to hand him to you, if you understand my meaning." Coralie rose from her chair, smoothing her titian hair back into its sleek chignon. "Give up."

"I think not," Harriet said quietly. "I am to sing at Lady Wynnstay's musicale a week come Thursday evening. And she has introduced me to a number of interesting people. I feel certain she will present me to more. And Mr. Andrews has declared himself to be my sympathizer, offering his help," she rashly insisted. "I understand he is everywhere accepted and has friends in the highest of places, including the Prince of Wales."

Coralie gave her little sister an arrested look, then made a dismissing wave of her hand. "Pooh, almost anyone can claim Prinney as a friend if he has enough money." A sly gleam flashed in her eyes. "Mr. Andrews is rich? Truly well to do?"

"I believe that is the case. Unlike you," Harriet said calmly, "I do not judge people solely by their bank account nor their social standing."

"How unfeeling you are! You just said he has wealth and Lady Wynnstay has social standing. Double-face!" Coralie stamped a dainty foot encased in the finest Morocco leather, glaring at her sister with narrowed eyes.

"I said that because I knew those things meant something to you, not because *I* find them important. They also happen to be warm, caring people whose company I truly enjoy."

"Ha! Ask me if I believe you. Better take what Papa offers, else he may consign you to Aunt Croscombe, and I suspect she may be worse than Lord Pomeroy!" Coralie sniffed, poked her beautiful nose in the air, and majestically swept from the room, total elegance in her every line.

Harriet turned to fondle Cupid's soft head. Gazing into those limpid eyes, she whispered, "I ought to have known better than try to reason with Coralie. She was ever like this. Perhaps it is not a blessing to be so beautiful if it hardens the heart to stone." But the very thought of being sent to live with Aunt Croscombe was enough to chill the blood. What a choice— smelly old Lord Pomeroy or a nasty-tempered harpy seemingly bent on making those around her as miserable as she was reputed to be.

Why Harriet might not simply remain at home with her parents she did not understand. But it appeared they wished her gone. Thus either she must find a husband on her own—Papa figuring he'd done all that was necessary with scouting out old Pomeroy—or find a means of escape.

Being ignored by one's family had certain advantages, Harriet decided later when she left the house with Cupid and Betsy for a foray to her favorite bookshop, Hatchards. No one asked her where she intended to go, nor scolded her for being bookish—which she actually was not since she did not count herself addicted to reading. But she did enjoy browsing through the shelves of interesting books, searching for something on a faraway place, or perhaps a new novel—one like *Sense and Sensibility,* for instance.

She espied Diana Oliver the precise moment that Diana spotted her. Diana joined Harriet in a swirl of elegant turquoise silk, the plumes on her bonnet waving frantically in the air as she hurried over.

"You are prepared to sing at Emma's musicale come Thursday next?" Diana asked breathlessly.

"I have selected my music and Signor Carvallo will coach me with my singing. Would Emma like him to come that evening to play for me? He sometimes does that for his pupils," Harriet said hesitantly, not wishing her hostess to be pushed into the role of accompanist again, especially if she had a large number of guests.

"I believe she would appreciate that. Yes, do ask him. You do not mind singing for so many people?"

Harriet gave her a look of alarm. "There is to be a crush?"

Diana shrugged, picking at the spine of a volume of poetry on the shelf at her side. "No more than usual. You surprise me. Most girls having their come-out are terrified. When is your ball to be?"

Taking a deep breath, suspecting what Diana's reaction might be, Harriet said, "I shan't have one. Mama said they had made their splash with Victoria and Coralie."

"How perfectly dreadful," Diana stated, then placed a gentle hand on Harriet's arm. "I am sorry. I have no right to criticize your family. It's just that you caught me so off guard. I did not expect such a reply. Well, we shall have to double our efforts to find you a husband who is worthy of your talent and beauty."

Harriet giggled. "Truly, you jest. But I do enjoy it. It is better than being told that if I don't accept what Papa offers I shall be shipped off to Aunt Croscombe in Little Munden— Hertfordshire, you know."

"I gather dear Auntie is a horror?"

"I fear she is. Now I must beg your pardon, for I ought not

speak of her so," Harriet said. "Come let us see what new books are on offer."

Wisely accepting the subject as closed, Diana drifted along with Harriet to view the latest in reading material.

Later, in Emma's morning room, Diana plopped her book purchases on a backless sofa covered in green-and-white striped satin and dropped beside them. "I saw Harriet at the bookshop and you will not believe what I learned!"

"I can see you are bursting to reveal all," Emma said with a smile.

"Her family is *not* giving her a come-out ball! Not so much as a party! All attention and money has been lavished on those gorgeous sisters of hers—who, by the way, are rumored to be cold-blooded beauties." Diana exchanged a significant look with Emma.

"We must inform Ferdy of this, would you not agree?" Emma asked in a guileless manner.

"Indeed," Diana replied, her eyes lighting up with sheer delight at the thought of his reaction to such neglect.

"It makes the necessity of vouchers all the more important," Emma said thoughtfully, sharing another significant glance with her sister.

"Indeed. What a pity we are not the sort to resort to blackmail. The trouble is, I do not have the vaguest idea what we might use!" Diana said with her infectious giggle.

"But we do have Ferdy," Emma said.

"True. If only our plans bear fruit."

"Harriet said she has a pretty forest green gown about to be delivered from Madame Clotilde," Diana said. "She'll need a proper bonnet for the dress—one with green feathers or whatever. She will wear them to the archery grounds."

Not seeming surprised at the turn of conversation, Emma nodded. "Shall you take her shopping or shall I?"

"I am in need of a new evening hat. I will take her as soon as may be."

Thus it was that Harriet received an invitation from the dashing and socially prominent Mrs. Oliver to go shopping.

When she entered the Oliver carriage and settled next to Diana, she thanked her benefactress for her kindness.

"Nonsense. I detest shopping alone and you have such excellent taste."

Harriet—who had been told from infancy that she was as dull as ditchwater in her choice of wearing apparel—gave Diana a suspicious look.

"Now, merely because you are not as flamboyant as your sisters does not mean you do not have taste," Diana scolded, rightly interpreting the expression on Harriet's face. "Ah, here we are," she said as the carriage drew to a halt before an Oxford Street shop that had elegantly beautiful bonnets and hats in the windows.

It was a distinct pleasure to select a wicked little hat bedecked with green leaves from behind which peeped a froth of green feathers. When Diana learned that the archery dress had sleeves slashed with white, she insisted upon adding a dash of white to the hat with a tiny rosette white riband.

"For you will not wear typical gloves, but a peculiar form of a glove with only three sort-of fingers—strips of leather with leather tips into which you insert your three fingers to protect them."

Harriet gave her an alarmed look. "I had no idea that archery is dangerous."

"It isn't. 'Tis simple good sense to protect the fingers from the lash of the bowstring."

This left Harriet in the dark and wondering what she was letting herself in for when she took archery lessons from Mr. Andrews. She could not permit herself to think of him as Ferdy, no matter that Diana and Emma constantly called him that and he had agreed that Harriet do so as well.

Upon entering the Mayne residence with Betsy trailing behind carrying the hatbox and a few other items Diana had insisted Harriet needed—such as a new evening hat and a pretty Norwich shawl—she was met by the housekeeper.

"Two letters for you, Miss Harriet," the good lady intoned, with the surprise she felt clearly in her voice. It was usually Victoria or the parents who received missives.

Absently thanking the housekeeper, Harriet wandered up

the stairs to her room, staring with curious eyes at the folded paper. Once in the security of her room, she broke the seal of the first and unfolded the paper to see that Ferdy had elected to give her instructions regarding her archery lessons. He would—if agreeable to her—collect her on the morrow, early in the morning.

The second letter was cleverly folded, quite as though it contained something inside. More than a little curious, Harriet settled upon the dainty chair near her window to break the seal on this missive, unfolding the crisp vellum to see that it indeed held an enclosure. Vouchers! The letter was a prettily worded invitation to join their select little group for a bit of dancing and refreshment.

The subscriptions were ten guineas for a ball and supper once a week for twelve weeks. The Wednesday evening tickets were nontransferable and Harriet wondered if her mother—whose name was inscribed on one of the vouchers—would condescend to attend with her youngest daughter. It would be nice to go there and it was indeed necessary for her prospects. The very best of the *ton* would be present, not to mention those gentlemen who might be looking for a wife. Although not all of those men were on the prowl for a spouse. Ferdy had promised to attend were Harriet granted the esteemed vouchers, and he was far too enamored of his opera dancers to think about marriage.

Harriet thought that a pity, for he was so charming with the children. And that they adored him was most evident.

Afternoon brought the delivery of her forest green gown Madame Clotilde had declared quite *comme il faut* for archery. The dress flattered Harriet's coloring, although it seemed that her hair had faded a bit. She summoned Betsy and they applied the infusion of mullein flowers and lemon juice to see if that might restore the golden gleam in Harriet's red locks.

When Lady Mayne learned that Harriet had been given the vouchers, she was uncharacteristically silent.

Her hair still slightly damp from the successful coloring, Harriet cast an anxious look at her parent. "I feel sure you will find many of your friends there, Mama."

"It is only ten evenings of balls, after all," Lady Mayne said with a sigh. "You have ordered enough white dresses? It will not do for you to be ill dressed."

"Yes, Mama." Harriet did not bother to explain that Madame Clotilde had decreed that her evening gowns would be the palest tints of peach or gold in silk jaconet, or lush cream satin. She doubted Mama cared as long as Harriet was decently covered and acquired a respectable number of partners at the assembly.

The following morning she donned the new green gown, with the upper sleeves slashed in white, the remainder, close fitting. Setting the wicked little hat on her head, she adjusted a few curls to caress her cheek, then made her way to the ground floor so to be there when Ferdy arrived.

Cupid pranced up to greet Ferdy the moment he stepped inside the house. A pert green riband adorned the dog's ruff and he looked quite proud of himself.

"Well, I am honored," Ferdy said reverently when he caught sight of Harriet in her splendid attire. "I shall be the envy of all my friends when they see us at the archery grounds."

"Not when they realize you have to teach me," Harriet shot back, bestowing an impish grin on her friend.

"As to that, you had best reserve judgment until after our lesson," Ferdy said with an answering grin that made Harriet more than a little suspicious.

The grounds, Ferdy explained as they jogged along in his carriage, had been moved a couple of years ago to the new location. When they entered, she found it was a lovely site with trees standing in the background like sentinels on guard. In various sections of the grounds, a number of targets had been set up awaiting the pierce of an arrow.

Ferdy's groom had followed behind with Betsy, carrying a large case that held bows and another smaller one holding arrows. Ferdy produced a number of other articles associated with archery and proceeded to explain their purpose, even as he placed them on Harriet's arm and hand.

"This first is a bracer, a protective device for your arm." He stood very close to Harriet as he strapped the leather, about eight inches long and finely crafted, around her left arm, just above her wrist.

She gazed up at him, noticing the laugh wrinkles about his eyes and the clean smell tinged with bay rum she associated with him. "I must say you look splendid in your green tailcoat and that feather in your hat is quite dashing."

He gave her a surprised glance and said, "'Tis standard wear on the archery green and we all abide by it."

"How fortunate you are that green becomes you so well," Harriet artlessly informed him. He merely grinned at her, his hazel eyes twinkling, a lock of his sandy hair flopping down over his forehead while he worked.

He pulled a strange glove from his pocket and proceeded to draw it over three fingers of Harriet's right hand. As Diana had said, it had leather tips into which she put her first three fingers, then Ferdy fastened the glove around her wrist with a leather strap.

All this necessitated his standing extremely close to Harriet, yet she felt there was nothing untoward in his behavior. It wasn't as though he flirted with her, using winks and leers and such. Oddly enough, for the first time in her life she actually wished a man *would* flirt with her, yet she doubted it would come about. He treated her like a sister.

"It is quite simple, actually," Ferdy began, capturing Harriet's wandering attention by handing her a bow. "You hold it thusly, the bow centered in your left hand. Then pull the string back with your right. Once you have nocked the arrow on the string, you merely take aim, using care to stand sideways to the target and in line with your point of aim. You aim at the center of the target," he added with what Harriet decided was a tinge of irony. It was not expected that a beginner hit the target in the center.

He picked up his own bow, a powerful-looking thing that he explained weighed a bit more than her lighter twenty-pound bow. Pulling an arrow from his quiver, he nocked it in the center of the string, then drew the string back toward his shoulder.

Harriet admired the picture he made in his green, the powerful bow in hand and him standing so tautly, concentrating on his mark. For all that he joked about his size, he was indeed a handsome gentleman. Or was she merely partial to sandy hair and hazel eyes in a man of great proportions?

She resolved that she would not only hit the target this morning, but that she would make that center area. She discovered she desperately wanted him to be pleased with her.

"In the reckoning, the gold earns you nine points, red earns seven, blue gains five, the black, three, and white, one point—this is part of the Prince's length and reckoning. You know, the Prince Regent was the one to standardize the distances, target size, colors, and values of hits. He was quite an enthusiastic archer and still comes once in a while—mostly to observe, but occasionally to hit a few. Of course, it is expected that men play, not women. I fear women are not taken very seriously as contestants."

"I expect we must work harder to prove ourselves . . . at least in archery. Show me again how it is done."

Ferdy obliged and Harriet watched closely. She held her bow in like manner, drew the string back, fumbling with her arrow a bit before she felt it secure. Then she let the arrow fly—and, to her great disappointment, it fell a yard short of the target.

"This time aim your arrow a trifle higher, as though you wanted it to go into the sky, creating an arc," Ferdy instructed patiently.

Firming her stance, Harriet pulled an arrow from the quiver attached to a belt that Ferdy had clasped around her waist and tried again.

"Gold? Nine points?" She couldn't believe her eyes. "That probably will never happen again," she said with a grin. "Beginner's luck."

"Maybe, and maybe not," Ferdy said, beaming at his apt pupil.

Harriet tried again, accustoming herself to the feel of the bow in her hand, the weight of the arrow, the pull of the string as she drew it back to her shoulder. She let the arrow fly and was disappointed, although not very surprised, when it hit the white portion of the target.

"Try again," Ferdy said after he demonstrated his stance and technique again.

Harriet obliged, then noted that several others had entered the grounds, carrying their bows, with quivers and other accessories at the ready. They greeted Ferdy, looking curiously at Harriet.

Taking their hints, Ferdy introduced her to each one as he came over. Taking pride in his pupil, Ferdy boasted, "She hit a gold on her second shot."

Harriet laughed and modestly added, "I doubt I shall duplicate that again anytime soon."

But the gentlemen seemed impressed and said so.

"Come, let us relax a few moments," Ferdy said when left alone, not counting Betsy and his groom, Norbert, who lingered a short distance away.

"All is going well?" he asked.

"Yes, your sisters are such dears. I know they are responsible for my vouchers for Almack's. Mama has agreed to go, for as she pointed out, it is for but ten weeks. Diana seemed displeased when she learned I'm to have no come-out ball, but I feel the vouchers more than compensate for that lack," Harriet said with more frankness than was her wont. With Ferdy, she found herself letting down barriers now kept stiffly in place around others. One could not behave the hoyden forever, especially when in Society.

"No come-out ball?" Ferdy said in surprise, fastening on the one thing that also displeased him. "I cannot think what they are about."

"Well, until you took me under your ample wing, I wasn't much to look at and scarcely merited such expense."

"I have seen the most platter-faced chits given balls, and you are far from that!" Ferdy exclaimed.

"Shall we continue?" Harriet suggested, unwilling to discuss the various balls given for ill-visaged young women.

"I must say, you appear to have a natural ability for the bow," Ferdy declared after she had shot a goodly number of arrows, hitting the target every time, although not in the gold again.

"Perhaps it is my love for doing things out of doors rather than being cooped in the house," she confessed.

"Emma said you are going to sing next Thursday at her musicale. I trust you are not anxious regarding it."

"You, too? Diana said much the same thing. I sing and they listen. If they enjoy my voice, fine. I refuse to allow the butterflies to overcome me," Harriet said, smiling at her friend.

At this point, just as Harriet was about to let fly another arrow, a party entered the grounds. The center of this group was an extremely large gentleman arrayed in the most resplendent of green garb imaginable. Harriet gawked, shutting her mouth just in time. "Who's that?" she whispered.

Ferdy failed to reply, doffing his hat and bowing low to the approaching gentleman even as he whispered, "Curtsy!" to Harriet.

Not stupid, Harriet sank into a proper curtsy after recalling what Ferdy had said about the Prince of Wales being a member of the Toxophilic Society. She just hadn't believed he was quite that enormous. It was a good thing that she had her bow for support, for the group paused before Ferdy and herself.

"You are enjoying a day in the sun with your archery?" the prince asked of Ferdy. "And who is this young charmer, may we inquire?"

"May I present Miss Harriet Mayne, Your Royal Highness," Ferdy replied. Then he added, "She is learning the sport and seems most gifted, having hit a gold on her second attempt."

Harriet flashed a minatory glance at Ferdy, but said nothing other than to murmur her pleasure at meeting the royal personage.

"Charmed, we are sure," his Royal Highness said, inspecting Harriet as though he intended to purchase her. At least, that was how she felt. "Not only is she pretty, she has a dog to match. Dashed clever of her, we'd say." He chuckled, then turned to the others, adding, "I feel that someday we shall welcome women into our ranks as skilled bowmen."

"Indeed, sir," Ferdy replied, looking amazingly at ease while conversing with the first gentleman of Europe, as he was often styled.

"Come, my dear, demonstrate Ferdy's ability as a teacher," the prince commanded.

Quelling resentment at being spoken to as though she were

beetle-headed, Harriet took proper stance, raised her bow, carefully nocked her arrow, and tautly drew her bowstring while saying a little prayer, held it a second, then let her arrow fly at the target.

"You may open your eyes now, for you hit the gold again," Ferdy said quietly, with a note of triumph in his voice quite as though he had been the one to hit center target.

"Capital!" the Prince exclaimed. Turning to the others in his entourage, he said, "You see, here is a woman with *possibilities.*"

They dutifully laughed at his sally, then drifted along to the other end of the grounds where they set up to shoot.

"I doubt I shall better that one, at least today," Harriet said once she had resumed breathing normally again.

"We shall make you a true Toxophilite, a lover of the bow," Ferdy declared quietly but fervently. "And with your obedient little dog at your heels, you shall create a niche for yourself."

"You do not think that word of this shall reach others?" she said in alarm.

"Of course," Ferdy said wryly. "The Prince Regent is a great gossip. I have no doubt that by tomorrow the word of your marvelous accomplishment will be all over London—at least the part that counts."

"Is that good or bad?" Harriet wanted to know, holding her bow against her as though it might ward off evil.

Ferdy didn't know how to answer her question. It all depended on what Prinney said and the inflection in his voice at his recitation of the event. Society might laugh at their fat prince, but he still had influence. "We shall see," he temporized. "At any rate, you will be certain to earn an invitation to the Toxophilite ball this spring."

"I shall like that. Do the ladies wear green then?"

"Of course. What else?" Ferdy said jokingly.

She assisted in putting things away, wanting to know the proper procedures for future use. From time to time she glanced at the prince's party, worrying a trifle about what the prince might say in regard to her shooting and having Ferdy as her mentor. Though she had her maid and his groom in constant attendance, it still could be made to sound *fast,* and no young woman making her come-out wanted that label.

"Will you come with me again?" Ferdy demanded as they walked to the gate.

"I hoped you might ask." She thought a bit and before entering his carriage she looked up at him. "Ferdy, I have a bit of money of my own and I should wish to pay my way," she stubbornly declared. "I'd not like to have it known that you purchased my bow and arrows. Moreover, I should like to join this club, if it is possible. Or must I come as your guest?" she wondered, knowing that many clubs forbade women members.

"Well, I'd like to make you a present of the equipment, but perhaps we may reach a compromise. Allow me to think about it? And I will look into the matter of club membership for you, if that is agreeable, Miss Independent."

"I'm sorry if I sound ungrateful or independent or anything I am not. Really, I am most appreciative. Archery promises to offer me an excellent opportunity to rid myself of blue devils. It must be amazingly refreshing to the spirits." She smiled at him, then prepared to enter his carriage.

As he assisted her into his landau, Ferdy wondered at the strength of his feelings regarding this young woman. Never before had it bothered him that a young lass be neglected by her parents. He wondered if perhaps they had merited the neglect. The Harriet he knew was a girl of rare courage and spirit, uncomplaining and kind. He resented her parents and Society for allowing such things to happen to nice people.

Joining her in the carriage, he glanced at her green-garbed figure, so slim and pretty, and resolved that he would make a difference in her life. Not that he intended to marry the girl, but he would see to it that she had a Season never to be forgotten!

The matter settled, he chatted with Harriet on the return to the Mayne house, covering topics of general interest, feeling enormously pleased with himself. This was going to be one excellent Season; he felt it in his bones.

Chapter Six

"**Y**ou intend to go to Almack's?" Emma cried, giving her brother a highly astonished look. "But you never go to Almack's. You said that those insipid young women gave you the headache."

"Well, when I told Sally Jersey that Harriet is making her come-out and I wanted to be certain that everything went well, she suggested that were I to be there in person, I would be able to vet her partners. And you must admit that with her dowry she makes a tempting target for a fortune hunter." Ferdy paced back and forth in Emma's pretty drawing room, while that surprised woman reclined on her backless sofa, hands in her lap, unable to move in wonderment.

"I have underestimated Sally," Emma murmured. "How utterly clever she is."

"Dashed right," Ferdy agreed, but most likely for a different reason.

"Did Sally suggest you lead Harriet out for her first dance—just to let those unsavory chaps know that she is protected?" Emma asked with a guileless expression on her face.

"No, but it might be a good idea," he mused. "Actually, there are a number of fellows who would make a dashed good husband for any girl. Of course, I don't know if they will attend come Wednesday."

"Well," Emma said in an offhand manner while pleating her muslin gown in studied disinterest, "you might drop a hint or two to your bosom chums."

"Just the ticket. I shall head off to the clubs at once. Say, I am glad we had this chance to talk. You know, you have a

pretty good head on your shoulders," he concluded with a hint
of admiration in his deep voice.

Emma laughed. "Well, after all, we are related."

Relaxed and feeling pleased with the world, Ferdy joined in
the laughter, then took his leave of his dear sister and whisked
himself off to his club, thinking that this time of day he might
know success.

He found almost every chap he wished to see at White's,
and the rest he casually happened on at Brook's and Jackson's.
Most of the gentlemen were good-natured enough to agree
without questioning; the rest either owed Ferdy a favor or
money. They could be counted for their presence without argument.

Thus it was that as the shy aspirants to the state of marriage
entered the sacred portals of Almack's that Wednesday
evening, they discovered a far larger than usual number of
gentlemen—men of excellent position not normally found at
the banal assemblies. They had only been sent tickets in the
forlorn hope they might grace the dances to augment the admittedly scarce ranks of superior gentlemen partners.

Harriet entered, made her curtsies, and privately thought
that Lady Jersey had certainly given her a strange look. Calculating? Harriet concluded that the lady was as shrewd as reputed. And she certainly had seemed at first oars with Ferdy!
Why, she flirted with him in the most outrageous manner that
Harriet thought quite dreadful. And she a married woman.

The lilting music of a reel ended and Harriet looked about
uneasily, wondering how long it would be before she had a
partner. Ferdy she discounted, for had he not mentioned that
he was not overly fond of dancing? Thus she was greatly surprised when he approached her mother with a request for Harriet's hand in the next dance.

"Well, are you pleased?" Ferdy said when it was possible.
"Your gown is smashing and I must say—you are in first
looks."

"It is lovely to be here," Harriet agreed, willing herself not
to blush. She had been delighted with her reflection in the
looking glass. The lush cream satin gown, its hem edged in
delicate scallops and trimmed with the tiniest of bows and silk

roses, with slightly larger roses nestled becomingly at the front of her bodice, became her more than any gown she'd ever owned. It seemed fitting that she wear it for such an auspicious occasion. "And I am pleased you like my gown. I hold you partly responsible, for it was Diana who succeeded in persuading Madame Clotilde to take charge of me."

"Word is out about your success at the archery grounds, you know," he confided the next time they drew close in the pattern of the dance.

"Is that good or bad?" she inquired uncertainly. For all she knew she could be in the soup for shooting so well before the Prince Regent. One had to be cautious about those things.

"Apparently His Highness did well enough at the bow and butt that he was not offended by your success. When he achieves a respectable score, he is in a good mood."

"Aren't we all?" she murmured, then laughed at Ferdy's grimace.

Those who had observed the outing with the children and the splendid sailboat, then heard about the rides in the park, culminating in the episode with the Prince Regent at the archery grounds, bent their heads together and gossiped. Sally Jersey drifted about the room, dropping her opinions here and there to stir the pot a bit. By the end of the first set, all the young men felt perfectly at ease in asking Harriet to dance, figuring she was as good as betrothed to their old friend.

Her coming-out at Almack's was a roaring success—to her mother's amazement. Not one dance was spent in pained seclusion against the wall of the room; Harriet whirled from one partner to the next in laughing confusion, vivid green eyes sparkling, her saucy golden-red curls teasing. If one of those men paid the slightest attention to the smattering of freckles on that adorable nose, it would have been a wonder.

Diana and Emma frequently consulted each other, exchanging congratulatory looks. They politely answered the questions posed by those gossips who sought their sides.

"We dearly love Harriet," Diana said when one madam dared to question the admission of an undistinguished redhead to the ranks of the elite. "And she has a perfectly lovely voice.

She is to sing tomorrow evening at Emma's musicale, you know."

Since everyone knew that Lady Wynnstay asked only those of highest ability to perform at her affairs, the gossips were suitably impressed and Harriet's stock rose a notch higher.

When Ferdy sought Harriet's hand for his second dance, he almost had to fight to reach her side. It was not surprising, since with her ready smile and absence of affectations, she was so unlike the pitifully shy and correct young maidens who frequented Almack's. Once the chaps clustered about her realized that it was Ferdy who wanted in, they fell back, allowing their large and powerful friend easy access.

"Oh, Ferdy," Harriet whispered, her eyes aglow as she walked at his side onto the dance floor, "this is far more fun than my sisters said. I do not understand why they insisted I would be miserable here. I adore it. Of course, I owe it all to you," she concluded artlessly. Ferdy looked alarmed until she added, "Had you not sought me out for the first dance, I doubt so many gentlemen would have asked me to partner them."

He relaxed and actually enjoyed romping down the line of a Scot's reel. He followed this effort by escorting Harriet to the refreshment room so that he might quiz her about her reactions to the various gentlemen.

However Harriet had no favorites; she simply reveled in the association with so many nice gentlemen.

"I fear I do not understand it in the least," her mother complained on their way home. "Neither Victoria nor Coralie had as many partners as you did on their first night at Almack's and they are incomparables. Gentlemen's taste must have altered this past year." That she revealed her partiality for her two eldest daughters with these words, so like her in character and looks, she seemed unaware.

"Be thankful I have been befriended by Mr. Andrews and his dear sisters. I owe them a great deal," Harriet concluded modestly. "I look forward to singing at Emma's musicale tomorrow evening—no, tonight, for it has grown late, hasn't it?" she said in wonder.

"*You* are to sing? I trust you will spare me the need for accompanying you. I always suffer the headache at those affairs." Lady Mayne gave Harriet a pained look.

Accustomed to being neglected by her family in any and all matters, Harriet pointed out that Lady Wynnstay would be with her, and leaned against the squabs to savor the success of her first appearance at the renowned Almack's. It seemed very likely that she would not be sent off to Aunt Croscombe, nor endure marriage to the offensive Lord Pomeroy if she would be able to capture the attention of one of those gentlemen she had seen tonight. She couldn't decide whom she liked best. She ought to consult Ferdy, for he would surely know.

Ferdy had been so thoughtful and attentive. How the other girls must have envied her. That he had not danced with any of them was puzzling until she realized that most of those creatures were mere dabs and most likely would have been lost beside the very large and possibly intimidating Ferdy. If only they might know what a marvelously gentle man he was. How fond she was of him—exceedingly fond.

For the Wynnstay musicale Harriet donned a new oyster white gown of embroidered glacé silk. The tiny puffed sleeves were especially pretty and the exquisite embroidery of white silk twist on the luscious fabric looked demure, yet ravishing, as Emma declared when she clapped her eyes on Harriet.

"I thought since the decoration was chiefly on the bodice that it would be a good gown to wear when I sing," Harriet explained, twirling about for approval. "It is always nice to perform when one believes oneself to be in first looks," Harriet confided brightly. Then she turned to greet her teacher, Signor Carvallo, a gray-haired, dark-skinned gentleman of short, portly proportions, immaculately groomed. He went immediately to the pianoforte to test the sound and touch of the instrument. He appeared pleased.

The gathering of musically inclined socialites filtered into the large Wynnstay drawing room at a desultory pace, more or less ignoring Harriet. Once settled on their gilt chairs, they listened raptly to the harpist who was first to entertain. That she was exceptionally skilled and played favorite pieces added to their pleasure.

The next to perform was the talented Felicia, Lady Entwisle, brilliantly coaxing music forth from the pianoforte with the skill of a professional pianist.

As she concluded her modest program, it was Harriet's turn. Butterflies rampaging through her stomach, she nevertheless posed calmly by the instrument, giving Signor Carvallo a nod when she was ready.

The pure tones of her exquisite soprano voice immediately captured all the attention of the musical devotees. Her first number was a simple piece composed by Haydn. "My Mother Bid Me Bind My Hair" had never had a better rendering in Emma's considered opinion. This piece was followed by "I Have a Silent Sorrow Here" from *The Stranger* with the music by Georgianna, Duchess of Devonshire and the words by Richard Brinsley Sheridan. It was not one of Emma's favorites, although those attending seemed to like it, perhaps with remembered affection for the duchess. Yet Emma admitted it was flawlessly sung by Harriet. Two selections by Charles Dibdin—"The Joys of the Country" and the soaring and technically difficult "The Soldier's Adieu"—concluded her program. Harriet prepared to return to her chair, accompanied by enthusiastic applause.

Emma hurried to her side. "You must sing another song, please, dear Harriet. I'd not have you disappoint my guests," she begged with an engaging smile.

Harriet turned to the signor with a questioning look.

"The Lucky Escape," he said quietly, referring to another favorite by Dibdin. He began the introduction, silencing the buzz of the group. Harriet lightly clasped her hands before her and lifted her head to sing.

In the shadows at the rear of the room Ferdy proudly surveyed the discriminating gathering of those who were of the highest musical taste. Had he produced Harriet Mayne from thin air he could not have felt more her creator. Golden-red curls framed a face that held a delightful sweetness and no one could detect the hated freckles with the dusting of powder Emma had suggested.

Harriet's lilting voice soared with seemingly no effort through the gay little song. Ferdy decided he could come to enjoy musicales were they all of this caliber. At the final note, the silence in the room was broken by spirited acclaim.

At the conclusion of the song, Harriet made her slow but determined way past the gilt chairs filled with appreciative listeners who demanded more. However, refusing with polite resolution to sing another song, she continued to the rear of the room, cheeks abloom with the heady acclaim.

That she was pleased her performance had been admired was unmistakable to Diana. A smirk of pleasure crossed Diana's face when she saw Harriet greet Ferdy at the back of the room. Harriet simply glowed with delight. Diana might have found even more cause for satisfaction had she overheard their exchange.

"Ferdy, you came." Harriet extended her hands to clasp his. "I am so pleased to see you," she added with an uncharacteristically shy drop of her gaze.

"Well, I am pleased to be here, I can tell you that. I had no idea what I would have missed had I gone to White's instead. You sing dashed well, Harriet."

Try as she would, Harriet could not prevent the blush that she felt flood her face.

"Now, do not go into a taking." Ferdy placed a brotherly hand on her bare shoulder, quickly withdrawing it as though burned. In addition to a deuced fine voice, Harriet possessed satiny skin that felt far too good to his fingers. His hand had brushed her curls, their silken strands caressing his skin, making him wish that he had a reason to explore those curls at greater length.

"Well, at least I didn't mangle the notes," Harriet said, peeping up at him with her winsome smile firmly in place.

Ferdy laughed, the odd stirrings he'd felt fading into the back of his mind. He stood close to her while they listened to the excellent rendition of a Mozart German dance arranged by Signor Carvallo for Lord Strahan, a talented flautist.

The gathering rose following this concluding music and drifted along to the dining room where a splendid collation was arranged for them. Ferdy and Harriet slowly followed in their wake, soon joined by Diana, Emma, and Lord Wynnstay.

"You are fortunate," Diana bubbled, "to secure the signor as your teacher. He is most skillful and I have heard marvelous things about his abilities."

"I hope you will favor us with your singing at the next of our musicales," Lord Wynnstay said, earning a pleased look from his wife.

"If you wish, I shall be happy to sing again," Harriet said simply, seemingly unconscious of her superb talent.

Ferdy, seeing how oblivious she appeared, reckoned her family had either never listened to her or not cared that she had a voice like an angel. He watched as she graciously walked to the signor, attending to him as though she were the merest cipher in the musical world instead of a promising soprano of remarkable gifts.

"You failed to tell me that your little protegé has such talent," Edmund, Lord Wynnstay, remarked to Diana and Emma.

"Well," Emma confessed after glancing at her sister, "we heard her sing but once, and that before a few ladies. We only hoped that she might do well before a large group."

"Heaven help us," he replied with a laugh. "Does she possess any other skills?"

"Dances like a dream," Ferdy unexpectedly offered. "She's as light as thistledown and much more fun."

The laughter generated by this remark drew a number of others to their group and the topic was necessarily changed.

By the time of her departure, Harriet felt as though she had been nicely accepted into the world of London's music lovers—at least those present this evening, and it was a very large gathering, so large that she couldn't begin to count those clustered about in the diningroom and spilling forth into the hall and drawing rom.

Signor Carvallo shook her hand in gracious farewell, saying, "You did exceedingly well this evening, Signorina Mayne. There is nothing like a sympathetic audience to bring forth the best in a performer."

"I have acquired some fine and generous friends, I believe," Harriet said modestly. She turned to find Ferdy at her shoulder, looking somewhat forbidding by means of his sheer size. Then he smiled and both the signor and Harriet returned that smile, for there was something infectious about Ferdy's pleasure.

"Your maid is here?" Ferdy asked once the signor had gone and they were relatively alone, if you discounted the people milling about the rooms.

"Yes, and Diana said she would drop us off on her way home. Your family is most kind," Harriet observed, not accustomed to a family which was other than self-absorbed.

"I would take you, but I fear it might cause talk."

Harriet giggled, slanting a grin at Ferdy. "Heaven forbid any more gossip than already floats about."

"You are becoming a minx," Ferdy admonished.

"Well, as I recall, I did tell you I was a horror as a child. You were warned," Harriet said, causing them to laugh together.

"I shall demand a round at the Archery Grounds on the morrow for that," Ferdy joked.

"I can't promise I shall hit the gold twice in one session as I did last time. But I would enjoy trying again if you are willing to teach me."

"Hah, you have natural ability, my girl," Ferdy riposted.

Harriet carried an inner glow all the way home. It lingered in her room at the mere thought of being Ferdy's girl, never mind that it had been said in jest. It was merely a very lovely thought, that was all.

Like many performers, Harriet was still in alt over the evening and her success in singing. She had never been in better voice, and she wondered a little at that. Perhaps it was as the signor said, she had sung to a sympathetic audience. If that was the case, she could only hope for more of such.

Once in bed with her head reclining on her plump pillow, she fell asleep dreaming of a smiling Ferdy, her own gentle giant.

The Archery Grounds were nicely groomed and had a smattering of bowmen at various points, bows aimed at the multicolored butts. The thunk of arrows echoed in the pleasant morning air.

Garbed in her hunter green dress Harriet, with Betsy in tow, walked beside Ferdy as he strode down the gravel path until they reached a vacant spot. His groom set out their bows and arrows while Betsy took a seat on a stone bench behind them.

"Do you think you can hit the target after your smashing success last evening?" Ferdy teased.

"I do not have a swelled head, if that is what you mean," Harriet retorted. She took her bow in hand, assumed the proper stance, nocked her arrow, and aimed.

"Blue," Ferdy said quietly. "Not too bad, five points for you." He proceeded to hit the gold center.

"We are keeping score this morning?" Harriet asked in mild alarm.

"Why not? It will put you on your mettle. You seem to like a challenge." Ferdy studied the trim figure in green, then added, "You did well last night, you know. Impressed ever so many of the musical crowd. Emma was in alt over your success."

"Well, and that is very nice of her. I feel privileged to be permitted to sing for such august company." Harriet raised her bow again to take aim. "Ah, red, this time. That gives me seven more points, I believe."

"Nothing wrong with your memory, is there?" Ferdy said, then took aim and also hit the red.

"Will you sing again?" He waited while Harriet took aim and noted that she hit black, earning but three points.

"Yes, I suppose so. Do you think I might look amongst that set for a husband?" Harriet asked as she prepared to take her next turn.

Ferdy's arrow missed the target completely and landed in the turf beyond the butt. He muttered something Harriet couldn't hear, which was probably just as well given his provocation.

"I thought I would seek your opinion, for you have a better notion of these gentlemen than I might," she continued. "I would ask George or Papa, but they seem to think I ought to be pleased to accept Lord Pomeroy and I'd rather run away than do that. And I *refuse* to go to Aunt Croscombe."

Ferdy selected another arrow as though it were a momentous matter, then looked at Harriet in a most considering way. "Just be careful. Don't choose some nodcock."

"Of course I'd never do such a thing deliberately," she countered, slightly annoyed that he might think her so shatter-brained. "I merely sought your opinion because it is important to me," she explained patiently.

"Important, is it?" Ferdy grumbled without knowing why he was irritated by the entire subject of Harriet finding a suitable husband. Naturally, he agreed that she must never marry that rank old fool Pomeroy. And he certainly did not want her sent off to a vicious harpy of an aunt. Yet, he confessed inwardly that he felt Harriet needed someone special, someone who could make her laugh, and do nice things for her. She had been given precious little attention in her young life to date. She deserved more from life than a humdrum marriage. It would take a bit of consideration, he decided and told her so.

"Well, I do not see why," she snapped back when he informed her that he had to think about it. "Surely there must be a gentleman you favor."

"Dash it all, Harriet, that is just it. Nearly every chap that comes to mind has some fault to him. Thought about Sir Percival Leadbitter, but decided you might not like the name—and the chap is a trifle dim, although nice enough. And there is Jason—Lord Titheridge, you know. But you might object to his voice—he's a tenor and squeaks and has an unfortunate laugh that I don't mind, but you might. You see how it is?"

"Could it be that you accept a man as a friend but cannot see him married? Especially to me?" she asked in a quiet little voice.

"Now I've done it," Ferdy said, disgusted with himself. "I've gone and hurt your feelings and I never wanted to do something like that. You must know that I'd sooner do anything than hurt you, Harriet?"

Not immune to a plea from nice hazel eyes that peered engagingly from under the sandy hair that flopped over his brow, Harriet smiled. Ferdy visibly relaxed.

She took aim and hit the gold again, sighing with pleasure when she saw where her arrow had landed. "I suppose I shall just have to follow my instincts."

Ferdy gave her an alarmed look before raising his bow to shoot. He hit the white band and lowered his bow in disgust. "I am not so sure about instincts," he cautioned. "I imagine they could lead you astray."

"Well, it was my instincts that told me to trust you," she countered. "And I am ever so pleased that I did for I met your wonderful nieces and nephews and your charming sisters and brother-in-law. He is quite elegantly smashing, you know," she confided.

"You like elegant gentlemen?" Ferdy inquired with a note of frost in his voice. He took aim and hit dead center.

"Not necessarily. I would prefer a husband with whom I might find many things in common and feel comfortable about. I am not elegant, you see, and I might not know how to act with a man like Lord Wynnstay. He is nice, but I wouldn't want to marry him."

She hit white, then Ferdy hit gold again.

At this point a gentleman chanced to come along who knew Ferdy and paused to chat, eyeing Harriet all the while. Of course, Ferdy felt obligated to introduce his friend. The chap was well to grass and fairly good to look at, he supposed. He certainly seemed to admire Harriet. Seems he had been watching from a distance.

"I say, Miss Mayne, you are a champion bowman. Ferdy had best look to his laurels," Mr. Tooke declared with admiration. "A bit of a contest, eh?"

"Well he is my instructor, so I had better not be horrid," Harriet said with a laughing glance at Ferdy.

"Never knew you to give lessons, old chap," Mr. Tooke said, looking from Ferdy to Harriet and back again.

"Well, she was interested and certainly has proven to be an excellent student. She may beat me yet." Ferdy picked up his bow and nocked an arrow in the string.

Mr. Tooke proved no slowtop and said good-bye, walking briskly along to his group. Harriet hit blue.

"Now we are in for it," Ferdy murmured.

"How so?" Harriet said quietly.

"That fool is the worst gossip I know. Word of our little contest will be all over London before you can say boo."

"I thought women were the gossips to fear?" Harriet said, looking to where Mr. Tooke now stood chatting with his friends.

"Don't fear Tooke, precisely. But it could cause you complications were your name to be linked with mine unduly."

Harriet considered what her friend had said and decided that she didn't mind that in the least, yet she didn't know how to tell him that without scaring him clear to the next county. "Well," she concluded at long last, "I would not worry about it. The worst is that we are a nine days' wonder." She took aim and grinned when she hit red.

Ferdy missed the target again and glared at Harriet as though it was her fault.

"Are you keeping track of our scores? I do believe I am ahead of you at this point."

"By two points," he admitted.

"See what a marvelous teacher you are?" she said with an infectious chuckle.

"I can only hope you pay attention to everything I tell you," Ferdy countered with a more serious look.

"We shall see," she countered, not promising a thing.

Ferdy frowned and took aim again.

Chapter Seven

"**Y**ou *must* learn how to waltz," Diana said giving a bounce on the backless sofa in her enthusiasm for the latest kick in dances.

"But the ladies at Almack's disapprove," Harriet objected. "Even I know you do not court their displeasure." She thought a bit, then asked, "Are you taking lessons?"

"Oh, both Emma and I know how, as do our husbands. In fact, Damon quite enjoys it. He never misses a waltz with me. Although he won't hear of me dancing it with anyone else," Diana confessed with a little smile.

The dangerous and wicked waltz had become more and more accepted at even the more proper balls. Countess Lieven was skilled in the dance, having brought her notions and abilities from Germany. But could she dare to introduce it to Almack's, that temple of Society? She had successfully introduced it elsewhere, but to persuade the other patronesses to permit waltzing at the snobbish establishment that considered itself the last bastion of British refinement seemed questionable. Rumor had it that Lady Jersey had her own ideas—and they didn't include the waltz.

Harriet had longed to learn the wicked dance, but her sisters declared it quite unnecessary, feeling it was unlikely that she would ever attend the *tonnish* parties and balls where it would be performed. Harriet turned to the more sedate Emma, raising inquiring brows. "Emma?"

"I agree. In fact, I thought you knew how to waltz as you skim through every other sort of dance with ease. It seems that being a hoyden as a child has a beneficial side, for you are indeed graceful. I shall have to remember that with Jane."

Glancing at Diana, Emma added, "Jane shows signs of incipient hoydenism."

"Good for her," Diana said, looking very unlike a young matron with three children. "I shall encourage Anne to do likewise. I detest these silly little girls with all their die-away airs and smelling salts."

"Society praises them, however," Emma reproved. "A bit of independence is not harmful. Yet one must not permit it to grow out of hand, that is all. Now, to Harriet. You are agreeable to lessons?"

"Does Ferdy approve?" Harriet said, then bit her lower lip in apprehension. "I will not do anything to which he objects."

The sisters exchanged glances, then Emma said, "Ferdy—my dear innocent—is the premier waltzer in the family. He may be a very large man, but he is very light on his feet, as you must have observed during that Scot's reel at Almack's."

"Well, then, I expect it would be most acceptable." Harriet looked from one sister to the other, not missing the impish gleam in Diana's pretty eyes, nor Emma's upward quirk at the corner of her mouth.

"We will consult our brother as to a suitable teacher," Emma said primly, setting her teacup on the table before her.

"You cannot teach me?" Harriet said warily.

"No, no, for a lady dances the reverse of the gentleman and it would not be at all the thing for one of us to practice that way—in fact, it might undo our skills," Diana explained readily.

Before Harriet could point out that they might stand side by side, thus eliminating the need to bother Ferdy or hire a teacher, the sound of steps on the stairs heralded the arrival of another guest.

Emma rose to cross to the door. A sigh of relief was detected when her brother entered the room like a wind from the east.

"What's afoot? Your missive indicated I am needed?" Then he caught sight of Harriet and his expression softened. "It is all over town that you beat me yesterday. You would scarcely believe the twitting I have had to endure since then."

"Poor man," Harriet said demurely. "What on earth did you say in reply?"

"I declared it was proof of my ability as a teacher!" he said in triumph. "Of course, now I shall have to endure all manner of fools wanting lessons."

Diana popped up from where she had perched and crossed in swift steps to confront her brother. "Speaking of teaching, we were wondering if you would recommend a good instructor for the waltz. Harriet has not yet learned it!" Diana declaimed these last words in horrified accents that made Harriet chuckle.

"It is not as though I cannot dance all the other required steps," Harriet objected, even though she dearly wished to learn the new dance.

"You cannot have just anyone teach you," Ferdy insisted, pacing across the room to lean his tall and considerable frame against the fireplace mantel.

"We would never dream of hiring someone of whom you disapproved," Diana said, that suspicious gleam still lurking in her eyes.

"Why do I not teach her? Emma can play a waltz on the pianoforte while I do the pretty with Harriet. She learns deuced quickly, I must say. Bound to catch on to the waltz in no time at all. What do you say, Harriet. Are you game?"

Considering the trouble the sisters had gone to arranging this lesson just for her, Harriet decided she had to accept. And besides, she wanted to. From what she had heard it might be scandalous, but it sounded like fun.

She rose from her chair and extended her hand. "Lead on, oh teacher of everything and anything. You did so well at archery, you must be smashing at the waltz."

Emma scurried over to the pianoforte and opened the conveniently placed music. In moments, the delicate notes of a very pretty waltz flowed into the drawing room in perfect tempo.

Ferdy ignored his sister's music to take Harriet by the hand and commenced explaining the basic idea of the dance. He then demonstrated his steps and showed her how she was to follow him. It seemed perfectly simple to Harriet—just one, two, three and circle around as you go.

She was wrong. Very, very wrong, indeed. For one thing,

she hadn't taken into consideration how close she would be to
Ferdy, nor the sparkle of mischief that lit those hazel eyes
when he looked at her from his great height. As for his arm en-
circling her waist, his hand holding hers ever so gently, and
her own reaction to all of this, well, it was a good thing she
was made of stern stuff.

"Now, begin again, Emma, and not too fast at first," Ferdy
ordered. "Now, my dear Harriet, off we go."

And off they went, slowly circling the room, Ferdy skill-
fully avoiding furniture he had instructed Diana to leave in
place, because they could serve as pretend couples.

Harriet scarcely knew what to think. Her wits were decid-
edly scrambled, but somehow the notion that she could happily remain in Ferdy's arms forever took root. She stumbled.

"Now, don't hit the white nor miss the target altogether,"
Ferdy admonished. "Aim for the gold, my dear, that's the
ticket."

Amused by his likening waltzing to archery, Harriet concentrated on her feet and the steps, feeling the rhythm and relax-
ing in Ferdy's light clasp.

"Lovely," he said softly. "I thought you would be a natural,
just as you are at archery. Clever girl."

Harriet felt as though she had just won a marvelous contest.
She was exhilarated and pleased that Diana and Emma had
cared enough for her to concoct this delightful afternoon.
When Ferdy at last ceased the slow, sinuous revolutions about
the room, Harriet clasped her hands and looked from one to
another.

"What can I say, dear friends? Thank you, very, very much.
Of course if I am sent off to Aunt Croscombe, I shan't need
this skill, but perhaps Lord Pomeroy shall prevail after all."
Her lightly spoken words were not dismissed by her friends.

"Your parents again?" Diana guessed, dropping down on
the backless sofa to stare at Harriet in dismay.

Harriet nodded. "In spite of my success at Almack's, Papa
brought up the matter at breakfast this morning. If I did not
know Papa was not a gambler, I would think he owed Lord
Pomeroy a vast sum of money and hopes to repay the debt by
sacrificing me on the altar of atonement."

"I will nose around to see what I might learn," Ferdy said. "Meanwhile, if things become pressing, either Emma or Diana will take you in, should you need a place to hide."

"Indeed," Emma quickly declared, "we have an empty guest room as does Diana. And neither of us could bear to see you bound to that nasty old woman in Little Munden—wherever that may be up north."

"I believe it is somewhere you would rather not go," Harriet said, forcing a light smile to her lips.

"Well, you had best practice once again before Ferdy takes himself off to his club."

"Perhaps Diana and I could demonstrate some of the more clever variations to the waltz, just so you might know they exist," Ferdy said with a glance at his sister.

"Damon doesn't mind if I waltz with you, Emma?" Diana held out her hands to her brother and they began the waltz the usual way, then proceeded to create the changes of position, hands high over the head, waltzing side by side, and another where Ferdy held Diana's waist with both hands and she casually draped one hand over his shoulder while she held the other gracefully away from her.

Harriet watched avidly, studying each change. When the music ended, Ferdy turned to Harriet, hand out.

"Now it is your turn."

"I do not know," Harriet said hesitantly. No matter that she longed to try the variations, they appeared very daring.

"Good heavens, girl, it is 1812, not the Dark Ages," Diana said with a chuckle. "It's naught but fun."

That settled it for Harriet; she'd not be thought a quiz. She extended her arms even as Emma began the irresistible notes of the waltz.

The variations proved more seductive than the basic dance. Ferdy twined her about in his arms, then grasped her waist with both his hands. She remembered to hold one of her arms out, while attaining a better clasp on his broad shoulders. It brought her even closer to him and she found it was not merely his size that overwhelmed her. It was Ferdy himself, that inner, most fetching man that captivated Harriet.

The dance was perfectly splendid, but she found herself

weak-kneed and breathless when the music ceased. How she longed to lean against that tall, large gentleman and restore her poise. On the other hand, that might simply make it worse! She thanked him, then retired to the closest chair with shaken sensibilities.

"I meant to ask you if you would consider taking the children on another outing," Diana said sweetly to her good-natured brother, with a quick glance at Harriet. "You have such a marvelous way with them, and with Harriet to assist you, it would be easily done. The children simply adore you and they always managed to have such a splendid time," she concluded in a rush.

Harriet knew that whatever was planned, she would agree to go along. It was the least she could do for these dear ladies who had befriended her. She looked to Ferdy as well.

Ferdy studied the guileless faces turned toward him and shrugged. "What is it this time?"

"It should be your idea," Emma declared generously.

"Boating, then? I'll rent a boat and take the older children along. I'm afraid the younger ones might fall in the water and neither Harriet nor I have any desire to plunge into the river to rescue them."

"I will find a treat for the girls. Just the boys, if that is agreeable?" Diana said, clapping her hands with delight.

"You will help, Harriet?" Ferdy asked hesitantly.

"Of course. I quite like Edward, Harry, Timothy, and William. I hope Jane and Anne will not be too disappointed."

"We will take them for ices at Gunter's," Emma decided.

The Thames was relatively free of traffic upstream, Harriet discovered as their pretty boat sailed along the river's winding path. The boys behaved quite splendidly, knowing that if they were naughty their Uncle Ferdy was capable of turning them over his knee.

Harriet held her parasol to shield her delicate skin. It was the large silk one that had the tilting handle and knot of fringe at the top. Her straw bonnet tied with moss-green ribands and adorned with a tuft of feathers nicely shaded her face as well. Thank goodness the sheer muslin gown spotted with moss-green dots that Madame Clotilde urged her to take was delightfully cool and most comfortable. Unfortunately, the boat was not, fitted with wooden seats and the merest of cushions.

In spite of the lovely outing, she was most uneasy. For some odd reason, things had altered between Ferdy and her following that foray into waltzing. Being held in his arms had made her more aware of him as a man. Now she must do all she could to conceal that interest. The last thing he would want is to have yet another young miss sighing over him.

"Sit quietly," she urged four-year-old Timothy, the youngest of the boys. "It cannot be easy for your uncle to row against the current. Did you know that your mothers have sent along what promises to be a sumptuous picnic? I venture to say that we shall all enjoy it immensely."

"I'm hungry now," Timothy said by way of reply.

Harriet looked at Ferdy and he shook his head.

"No, dear, it isn't time yet."

"I am hungry *now*," Timothy said stubbornly. "And I wish to stop over there. That looks like a smashing place for a picnic and I cannot see why we can't stop *there*."

"Your uncle has made plans and we are not going to alter them. I happen to like his surprises and I'll not wish to spoil this one," Harriet said firmly.

Timothy gave her a surprised look. "Do you have a little boy?"

"Not yet, but I hope to have a little boy some day. And I intend to treat him as firmly as I'm treating you," she added.

Timothy thought over this bit of information, casting appraising looks at Harriet from time to time, then at last said, "I am *still* hungry."

Cupid nudged Timothy's knee, looking up at the boy with hopeful eyes. With a glance Timothy sought permission to pet the dog. Then after Harriet's nod, he proceeded to run his fingers through Cupid's ruff, scratching behind his ears.

"I am still hungry," Timothy grumbled.

"Aw, wait a bit," Harry said without mercy for a starving cousin. "I know there are ginger biscuits in the hamper and you wouldn't want to miss those," he said, subtly reminding

Timothy that were he punished, he might well lose out on a treat.

They rounded a bend in the river to reach a placid stretch of water with a grassy knoll to one side crowned with a splendid oak, a few apple trees behind it. In the distance a pleasant village could be seen. A bridge spanned the river there; carriages, drays, and riders busily crossing.

"Here we are. Now, Timothy, it was not such a horrid wait, was it?" Ferdy inquired as he nudged the boat to the shore. He clambered out, tugging the craft to a firmer rest. Harriet remained to assist the boys out one by one; then she handed the hamper of delicacies to Ferdy before holding out her parasol. She couldn't envision coping with exiting the boat and managing the parasol at the same time.

The very moment that she rose to step onto the shore, Cupid decided to jump overboard. The boat rocked just enough so that Harriet lost her precarious balance and over she went with a small scream.

She splashed into the cool water, sinking to the sandy bottom, feeling the pull of the current as it tugged at her, drawing her from the boat and the safety of the shore. The chill shocked her sun-warmed body and for precious moments she found it difficult to respond.

Then her lungs demanded air; her limbs propelled her upward to the surface where she floundered, trying to obtain her bearings. Her gown and petticoats tangled about her legs, making it far more difficult to swim than when she had enjoyed the shadowed pond on the Mayne Country estate clad in nothing more than her shift.

On the bank she could see Ferdy pulling off his boots. His coat lay discarded on the ground.

"For heaven's sake, do not jump in after me," she called to him when she could gather sufficient breath. "I can swim, if I can manage to cope with my clothes and bonnet." Her beautiful bonnet, she silently mourned. It had been so perfect for this dress. Ruined, as might be the spotted muslin, given the propensity for fabric to shrink at times. Her shawl had drifted off with the current and goodness knew where it might end up.

She didn't bother to untie her bonnet; it dragged behind her, held by its ribands. Rather, she concentrated on stroking her way around the boat and to the shore. The only problem with this plan was that a fairly strong current beneath the deceptively calm surface persisted in trying to carry her downstream. It proved difficult going, and by the time she struggled to climb from the river, she was exhausted. And dripping wet. And muslin was not known for its concealing properties.

Fortunately Ferdy had the presence of mind to be ready with a large blanket, holding it out as she managed to stand. She noted the expression on his face and rued her foregoing her stays today. It had promised to be an exceedingly warm day and with the thought of exercise, she had thought the freedom from the constricting stays would be welcome. Now, she was well aware that too much of her might be on view.

Quickly wrapping the blanket about her body under her arms, tucking the ends inside, she then untied her bonnet ribands and tossed it aside, consigning it to the rubbish heap. Her hair dripped down her face and she knew she looked an utter fright.

"Thank God you know how to swim," Ferdy exclaimed, wanting to hold the trembling Harriet in his arms, if only to warm her. She looked chilled to the bone and he could only hope that his sisters had included a beverage more potent than lemonade.

"It's a bit different than swimming in a pond," Harriet observed, not wanting to frighten the boys.

"You truly know how to swim?" William demanded.

"Had I not, I'd have either drowned or your uncle would have had to pull me out like a half-drowned cat," Harriet said lightly.

"I wish I knew how to swim," Edward said reflectively. "I mean, what if one of us had fallen? Why, we would have been halfway to the sea in no time."

Ferdy had found a towel tucked about some sandwiches and he used it to dry Harriet's curls. Within a few minutes his efforts, combined with the sun, had her hair reasonably dry, and curls tumbled over her head every which way in a manner that would have made Betsy shudder. The sun also served to bring out every freckle on Harriet's face, now free of its dusting of tinted rice powder. She looked like an adorable sprite.

He had wanted to touch her hair and this was an unexpected opportunity. Her curls were soft and springy, yet surprisingly silky. And this close he could count the freckles on that little nose of hers, given time. He dare not, but the notion intrigued him.

She seemed to be impervious to his touch, sitting calmly with an occasional shiver, which was quite understandable given her plunge into chilly water on such a warm day.

Harry studied her for a time, then said, "I should like to know how to swim, too. If we found a pool, could you teach us?"

At this, she looked up to meet Ferdy's gaze, giving him a helpless look. "I could teach, but I fear it would be rather improper, given one thing and another. Even if I could obtain a bathing costume, I understand there are none for gentlemen. Perhaps your uncle might find a way?"

Ferdy struggled to pull his mind from the image of a shapely Harriet clad in a shift—which is all she could have worn swimming, since she admitted she didn't own a bathing costume such as were used in the bathing machines at the seaside beaches. How fortunate that he was in the sun, and could attribute any coloration of his skin to its warmth.

"I shall put my mind to it and you will learn to swim before this summer is out, I promise."

"I am still hungry," Timothy reminded them. "Could we eat now?"

"Of course," Ferdy said briskly. "And I shall find something to warm Harriet—that is, Miss Mayne." Rummaging in the hamper, he came up with a flask of lemonade and a bottle of white wine.

Reaching for a glass, he poured out some wine, then thrust it into Harriet's still-cool hands. "Drink this while I see to the food."

The boys gathered around, each doing some little task. Soon a cloth was spread on the grassy slope beneath the oak tree and the china set out. Harriet sipped her wine while she watched, feeling as though she ought to help, yet knowing that given her garb and still-shaken state, she was better off just being quiet.

Leaning against the sturdy tree trunk, she feasted her eyes on Ferdy. Although he had not plunged into the river to pull her out, he had been prepared to do so. Didn't that make him some sort of hero? And he'd said nothing suggestive about her most likely shocking state when she'd emerged from the water. He was a gentleman, through and through. She'd trust him with her life, she realized.

Alas, she was nothing more than a burden to him. He'd picked her up like a stray kitten that needed a bit of care and feeding. He'd taken her to his sisters, taught her archery and waltzing—in aid of finding her a husband. And she in turn had grown far too fond of him.

But, she comforted herself, he was such a dependable, cheerful sort of man, concerned for her far more than her brother had ever been.

"At least this lovely parasol didn't end in the river," Ferdy said in an attempt to console her.

"I shall look a fright when we return," she observed, concerned as to what might happen when she entered her home looking like a drowned cat or worse.

The boys had quickly stuffed themselves, neither Ferdy nor Harriet having the energy to scold them for it. Now Ferdy glanced at where the lads were playing not far from the riverbank, yet not too close.

"Tell you what," he said quietly, "I will walk up to the village and see if a bonnet can be found, perhaps a shawl. If I am able to find a large one, we might be able to sneak you in the house with no one the wiser. Or for that matter, we could see what Diana or Emma can do."

"They have done so much for me already," Harriet objected, thinking of the many kindnesses from his sisters.

"Well then, I shall have a look around." He rose, then walked down to inform the boys of his plans.

The boys decided they wanted to explore the village and, with the boundless energy of children who have escaped the attentions of their nanny and are off with their favorite uncle, they scampered along at Ferdy's side toward the bridge that led into the village on the other side of the river.

The sun filtered through the wind-tossed leaves of the oak tree and the quiet gurgle of the water rushing past the pleasant and very private spot created a soothing sound. In short order, Harriet had snuggled into the blanket and fallen fast asleep.

When Ferdy returned, bonnet and scarf triumphantly in hand, he found her still sleeping, looking most vulnerable. Her surprisingly dark lashes fanned sweetly over her freckled skin and her rosebud mouth drooped slightly. He was tempted to drop a kiss on those delicious lips, usually tilted in a smile and now still. Then he remembered his young charges, and that he was nothing more than a guardian and benefactor of sorts to this young woman.

Unaware that she slept, the boys found a ball and began a noisy game. Harriet's long lashes fluttered, then flashed open to reveal startled vivid green eyes gazing up at Ferdy with an intensity he couldn't identify.

"Oh, I must have fallen asleep," she said needlessly, looking away in confusion. She pushed herself to a sitting position, then observed his purchases. "You found something!"

"There were two bonnet shops and this one looked like you," he said diffidently.

He produced the bonnet with the air of a conjurer. She exclaimed over the pretty straw trimmed in green ribands and yellow roses, insisting on putting it on her head at once. When she smiled up at him, looking well-pleased with his surprise, he brought the enormous shawl from the depths of the bag clasped in his hand.

He had happened on a little shop that catered to travelers. It carried valises, trunks, all manner of traveling impedimenta, and it also had a number of shawls on display. Why, Ferdy couldn't imagine. However, he was grateful and immediately bought the largest one. It was cream-colored and embroidered with pretty peach and salmon roses. On Harriet the shawl ought to be something special indeed.

She stood, examining the skirt of her gown, which was rumpled from being crushed while drying. Smoothing down her still faintly damp skirt, she said, "It could be worse, I suppose.

I believe this shawl will conceal the worst of me. Thank you so much for finding it."

Ferdy picked up the blanket where it had fallen. Worst of her? Somehow, he doubted if there was a *worst* side. She was a sprite, and that mischievous smile she bestowed on him suddenly made him want what he might not have.

"I'm pleased my parasol survived," she said, picking it up, opening it and twirling it behind her head.

"You make a lovely picture," Ferdy said without thinking.

That painful pink blush stained her cheeks as she looked at him, then down at the ground.

"You need to learn how to flirt," he exclaimed.

"I'm not the sort to flutter eyelashes," she shot back.

"Use your parasol," Ferdy replied. He explained what he had learned from his sisters when they were attempting to flirt. "They practiced on me. You may as well."

Giving him a dubious look, Harriet tried several of the things he mentioned, then peeked around the brim, shook her head, and collapsed on the ground, laughing. "I shall never be a flirt," she gasped when she might speak. Bestowing an engaging grin on her escort, she stared at him, blinked twice, and her laughter subsided. "And what is more, I do not know if I truly want to flirt."

He wondered if she knew that placing the handle on her lips, just as she did now, meant that she wished her escort to kiss her. He would be happy to oblige, were it true. Alas, he feared it was otherwise.

At that moment Cupid dashed up to his mistress, having enjoyed the walk to the village with the males and now wanting her attention. Then Ferdy turned away to speak to the boys and the moment was lost.

Harriet watched her gentle giant, as she thought of him, when he tossed the ball to Edward. There was a reason she wouldn't learn to flirt, but she refused to admit to it. It was far too shocking.

Chapter Eight

Both Emma and Diana were properly horrified upon hearing of the accident that had befallen Harriet.

Diana looked especially crestfallen and her brother, knowing her all too well, said, "You seem rather dismayed. Anything in particular?"

"No, that is, I feel dreadful over what happened to Harriet." Then she brightened, "But how fortunate you found her such a dear little bonnet and a marvelous shawl! Well!" She paused, giving him an appraising look. "It is just that I . . ."

"That you what?" Ferdy prodded in a deceptively lazy manner.

"I had so wanted the boys to go fishing again," she said in a rush. "When Harriet mentioned what fun it was, the idea took root and I had hoped that they might experience the joy of having their favorite uncle take them with him at least once more. And Harriet, of course." She slanted a glance at him and he didn't miss the impish gleam in her eyes.

Since Ferdy didn't mind taking Harriet anywhere they wished, he shrugged and said thoughtfully, "I suppose I might. But do not consider making a habit of these excursions. I do not propose to take over Nanny's job. Also, I would have to guarantee Miss Mayne that she wouldn't fall into the stream. And you had better make Timothy understand that a jaunt such as this is not simply a means of stuffing his face."

"No, he did not do such a thing! Really? How like his father," Diana said, gurgling with laughter.

Ferdy might have inquired why said father couldn't take the boys fishing, but since the outing suited his purpose so nicely, he ignored that bit to concentrate on the necessary. "Large hamper of food? A change of clothing should they take a tumble? Oh, and by and by, I am to also teach them how to swim—at their request. I shall investigate the Peerless Pool here in London. As to the fishing, just let me know a day in advance and I will make suitable arrangements."

"You are the dearest of brothers. Just think of what happy memories your nephews will have of this summer when they grow up," Emma said, giving her brother a hug.

Diana, not to be outdone, also danced up to give her sibling a devoted squeeze. "We are terribly grateful. To both of you."

"The girls will not mind?" he said, having a hunch that the girls had not complained about ices at Gunter's.

"Well, Jane longed to go fishing, but I explained about worms and she changed her mind," Emma said with a smile.

"Ladies, I bid you adieu until the morrow—when I expect you will find something else that needs my attention." He left the room, running lightly down the stairs and whistling as he went, then shutting the front door firmly behind him.

"He was smiling. That means he truly does not mind," Diana pointed out to her frowning sister.

"Well, I am suspicious. Why doesn't he complain? I should think he might suspect something by this time. Ferdy is certainly not stupid! I'll warrant he hasn't had much time to devote to his latest opera dancer—a beauty whom I believe is called La Fleur according to the gossips. Moreover, I know I'd never persuade Edmund to spend so much time with the children."

"I do not feel guilty in the least," Diana declared with a righteous tilt of her chin.

"Do you ever?" Emma said, smiling at her peagoose of a sister.

"And as far as La Fleur is concerned, let her find another dupe to support her," Diana said with a flounce. "I believe our brother's money could be spent in far better ways. Did you notice the bonnet he bought for Harriet? It was utterly precious and went very well with her dress. And that shawl—well, should Damon bring me something that lovely, I would be terribly pleased."

"I think Harriet seems happy—in spite of her dreadful tum-

ble into the water. It was the dog, you know. The silly animal
was just fine." Emma gave her sister a concerned look while
clutching her hands together in apprehension. "You do believe
it is acceptable for us to do . . . what we are doing? I mean, we
are rather devious."

"Look at it this way, we are merely giving two charming,
dear people a chance to spend some time together. If they happen to fall in love, or even just fondness, it is up to them, not
us. We are totally innocent, dear Emma."

"Quite so," Emma said with a relieved sigh. "Can you think
of anything we might encourage following the fishing expedition? How about tennis?"

"The children are too young for that," Diana pointed out reluctantly.

"What about a balloon ascension?"

"True, they would all enjoy that. Watch the papers to see if
one is planned soon." Diana walked over to peer out the window, then turned back to her sister. "I think they are to practice archery tomorrow. When you chaperon Harriet at the ball
this evening, you must try to see if she has any feelings at all
for Ferdy."

"How can she not?" Emma cried. "He is one of the best of
men."

"True," Diana said complacently. "What a pity Harriet has
such a nasty family. Can you imagine a mother not wishing to
oversee her daughter's come-out? Poor dear. However, it
works to our advantage, so here's to the selfish, snobbish Lady
Mayne!" Diana said, raising her hand in a mock toast.

Harriet walked at Ferdy's side in the cool environs of the
archery grounds until they reached a vacant place. The groom,
Norbert, set down the bows and arrows while Betsy seated
herself nearby, looking pleased that her mistress had such a
nice gentleman for a beau.

"There is going to be a contest come Saturday and I need a
bit of practice," Ferdy explained as he took his bow from Norbert and prepared to shoot.

"I do not suppose females are permitted to enter?" Harriet
asked in a manner that made it clear what reply she expected.

"I fear not," he said, seeming to understand Harriet's disappointment.

"It would be nice were they to have a contest that ladies might enter—just for their own amusement," she ventured.

He paused, giving her an arrested look. "I will suggest that to the chaps who are in charge this year. If not this year, perhaps next? Excellent idea. You had best practice as well if you entertain ideas of entering a contest," he suggested.

She fell to the task with a will, thinking that Ferdy Andrews had to be the nicest gentleman in all of London. She was intent on shooting when a friend of his joined them for a moment, chatting quietly with Ferdy off to one side. That it was a teasing, jocular conversation was easy to tell. What they said could not be heard from where she stood, and besides, she'd never eavesdrop. But she did wonder what had been said, given Ferdy's sudden look of annoyance and flush of anger.

They had been at the archery grounds for an hour and a half when Ferdy checked his watch. "We had best leave now. I'd not want to monopolize your time."

Since Harriet liked nothing better than to be with Ferdy, but couldn't say such a thing, she merely smiled and handed her bow to Norbert.

They drove back to the Mayne residence in an odd silence. Harriet was positive that the friend—whoever he was, for Ferdy had not introduced him—had said something to greatly upset Ferdy. He hadn't shot well, preoccupation most likely putting off his aim.

"You do not mind going fishing with the boys again, Harriet?" he asked when the carriage had come to a halt. "They are a handful, but my sisters seem to think this will be a summer they shall always remember—not to mention the uncle who made it possible for them or some such nonsense."

"I should like to go fishing with you—all of you, that is. The boys are great fun," she concluded, then hastily exited the carriage with Betsy hurrying after her. Harriet had the strangest feeling that while Ferdy was being polite, he was impatient to be gone, as though he had a pressing engagement he couldn't reveal to her.

Once inside her room, she thoughtfully took off her neat little hat trimmed with the green ribands and feathers. Handing it to Betsy, she said, "Did Mr. Andrews appear to be in a rush, did you think?" Normally she would never gossip with a servant, but Betsy had been there and she possessed a keen pair of eyes.

"Well, after what that gentleman said to him about some La Fleur being mad as hops at him, I guess he needed to mend his fences, he did." Betsy put away the hat and helped Harriet change her gown into a pretty cream sarsenet trimmed with green ribands.

"Oh!" Harriet had never heard of anyone called La Fleur, but she was not stupid. The name sounded much like something given to an opera dancer, and she would bet her next quarterly allowance that this particular opera dancer was the one in Ferdy's keeping. "I wonder what she looks like?" she mused out loud.

Cupid, delighted his mistress had returned, demanded her attention and a walk, not necessarily in that order. Giving him an affectionate caress, she affixed his leash and turned to her maid. "We had best be off. Perhaps we will see something of interest while we walk this animal. I vow I am tired of nursemaids and nannies, not to mention crying children."

They entered the park through Grosvenor Gate, then strolled toward the Serpentine, with Cupid making frequent pauses for investigation. Once they had reached the area of the Serpentine, Harriet allowed Cupid off his leash, for the park here was very quiet, nursemaids and nannies seeming to prefer Green Park that day. She found a pleasant tree under which she was content to sit with the book she'd brought along. Accustomed as she was to being on her own without benefit of her family's interest, she had developed a number of agreeable pastimes. Reading in the park was one of them.

She had become totally absorbed in a Gothic tale that was rather implausible, but vastly amusing, when she was disturbed by Cupid's barking. Rousing herself, she murmured to Betsy, who was half asleep at her side, "Whatever is that dog up to now, I wonder?"

It took but a moment to discover what was afoot. On the road that wound through the park a carriage had drawn to a

halt with Cupid dancing dangerously close to the horses' flashing hooves, then dashing back to the carriage. Harriet did not
have to look twice to know the identify of the carriage and
driver. It was Ferdy Andrews accompanied by an utterly gorgeous young creature.

Raven black curls peeped from beneath a fetching bonnet
the ribands of which matched the sky blue pelisse she wore to
great advantage. Her heart-shaped face wore a look of amusement, as well it should with Harriet as a contrast to her own
perfect image. Harriet wagered the woman had blue eyes to
match the pelisse and wondered if she could sing as well. But
she danced, there was little doubt of that. She had to be the
opera dancer La Fleur, or Harriet was certain she'd have seen
such a beauty at Almack's or one of the *tonnish* parties.

Harriet approached the carriage, calling for the dog even as
she mentally prepared herself for the inevitable.

"Good day, Mr. Andrews," she said with civility and not
looking directly at Ferdy. "I must apologize for Cupid's bad
manners."

"Cupid?" the precious voice trilled in what was easily recognized as a fake French accent. "'Ow quaint. And he matches
your 'air! 'Ow clever." She leaned against Ferdy as though to
claim ownership. Harriet could scarcely blame her. She'd have
liked to have done the same.

"Indeed," Harriet said, still not looking at Mr. Andrews. She
did not want to see what was in his eyes. *Traitor!* she wanted
to cry, but of course she said nothing. She merely clipped on
Cupid's leash and spun about to leave this dreadful spot as
quickly as possible.

"Miss Mayne," Ferdy called.

She pretended she did not hear him. Thus, there was nothing
he could do about that short of abandoning his precious La
Fleur, and after seeing the creature, Harriet knew that to be an
impossibility.

What a little fool she had been. What had made her think
that a man such as Mr. Andrews could possibly be truly interested in her, plain Harriet Mayne? She was his charity case; he
merely felt sorry for her. And she, silly idiot that she was, had

gone along with every single scheme he proposed, thinking he might enjoy her company just as much as she welcomed his.

The worst of it all, she acknowledged, was that she'd fallen in love with the gentleman. Some gentleman. Of course, they all kept beautiful women, did they not? While worthy girls like Harriet sat primly at home, awaiting a scrap of attention, the men favored these creatures with lavish gifts and their time. Oh, her blood fairly boiled. And she loved the dratted man!

Fat lot of good this had done her, she gloomily thought, sinking down beside Betsy, absently scratching Cupid's head while she contemplated her future. If she couldn't come up with a suitable husband, it was either Aunt Croscombe or Lord Pomeroy. The worst of it was that she truly did not know who would be the more dreadful of the two.

"Mr. Andrews had a lady with him," Betsy observed quietly when she saw how downcast her mistress had become.

"That was no lady. It was La Fleur the opera dancer and Mr. Andrews's latest. She remains a mystery no longer. I am a silly ninnyhammer, Betsy. What man would look at any other woman, particularly one like me, when he has her?"

"Well," Betsy observed, "he can't marry her. You have a good name and a good heart, and I doubt she has either."

Harriet reached over to pat Betsy's hand in appreciation for her championship. "I had best put forth more effort in finding a husband other than Mr. Andrews. Perhaps Lady Wynnstay will guide me to a proper choice. I am to go with her this evening to a party at the Nesbit home."

"You surely don't want that old Lord Pomeroy," Betsy declared stoutly, having been told all about the old reprobate by the other servants, not to mention the threat he posed to the best of the Mayne family. None of the servants could understand how a father could condemn his daughter to life—however brief—with a man like that. But then, the Quality had odd ways.

Having lost all interest in her book, Harriet murmured an agreement of sorts, gathered her things and tugged Cupid with her, Betsy trotting along as well. Within a short time, they had reached the Mayne house, intent on preparations for the coming evening.

Ferdy grimly tried to entertain the delectable La Fleur, knowing there were a number of chaps who sought her favors as well. He'd been a lucky fellow to win her, he knew, but of all days to take her to the park! And to encounter Harriet! She hadn't even so much as looked at him. She'd swiftly appraised La Fleur, then concentrated on Cupid. Harriet had never seen his beseeching look. But how could he blame her? She might have been a hoyden, yet even Harriet would not be best pleased to see her friend with his opera dancer.

From her forbidding expression he surmised that Harriet had guessed the identity of his companion. Considering how the gossips liked to spread any scandalous bits and scraps of news, it was highly likely. This probably put him back to the beginning of intent regarding Harriet Mayne. She would consider him beyond the pale now, her innocent mind rejecting him out of hand. He wondered if the fishing expedition was still on.

"You are very quiet," La Fleur said, sensing something had occurred to displease her patron, something to do with that redhead who had the dog that matched her hair. A novel idea, that, one that the dancer intended to remember.

"Well, I have had to shift some plans. Hadn't intended to go out this evening but I just remembered my sister Emma asked me to attend her. Some party or other," he invented. He thought Emma was to chaperon Harriet this evening and if so, he might mend his fences there. The sooner, the better, that was his motto.

More intelligent than most suspected, La Fleur guessed that Ferdy had important business to handle, something to do with that young redhead. She was not about to lose the nicest protector she'd ever had by kicking up a dust over a missed evening.

"You are very good to your sister. I approve of zat. It is one of zee many things I like about you, Ferdy," she said, her accent giving the words a particular charm. "You are a wonderful man." These words were spoken in a soft, seductive voice that promised a great deal.

Ferdy decided that he really didn't have to be at Emma's house terribly early. And so he continued through the park, then on to Half Moon Street where La Fleur had a cozy little house all her own.

"Never tell me that Harriet saw you with your opera dancer?" Emma whispered, utterly furious. Now what were she and Diana to do? All their careful plans ruined—by Ferdy's stupid opera dancer, no less.

"I did not want to tell you, but if you are to be with her this evening, she might say something about seeing me this afternoon with an unknown woman and wonder about her," Ferdy said while pacing back and forth before the drawing room fireplace. He halted and looked down at Emma. "However, I suspect she knew the woman's identity. She refused to look at me. Her most civil greeting might have chilled Gunter's ices."

"Really?" Emma took heart. Perhaps all was not lost. If Harriet was so disturbed about the sight of Ferdy with that creature, it could mean her affections were engaged.

"Would it be amiss if I escorted you this evening?" he asked in an offhand manner.

"Actually," Emma said with great pleasure, "Edmund is taking us. But you are welcome to join our little trio. Just do not be surprised if Harriet is a bit cool."

"If she is only cool that will be an improvement, believe me," Ferdy vowed, ranking his fingers through his hair, totally destroying the artful style his valet had worked so hard to achieve.

"Must you associate with that woman, dear brother?" Emma asked softly. She had never uttered one word about his opera dancers, although gossips had been only too glad to keep her informed about each and every one of them.

"Every fellow has a woman in his—that is, I have always had a—er . . ." he muttered, obviously trying to spare Emma any blushes.

"What you mean to say is that you believe that every gentleman has an opera dancer or a pretty woman in his keeping. I doubt Edmund has. Or if he does, I can't imagine when he sees her, for he certainly seems devoted to me," she retorted gleefully.

"I'd kill him," Ferdy quietly threatened.

"Then you may understand how Harriet might feel. I know I do," Emma declared. "Have you forgotten the threat of Lord Pomeroy? And we must not disregard the formidable Aunt Croscombe in Little Munden. Dear Harriet. She is such a brave girl, declaring she will run away rather than give in to the family demands regarding either of those two."

"How would she survive? Somehow I cannot see Harriet as a governess. I have seen her attempts at watercolors, needlework, and heard her try the pianoforte, you know. Believe me, she is not qualified to teach any of those."

"And those skills are the foundation of teaching young girls today," Emma said reflectively. "We shall just have to find a husband who will treasure her and *not* be inclined to opera dancers or the like. While I believe that knowledge might be tolerated by many women, of the *ton*, I fear it would break Harriet's heart."

Emma bestowed a sidelong look at her brother, who appeared to be deeply in thought as he lounged against the fireplace mantel.

The entrance of Edmund, Lord Wynnstay, ended this particular conversation. The three enjoyed a lovely dinner with very circumspect conversation which never once mentioned the opera house or the dancers there.

When Harriet descended the stairs to go with Emma to the Nesbit party, the last person in the world that she expected or wanted to see was Ferdy Andrews. Yet there he stood, resplendent in evening dress. A corbeau coat over biscuit satin breeches with a matching waistcoat looked far too good on the man. The emerald nestled in his cravat winked at her and she frowned back.

"Good evening, Mr. Andrews. How is it that you happened this way?" she said with chilly civility. "Could you be lost, perhaps?" She stood, politely waiting for his reply while her heart sank to her toes and she felt a lowering of her spirits. He

was so dashing and handsome and so very dear. He was also a
cad who kept a gorgeous opera dancer.

"I am part of your escort this evening, Harriet."

"How distressing," she murmured, then sailed past him, the
lovely, large shawl that he had bought her draped over her
cream satin gown with the embroidered bodice and sleeves.

At least she hadn't tossed it away, Ferdy thought, tena-
ciously following Harriet to the carriage, where they joined
Emma and Edmund. Harriet carefully studied the pretty gold-
mesh reticule in her lap all the way to the Nesbit house. Ferdy
managed a quiet chat with Edmund, a continuation of something discussed at dinner.

"Cheer up," Emma whispered to her as they exited the carriage once they had reached their destination. "I have a plan."

Curious what Ferdy's sister—and Harriet must remember
those two were related, as was Diana—might have on her
mind, Harriet followed her into the lovely home before them.

The double doors between the drawing room and dining
room had been opened up to allow free passage for the guests.
Fortunately, the crowd was not overwhelming. Harriet and
Emma found a pleasant place to chat after greeting their hostess. That good lady might have been surprised to see Ferdy
Andrews, but any unmarried gentleman of wealth and position
was always welcome to any party, large or small.

"I understand you went to the park today," Emma began
once they were seated on a pair of pretty gilt chairs.

"He *told* you?" Harriet softly demanded, mindful of the
throng about them.

"He confessed his transgression because he was very distressed at your seeing him with that creature and he was
keenly aware of your obvious displeasure," Emma explained.

"Yes, I saw them. I am so embarrassed," Harriet said quietly. "Somehow this does not seem at all the proper topic for
conversation."

"It is not," Emma said a bit sharply. Then she quietly added,
"Therefore I have a plan. I am going to insist that Ferdy find
you a very nice gentleman who is bound to make you far hap-
pier than he could—someone who does not have an opera
dancer in keeping."

"You would never dare!" Harriet said, utterly aghast.

"Just watch and see," Emma said, firming her mouth before she rose to confront her dearest and only brother, whom she loved with a generous part of her heart. "Nodcock," she muttered as she joined Ferdy and her husband.

"There is a delightful musical group playing in the far end of the other room, my love," Edmund said, recalling how he had been prompted earlier.

"I would not wish to leave Harriet alone," Emma said demurely. "Ferdy, would you be so dear as to nudge a good, kind man in Harriet's direction. Mind you, I do not want a man who is given to flouting a mistress for one and all to see. Find someone honest and decent, if you can," she added before gliding off on her husband's arm.

Harriet felt lost and abandoned. However, since that was hardly an unusual state for her in her young life, she kept a serene countenance, allowing a pleasant smile to hover over her sweet lips.

"Harriet, I wish to dance with you," Ferdy insisted.

"I cannot see why," she said, giving him a direct look. Then her sense of humor reasserted itself and she smiled. "Ferdy, how can you tolerate being seen with me when you have that absolutely glorious creature at your disposal?"

"Harriet! What an improper thing to say," he said, looking shocked.

"Don't be stuffy," she riposted.

Harriet rose to accept his arm and walked at his side while wondering if she was stupid or merely desperate. "I need to attend to my future," she said during the dance when they stood side by side. "Lord Pomeroy has not gone aloft, and Mama received a letter from Aunt Croscombe to the effect that she had not been able to find a replacement for her companion and wants me to come. Mama gave me a significant look. My free days are limited."

"I had no idea it was quite that serious," Ferdy said, frowning intently.

"Mama never does jest, you see. Nor does my father. In fact, I believe I am the only one in the family who has a sense of humor. I have often wondered where it came from. George insists I am a changeling. Only my red hair saves me from being put out of the family altogether, I suppose."

"And now you must find a husband on your own." Ferdy shook his head. He enjoyed Harriet's company very much and would miss it were she to become engaged to another. He wished there was not this pressure, so he might enjoy her companionship. But she had no time. He looked about him.

"Emma said you might help me this evening," Harriet said primly. "Perhaps you know of a gentleman who would appreciate an ample dowry and not be dismayed at red hair and freckles? Someone present here tonight? I fear I *am* in a bit of a hurry to marry."

"I know. You have mentioned it before," Ferdy muttered as he led her out in the next figure of the dance.

"Well, we do not all have leisure in our pursuits," she responded sweetly.

At the conclusion of the dance, Ferdy espied a good friend of his, a shy baronet who had a faint lisp. He was well set up with sufficient funds and not bad looking. Trouble was, he was most likely the sort of chap Harriet would dote on. Ferdy couldn't explain it to himself or anyone else, but he did not like the idea of Harriet being married. He didn't want her for himself, but he didn't want anyone else to have her either. Against his best judgment, he led her in that direction.

"Harriet, may I present Sir Basil de Vere, a good friend of mine," he said when he confronted Basil while dragging a reluctant Harriet on his arm willy-nilly.

"Sir Basil," Harriet said sweetly, "how lovely to meet you."

"Delighted," Sir Basil said in reply, having long ago found that the less he said, the better.

Ferdy watched the two walk off, noting that Harriet was obviously charming his friend and hadn't so much as glanced back at himself.

"Well, I believe you just may have found the ideal man," Emma said in triumph. "I ought to have thought of him, for he is a pleasant man and I have never heard that *he* has a woman in keeping."

"Emma, please," Ferdy said, glancing about them, hoping no one was listening.

"Yes, I am pleased, particularly with you. You may go, for you have done your duty. Oh, and I suppose I might consider asking Sir Basil to escort Harriet so she need not go fishing with you."

"No Harriet, no fishing," Ferdy said firmly. A chap could be expected to give up just so much.

Chapter Nine

Harriet quite enjoyed the company offered by the shy Sir Basil. They conversed—mostly Harriet, once she perceived his difficulty. They also joined in a country dance just sufficiently spirited to require a refreshing glass of lemonade afterward.

They were standing to the side of the drawing room, chatting over the lemonade when the oddest thing occurred. A late-comer paused in the doorway, then made his way through the room, people falling away before him like a wave. His progress was impressive and she wondered who this man might be. She soon found out.

"Lord Pomeroy, as I live and breathe," murmured Sir Basil before simply fading into the wallpaper.

Harriet wasn't skilled at fading so she stood her ground, facing the man who approached her while wondering what in the world had brought him here this evening. It was said that he seldom graced the *ton* parties.

His skin looked rather gray, as though he had indeed not bathed for some time, but his clothes seemed reasonably clean, so perhaps someone had persuaded him to change for the evening.

"Miss Harriet Mayne, I believe," he said confronting Harriet. It was true. The man did not bathe; the smell reminded her of very unpleasant things she would rather not consider.

"I am." She curtsied as was proper. After all, the man was supposed to be ninety—if a very hale and hearty ninety. He was due respect for his age, if nothing else.

"Your father said you would be here this evening and I'd a fancy to meet you. I'm Pomeroy," he concluded arrogantly—as though Harriet hadn't figured that out.

"Good evening, my lord," she replied, wishing that people would look elsewhere. It was unsettling to be the cynosure of all eyes.

"Not bad. Good teeth, from what I can see. Figure nice, even if you have awful hair. Don't see that once the candles are out, ha ha." He leered at her and Harriet tried not to cringe. His teeth seemed to be the latest thing from the Wedgwood manufactory and they tended to clack when he spoke, although they certainly gleamed brightly.

"Come, have a dance with me. I'm still very much a man, my dear, as you shall see." He raised a brow at her, then moved toward her.

The odious gentleman grabbed her hand and tugged her toward the center of the adjacent room where a country dance was forming. In moments, she found herself with the most unlikely partner, vigorously prancing up and down the line, while wondering if the old man would collapse. Yet, he seemed amazingly robust for a person of his reputed age.

When the dance concluded, he mopped his forehead with a none-too-clean handkerchief. "You see, my girl, you would not be wedding an old fellow who would be incapable of being your husband. Think on it." He leered at her again, looking foolish as well as dirty.

Harriet wondered if it was possible to be more embarrassed than she was at this moment. If there was anyone close by who had failed to hear his words, she knew they would soon be shared by those who had. It was simply too good a story to keep.

It was then that Ferdy strolled to her side. She had never thought she would speak to him again, let alone have cause to be grateful to him for his support.

"Good evening, Lord Pomeroy. It is a surprise to see you here this evening." Ferdy took Harriet's unresisting hand and placed it on his arm with a proprietary air, as though he had every right to do that and more. Lord Pomeroy did not look pleased.

"Who are you, you upstart, to interrupt a gentleman conversing with a young lady?"

Ferdy's smile had the look of a terrible cat about to pounce on an insignificant mouse. "I am a friend of this young lady, a very good friend. Name is Andrews."

Apparently even Lord Pomeroy knew of the wealthy Mr. Andrews, for he gave him a respectful nod. "Heard of you," he admitted.

"Miss Harriet promised me the next dance. Please excuse us," Ferdy grandly declared.

Harriet was certain that for those watching the scene was as good as a play; the contrast between the handsome young man and the elderly fool was almost theatrical.

Pomeroy nodded sourly, waved a dismissing hand, and said, "I got what I came for, but we'll meet again." His laugh was more like a cackle, Harriet decided. He then turned and marched from the room, after which it seemed as though a collective breath was drawn before the buzz of gossip began.

"Shall we?" Ferdy advanced to the other room, her hand still on his arm. The musicians struck up a waltz and Harriet began to regally circle the room with him.

"I believe you just saved me from utterly disgracing myself. I was about to tell that disgusting creature to go to Hades or worse," she observed, peeping up at Ferdy with reluctance. He looked just the same as he had before she had seen him with La Fleur. Only Harriet's perspective had altered somewhat.

Ferdy chuckled. "I admire your backbone. Not many women would stand up to him as you did, nor survive such a meeting with the poise you maintained. I cannot think what your father is about. I inquired, and it is true that your father does not gamble. Thus it is beyond belief that any parent would countenance such a union as proposed."

"Lord Pomeroy said he would see me again, but not if I can help it," Harriet said feelingly. "I will not marry that man."

"You must find someone," Ferdy said most unhelpfully.

He didn't suggest Sir Basil, and truth be known, Harriet had been disappointed when that gentleman had failed her by disappearing when Pomeroy had arrived. It showed a lack of fortitude.

"I shall, never fear," she retorted with more optimism than faith.

"You are still going to the Archery Breakfast and Contest

with me tomorrow, are you not?" Ferdy inquired, after he had twirled her through one of the variations he'd demonstrated the day of her dancing lesson.

Breathless and appreciative for what he had done, Harriet would be the veriest wretch to say no. "I have not forgotten, sir. I shall attend with you—if you still wish my company," she said, thinking of La Fleur. He couldn't take that woman, but he might not truly want Harriet as a substitute. Perhaps he was merely being polite?

"Naturally." He seemed pleased, which in turn made Harriet feel far better about the horrible evening.

Before long, Emma and her husband came, whisking them all to the waiting Wynnstay carriage and along to the Mayne house. Emma was all soothing words, and Harriet was made to feel a heroine.

"The thing to do," confided Emma to Diana in the peace of the Wynnstay drawing room, "is to encourage Sir Basil and Harriet without discouraging Harriet and Ferdy."

"I do not see how you intend to do that," Diana said, giving her sister a highly dubious look.

"We shall think of something," Emma replied serenely.

"And I thought I was the shatterbrained one of the family," Diana murmured.

"Well, she mentioned a Captain Benwell and I do not know a thing about him," Emma said with an inquiring look at her sister.

"I do. He is a fortune hunter and up to no good. Damon said he gambles a great deal. The captain is handsome and has a devilish air about him, though. Surely Harriet has more sense than to turn his way." Diana looked horrified at the prospect of Harriet linked to Captain Benwell in any manner.

"He would probably appear in a better light than Aunt Croscombe or Lord Pomeroy if a choice had to be made," Emma declared emphatically. "You should have seen that man last evening. He is even worse than reported. I vow he gave me the shudders. She *cannot* be permitted to marry that creature, especially when we have a better candidate in mind."

"True." Diana shifted about on the sofa, then asked, "Did

Harriet tell you that her aunt cannot find a companion and now demands that her niece come to keep her company?"

"Indeed. What a gruesome prospect for any young woman." Emma exchanged a significant look with her sister.

"We must prevent it," Diana said with a nod. "It is our duty."

"Well, there is one hope. Ferdy mentioned some archery thing they'll attend together today, and he insisted that Harriet must go with him on this fishing excursion that we cooked up. Thank heavens the boys are agreeable to anything their uncle does."

"That is a plus," Diana agreed. "Oh, those two are so right for each other, but I wonder if we shall ever see it come about, given Ferdy and his bachelor ways."

"Certainly Harriet was not pleased to learn about La Fleur. Nor would I be," Emma said with a glance at the door. Lowering her voice she added, "I am sure that Edmund does not stray. At least I strive to keep him happy at home, if you take my meaning."

"Oh, yes," Diana nodded confidently. "Damon needs little prompting, but I agree. Did I show you the nightgown that Madame Clotilde made for me? It is blush peach and the sheerest batiste that ever was woven. Damon likes it," she said with a pert smile.

"Edmund would as well," Emma said with a chuckle.

They continued to discuss this delightful topic before returning to the matter of Harriet. By the end of the afternoon, they had a plan all thought out. Now all that remained was for Harriet to cooperate and Ferdy not to mess things up again.

The Archery Breakfast was to follow the contest. Harriet had agreed that she would attend both, and even after the confrontation with La Fleur and Ferdy in the park, she kept her word. Since Ferdy saved her from Lord Pomeroy last evening, she could not honestly think of an excuse to back out.

Norbert and Betsy trailed closely behind Harriet as she moved to the spot designated for Ferdy to shoot. After seeing La Fleur, Betsy was not about to permit her dear mistress to be alone with *that man*, as she referred to the once admired Mr. Andrews.

Upset more than he would have believed by Harriet's chilly reception and her apparent enjoyment of Sir Basil's company, Ferdy was certain he would make a hash of the contest.

Apparently, Harriet sensed his apprehension. She stood quietly at his side, holding his arrows, watching as the first contestant began his shoot. He hit three gold and one blue.

"He's good," Ferdy murmured gloomily.

The second contender hit three gold and one red.

"He is good as well," Harriet pointed out quietly. "But you are better than either of them, you know. You must believe you can do it—hit all four gold. You can do anything if you want," she whispered passionately.

Ferdy was much struck by the intensity of her words, the sincerity of her expression. She truly cared that he won, even though she had espied him with La Fleur. He feared he had blotted his copybook beyond redemption. But perhaps there was hope. Of course, he didn't plan to marry the lass at his side, but he certainly did not want her ill opinion. She was quite a girl, one he was proud to know.

At last it was his turn. He had to better the chap who had hit the three gold and one red. It meant all four arrows must hit the center of the target, preferably as close to one another as possible.

"You can do it," Harriet whispered as she handed him the arrows. He put them in his quiver, then drew the first out, nocked it, and let fly. A gold.

The second also hit dead center, as did the third.

"You are the best here, you can do it," Harriet whispered again, then became silent when he drew his last arrow.

The air was thick with tension; the gentlemen, lounging along the perimeter of the grounds, straightened, watching intently. Even the ladies who had elected to attend the match became silent, observing Ferdy nock his arrow, then raise his bow.

Harriet said a little prayer. Ferdy had been very kind to her. If she minded his attention to that gorgeous opera dancer, it was her problem, not his. She really wanted him to win and concentrated on that. Win! Win! Win! she chanted silently.

He let the arrow go and it arched high in the air, coming to rest dead center of the target, its *thunk* as it hit the butt resounding throughout the grounds.

"You did it!" Harriet cried with joy. She was so elated that he had won that she threw her arms about him to give him an enthusiastic hug and a kiss on his cheek. Only it didn't turn out quite that way. He turned his head slightly and her kiss landed on his mouth instead. It was but a moment, and she doubted if any had actually seen what had happened. But as she looked up into Ferdy's hazel eyes, she knew he'd been very aware of her kiss, as aware as she had been.

"Thank you, Harriet, for your, ah, support," he said in an oddly strangled voice. The officials of the archery contest marched up to congratulate Ferdy on his fine shooting, carrying him off to the front where Ferdy was to receive a trophy of sorts.

He glanced back at Harriet, and she gave him what she hoped was a reassuring smile. What must he think of her now, wantonly kissing him, and not on the cheek but on the mouth! And in public! It had been rather nice, she admitted, but scandalous. She was little better than La Fleur, throwing herself at poor Ferdy.

The breakfast went extremely well, all things considered. Ferdy was kept so busy talking that he didn't have a chance to vex Harriet about that infamous kiss.

Harriet was able to nibble a lovely selection of foods, while remaining far in the background. Several ladies queried her about her interest in archery and before she knew it, she was involved in a pleasant discussion. It took her mind off her disgrace.

But eventually she had to face him. Long before she wanted, the time came to depart. Nearly all of the others had left; Ferdy had remained, supposedly to discuss some details with the head of the organization. Norbert carried the trophy to the carriage. Betsy followed him, carrying the bow and arrow plus a few other items. Ferdy marched up to join Harriet.

"Thank you for all you did, your support, for being so gracious to the other ladies present," Ferdy said with a wary look at Harriet, quite as though he was not certain what she might do.

"I did not mean to kiss you like that," she blurted to him, her face as pink as an exotic petunia from Peru. "I mean, I intended a mere kiss on the cheek, as I might kiss my uncle, you see." Her voice faded as a wicked gleam danced in his eyes.

"However, I am not your uncle, am I?" he said mildly.

"No," she agreed in a choked voice.

"We could try again, just to see if what we experienced before could be repeated."

"Ferdy Andrews, you are a scamp," Harriet declared.

"No, a solid citizen," he countered. "You can tell by touching, you see." He placed her hand on his heart and to Harriet's everlasting shame, she thought it was a marvelous sensation—the solidity of that comforting male chest, so reassuring, so very masculine.

"Harriet, you restore my faith in women," he said with a grin.

She thought that odd; had he no faith in La Fleur? She certainly seemed to have confidence in him. Harriet thought the entire matter most peculiar.

They were momentarily alone. Ferdy glanced about, then swooped down to steal another kiss, only this one was quite on target and delightfully longer than their first tentative touching of lips. When he at last drew away, he gazed at her and looked rueful.

"I suppose I ought to apologize, but I'll be darned if I will. You are one in a million, Harriet, as was that kiss." With those words he removed his shooting glove and brace, carrying them in one hand while he guided Harriet along with his other.

It was a good thing he led her from the grounds to where the carriage waited. Harriet suspected she'd be too dazed to make her way on her own.

Now *that* was a kiss, she decided. Other gentlemen had attempted kisses, but their attempts paled in comparison to Ferdy's touch. Whatever was she to do about her feelings for him? Love was such a foolish thing. What was she going to do now?

Ferdy helped Harriet into the carriage, then reclined at her side while Betsy stared at her with curious eyes. Could the maid possibly guess that Harriet had experienced such a shattering kiss?

They rode along in splendid silence for the most part, at least as far as Harriet was concerned. Ferdy offered a variety of conversations to which she managed to murmur vague sounds.

When they reached the Mayne residence, Ferdy assisted Harriet from the carriage, then walked her to the door. He propped himself against the door surround, effectively preventing her from entering.

"I believe we are to go fishing tomorrow. If I promise to behave, will you still come with us?" He looked at her, but she rather thought he focused on her mouth, not her eyes.

For one wild moment Harriet actually contemplated telling him that she would far rather he *mis*behaved. Saved from such disgrace by her common sense, she nodded. "I said I would and I do not break my word."

"Ah, my sisters will be relieved. They look to you to preserve their darling sons from mishap."

"Are they often given to such when they are with you?" she asked, curious about his relationship with his nephews.

"I don't know. I haven't had them that often. My sisters seem determined to give us all an improving course in togetherness."

"I shall see you early in the morning. And Ferdy . . . congratulations," she whispered before she slipped beneath his arms to open the door. Betsy left off chatting with Norbert and hastily followed her mistress, dashing past Ferdy as though he were some manner of devil.

"Norbert, I believe I have won the day," Ferdy said grandly, while reclining at his ease in his landau.

"Indeed, sir," the very wise and observant groom replied.

Ferdy did a considerable amount of thinking that evening after he left Harriet, dined at his club, then sat back at his ease, allowing the conversation to drift around him. He ignored it to concentrate on Harriet and what to do about her.

That innocent little kiss had affected him far more than he had expected it to when he lightheartedly bussed her. It was probably like being struck by lightning. His emotions had been knocked as severely as if mown down by Gentleman Jackson. He could see it had moved her as well. In his experience, a woman who looked that stunned had been touched by something, and in this case, a kiss.

So, now what did he do? She had been hurt—even he had seen that—when she encountered him with La Fleur. Drat it all, he simply did not want to give up his comfortable life because kissing Harriet had turned him upside down. If he was patient, maybe it would all go away. Disappear. He'd find her a decent husband and he could go back to living as he had before. Then he wondered why that seemed rather unappealing.

His brother-in-law, Damon Oliver, strolled over to his side and prodded his arm. "Troubles?"

Ferdy merely sighed, the gut-wrenching sort that came from his very bottom.

"That bad, is it? I understand you are taking William, Timothy, and the cousins fishing tomorrow. Miss Mayne as well. Diana rope you into that?"

Ferdy merely looked at him and nodded.

"She is very fond of Miss Mayne. I am too in a way. Pity if her father forces her to marry that old quiz Pomeroy," Damon observed.

"Can't do it," Ferdy said in a determined voice. "Criminal to marry a girl to that stinking old goat."

"I agree." Damon appeared to think he'd said quite enough and left the club.

Ferdy left shortly after, returning to his rooms instead of going to see La Fleur. He needed his wits about him if he was spending the day with Harriet. A good night's rest was essential.

When he had said early, he had not been making idle remarks, Harriet decided the next morning. How fortunate she had been dressed and in the breakfast room when he arrived. But why was he there? What did he wish of her?

"I wanted to see you first before we pick up the boys," he

said quietly, with respect for the rest of the family who still slept abovestairs.

She cast him a wary look, then dropped her gaze to the table. "Have a bite of eggs and toast, do. I have yet to eat anything." Not that she was the least hungry now. Her appetite had fled when he entered the room.

He helped himself to ham and browned potatoes, toast and jam. Then he pulled out a chair next to Harriet.

"I thought you might sit over there."

"Why? I'd rather sit next to you," he said reasonably.

"Ferdy, do not tease me," she suddenly pleaded. "I do not think I am constituted to be teased."

"Is that so?" he said between bites of succulent ham and delicious browned potatoes.

"You wished to speak with me?" she said cautiously.

"Nothing that cannot wait," Ferdy replied, apparently changing his mind about whatever it was he intended to say. He looked ill at ease, seeming uncertain what to do. He applied himself to the food, which rapidly disappeared.

"Well, we had best go," Harriet said tentatively after nibbling her toast.

"The boys will be waiting," he agreed. He rose, assisted Harriet from her chair and then stood looking at her. She was so fresh and sweet, her vivid green eyes gazing at him with trust and something else he couldn't identify. More confused than he cared to admit, he took her arm and tugged her along with him outside. He'd intended to discuss that kiss, then found it impossible.

The landau held an assortment of fishing gear and Norbert sat with Betsy on the far side of the carriage until they reached the Wynnstays. Once the two little boys piled into the vehicle, everything seemed to settle down and Ferdy decided that he had imagined his entire problem.

"Uncle Ferdy, why do you have all those funny-looking hooks in your hat?" Harry said.

"They are flies, silly," the older and wiser Edward said. "You use them for fly-fishing. Just like he wears a black fishing coat and hat because he's fishing. Papa said we have to be very quiet. Why?"

"The fish can hear you talk and it frightens them away," Ferdy said, more comfortable talking about fishing than thinking over his feelings toward Harriet Mayne.

Harriet gave Ferdy a disbelieving look and hid a smile behind a gloved hand.

"Really?" a wide-eyed Harry demanded. When they picked up the Oliver boys, he shared this information with them.

The remainder of the trip to the stream where Ferdy liked to fish was given over to a detailed explanation of the skills involved in fishing.

Harriet listened with half an ear, turning her thoughts back to when Ferdy sat beside her at the breakfast table. What had been on his mind? He certainly did not appear to have lost any sleep last night, as she had. Most likely he had gone to the opera and flirted with La Fleur. That notion so depressed Harriet that she returned to her original consideration. What had he intended to tell her when he came into the room? The puzzle nagged at her like a thorn in her flesh.

She was never to learn, because when they reached the chosen stream, she and Betsy set about arranging the picnic hamper and a large rug upon which to recline. The boys immediately took off with their uncle and before long, they were being initiated into the mysteries of fly-fishing.

" 'Tis a good thing I brought a book with me," Harriet grumbled.

"You might drop a line into the stream up a ways, miss. There be dace and trout in it and they are good eating Mr. Norbert says," Betsy informed her.

Deciding she preferred to sit on a bank to fish rather than poke her nose in a book, Harriet did as suggested and wandered along until she found the perfect spot. It wasn't long until she dozed off, only to be awakened by Ferdy shaking her arm.

"You had a fish on your line. Some fisherman you are." He expertly removed the fish and placed it in his creel. He gave her an odd look that might have meant anything, but confused her greatly. It was the expression in his eyes, actually—warm, probing, perhaps caring?

She was startled more by her reaction at seeing his face so

close to hers than being rudely awakened. A jolt of pleasure shot through her. She knew a wanton urge to touch him—caress him—so strong that she controlled it with difficulty. She walked back in a daze with him.

The boys consumed the picnic with the hearty appetite of those who had spent hours in the fresh air, wandering along the banks of a stream in search of fish. Harriet merely nibbled, reflecting on her wayward thoughts.

"You slept well last night?" Ferdy said quietly while Betsy was separating Harry and William, who were arguing over who had caught the larger fish.

"Not very. I suppose I needed the sleep now," she admitted, hoping she hadn't betrayed her reaction to him.

"I saw Damon at the club after dinner, then I went home as well, hoping for an early night," Ferdy offered a sandwich to Harriet, then took one for himself.

Those words pleased her enormously, more than anything she could imagine. When they at last left the stream, she felt happy, if not totally content. He hadn't seen La Fleur last evening, he had gone home to sleep. How lovely.

She parted from the group first, not wanting Ferdy to have to go the extra distance from the other houses back to hers. Bemused, she stood to watch as the landau with its parcel of children, fish, and a very handsome gentleman disappeared down the street.

Just as she was about to enter the house, feeling somewhat foolish to be standing with her maid on the steps, staring after a carriage, she caught sight of a familiar face. Approaching her was Captain Benwell.

"Miss Mayne, what a happy surprise. It is very nice to see you again," the captain said, giving Harriet what she could only describe as a searching look.

"Goodness, I must be a tangle," she murmured, thinking that the sleep on the bank of the stream had likely mussed her hair and clothes. "I have been on a picnic, you see."

"Ah, fair lady, you look a treat to these eyes, I assure you. I should like to offer you a picnic one of these fine days, if I may. Perhaps get up a little party?" the captain said with a roguish grin.

His extravagant speech brought a smile to Harriet's face. "Perhaps," she allowed, not taking him seriously.

She entered the house with Betsy, closing the door on the improper captain, who had spoken to her when he ought not.

The captain, on the other hand, had taken a hard look at the redheaded chit with the ample dowry. He was being pressed and dunned for money, for he owed everywhere and his creditors were losing patience. Perhaps it would pay him to give Miss Harriet Mayne more attention?

Chapter Ten

Ferdy left his nephews at their respective homes, then rode in silence to the Albany, where Norbert and his driver let him off before continuing on to the mews where his carriages were kept and horses stabled.

Thankful to be alone with his thoughts, he ambled up the stairs into his rooms. Crossing to the window, he stared at the street below.

The fishing expedition had turned out rather oddly, to his way of thinking. He couldn't shake the image of Harriet asleep on the bank, one hand on that fishing pole, the other curled on her lap, her head leaning to one side. Her lashes had been fringed fans sweeping over her freckle-dusted satiny skin. And her mouth had looked soft and inviting—quite as it had the other time he'd come upon her when asleep. Ferdy was not given to poetical notions, but when she had given him that startled look, her vivid green eyes had seemed like deep, mysterious pools that lured, invited him to fall into their depths. No, he admitted, it wasn't precisely her image—it was his reaction to her that had shaken him.

They had been totally alone, the boys having elected to stay with the food. He had made his way along the stream until he'd come upon the sleeping girl and the fool pole, one end bobbing in the water.

Harriet had looked so sweetly vulnerable, so infinitely fragile. He was accustomed to considering her as a sturdy girl, one who could do anything—including a dab hand at a twenty-pound bow. But she had looked so in need of protection, and he had felt this strong urge to gather her in his arms and take care of her, comfort her. While he knew she was in danger of being forced into an unpleasant life and he had desired to assist her, he had not felt such a strong compulsion to help her until now. It troubled him a little. What was happening to him? He felt threatened, yet couldn't say by what.

His ruminations ceased when his man ushered in his good friend Val, Lord Latham. Ferdy smiled in welcome, for Val looked like a particularly contented cat—sleek and well-fed and pleased with the world.

"Marriage to Phoebe seems to agree with you. How are she and the twins?" He gestured Val to sit, and joined him in the comfortable chairs by the fireplace.

"All are well. Phoebe and I came to London to do a bit of shopping and catch up on all the news. You look pleased with the world."

"Won the archery championship the other day."

"Phoebe saw Diana and your sister said something about you being on a rescue mission?" Val gave his old friend and one-time beau of Phoebe's a searching look.

"Long story."

"I have time. Phoebe is at Madame Clotilde's selecting a few things. Well?"

"There is this young woman—name of Harriet Mayne—who I thought was about to jump into the Serpentine—only she wasn't. But she did need help of a sort. Father threatens to either marry her to old Pomeroy or send her off to a dragon of an aunt if the chit doesn't find a suitable husband—all on her own, mind you, without the help and support of her not-so-loving family."

"So you elected to assist her? From the somewhat garbled account I received through Phoebe it sounded as though you have spent more time escorting her about than rounding up a likely candidate for husband."

"Well, m'sisters keep thinking of places to take their brats and Harriet goes along to help. You see how it is." Ferdy stared into the empty fireplace, thinking that Val couldn't possibly see how it was unless he met Harriet and saw how badly she needed his protection and help, poor innocent that she was. "However, she is most proficient at the archery grounds. She'll handle a thirty-pound bow before long, if I don't miss my guess. Natural bowman. I've been teaching her," he concluded modestly.

"*You* are teaching her?" Val said, sounding more than a little surprised. "I'd like to meet this girl—Phoebe would as well."

"Saw to it that she received vouchers for Almack's, and she is to be there again on Wednesday. The next evening I believe she has the Sefton party. Emma and Diana take turns in chaperoning her as her mother frequently has the headache. Dash it all, it's as though they *want* her to wed that smelly old goat, Pomeroy."

"He's as bad as ever?" Val inquired, placing his elbows on the chair arms and steepling his fingers before his face.

"Worse. Presented himself at the Nesbit party and confronted poor Harriet. Leered at her in a disgusting manner, told her he thought her ugly but it wouldn't bother him in bed once the candles were out." Ferdy clearly revealed what he thought of this behavior.

"Why, the chap is an out-and-outer," Val said with distaste. "I can see why you feel an obligation to help the girl. Is she really bad to look at?"

"Not really," Ferdy said, flashing a grin at his friend. "Has red hair, now with golden tints—thanks to Diana's abigail. Couldn't do anything about her freckles—but they are rather fetching in a way. Lovely green eyes and softest skin ever. Good figure and dances like an angel. Sings like one, too. Good with the children—they adore her."

"Sounds to me like she would make some lucky man a good wife," Val said, giving his friend a searching look. "Can't think of anyone good enough?"

"That's it, drat it. Every one of them has a flaw. She looked to be interested in de Vere, and then he melted into the woodwork when Pomeroy imposed his pungent self at the party."

"Who came to her rescue there?" Val said, tilting his head and compressing his lips as though to prevent a smile.

"I had to, of course. Couldn't let a creature like Pomeroy think the girl was without support."

"Emma and Edmund along at the party? You did say one or the other of the girls accompanied her?"

"Indeed, but you know how Edmund is. Nice fellow, but hates to have his cravat mussed."

"Hmm," Val agreed. "Well, we shall drop in at Almack's and I feel certain we can manage a late invitation to the Sefton do. Perhaps we can offer our help? The girl must be special to obtain the assistance of three of the Andrews' family."

"Oh, she is that," Ferdy replied absently, thinking again of the view of Harriet on the bank of the stream, leafy shadows from the overhanging tree dancing over her features, the sound of the rippling water—and her startled eyes when she'd gazed up at him. He realized at that moment he would have liked nothing more than to kiss Harriet again. "In fact, she is downright dangerous."

This obscure remark was not questioned by Val. Rather, the topic was changed and the old friends caught up on news of those they both knew.

Diana had gone with Phoebe to Madame Clotilde's establishment to shop. They had become fast friends after Val and Phoebe married, although Diana had wished Phoebe for a sister-in-law and had lamented her loss.

"I do believe we shall have a nice sister-in-law after all," she concluded, following a recital of all that had taken place regarding Ferdy and Harriet. "If we may only persuade Ferdy that Harriet doesn't just need any man for a husband—she needs *him*."

"Is the prospect a trifle daunting?" Phoebe inquired, looking over her shoulder as Madame pinned her into a swath of blue jaconet.

Madame entered the conversation at this point, a thing she rarely, if ever, did. "Miss Harriet Mayne is a sweet girl and has a lovely figure—splendid bosom and excellent posture. She is considerate of the staff—which is more than one may say for many ladies—yourselves excepted, naturally."

"You see? Everyone who meets her falls a little in love with her—just wait until you hear her sing! Only her family are fools. I truly cannot understand such people—as though freckles made one less of a person! Disgraceful, I say." Diana changed the subject, enjoying a good gossip.

Harriet, one of the objects of all this speculation, was blissfully unaware of the deep concern for her welfare. Indeed, although grateful for whatever guidance and help she received, she felt quite alone in working out the solution to her problem. She *had* discovered that one of the best things she could do was to avoid her family, particularly her father, at all costs.

Cupid on his leash, she was sneaking from the house when her brother caught sight of her about to open the door.

"You still live here? I haven't seen you in days. I hear that you have captured the attention of several gentlemen. Anyone come up to scratch yet?" George asked as he picked at his teeth with the silver toothpick he carried in his pocket.

"What an odious term—come up to scratch, quite as though he were a rooster. And, yes, I am pleased to say I have met several very nice gentlemen. And, no, none of them has asked for my hand in marriage. Yet." She placed her hand on the handle of the door, preparing to escape.

"Not Andrews? Rumor also says he is forever at your side. No title, but pots of money. You could do worse."

"Indeed," she snapped in icy tones, "Lord Pomeroy is the first to come to mind there. How Father could—" and she ceased speaking, for she suspected George cared only to twit her about the gossip he'd heard and not for her difficulties.

"He *is* a peer, and at his age, he shouldn't live long," George said with utter indifference.

"I care not for titles, but for the person," Harriet said, not particularly concerned if her brother understood or not. She had decided long ago that they would never comprehend one another.

"Amazed that there are those who do not mind a bran-faced chit like you," George said consideringly without any regard for his sister's feelings.

"There is more to a person than freckles." Harriet decided she had endured quite enough of her brother and whisked herself around the door. She walked toward the park, Betsy scurrying to keep pace with her.

"Why could I not be blessed with a family like Diana and Emma and Ferdy?" Harriet said softly.

"Well, miss, 'times it seems as if they've adopted you," the maid replied quietly.

"If only they might," Harriet replied with a sigh.

Nursemaids and nannies decorated the park with colorfully garbed children at play. A ball bounded past Harriet and Betsy. Cupid strained at his leash and succeeded in breaking from Harriet's loose clasp.

"That dog!" she said in wry acceptance of his love to run. Eventually, he came trotting back, ball in his mouth, running to the child who had tossed it. Once the ball had been restored to the grateful child, Cupid returned to Harriet, looking up at her as though waiting for praise.

"He is a clever dog," Sir Basil said, strolling up to join Harriet and her maid.

"He is naughty, but I do enjoy his company."

"I hope I may join you on your walk?" Sir Basil looked much as he had the night of the Nesbit party when he had disappeared just as Harriet had need of him.

Deciding to be charitable—for after all, Lord Pomeroy was a trifle overwhelming in many ways—Harriet nodded.

"Have you been enjoying your stay in London? This is your come-out, is it not?" he asked when he had adjusted to her pace, a wry eye kept on the poodle at all times.

"I have been pleased to meet so many fine people," she said, not answering the part about her come-out. That might bring an inquiry about her come-out ball, and she'd rather avoid admitting her family refused to present her at one.

Mr. Tooke pranced up to join them, obviously figuring that anyone the quiet Sir Basil was comfortable with might be worth pursuing. Harriet welcomed his presence, thinking there was safety in numbers.

Across the way Captain Benwell observed the bran-faced Miss Mayne surrounded by smiling gentlemen and was shocked. He had counted upon snaring her interest without any competition. How could a woman with those freckles interest those chaps? He preened slightly, then rode up to join them.

"Gentlemen, do you know Captain Benwell?" Harriet said while admiring the sight of the captain on his steed. He might be a bit showy, but she had not crossed him off her prospective husband list.

Mr. Tooke nodded politely, while Sir Basil gave the captain a chilly greeting.

Harriet felt a need to defend the captain against the cool reception from the other men, so she smiled at him warmly, certainly more warmly than she felt.

The captain gave her a confident look, then began a trivial conversation centering around himself and his interests. Harriet listened politely, if absently. She thought the captain rude to ignore the other men, but there was nothing she might do about that. She did insert a few words, changing the topic to a more neutral one.

The other men closed ranks about her, refusing to give an inch to the dashing captain. This suited Harriet, in that she wished to have as many gentlemen as possible to study. As long as she could evade her family, she might postpone the day of reckoning. Out of sight, out of mind had become her motto in dealing with her relations. This gave her more time in which to search, encourage a proper gentleman, and learn more about those who could see past her freckles—much like Ferdy did.

Why freckles should be so damning was beyond her. She accepted that it was so, but it puzzled her that Society should be so shallow in judging a person's merit.

They drew close to the carriageway and Harriet was delighted to see Diana approaching with a very stylish young woman in her carriage. She smiled in greeting, pulling Cupid to a stop when it appeared that the carriage would halt so they might chat.

"Harriet, this lady is someone you must meet, for her husband is Ferdy's best friend, Lord Latham. Phoebe, *this* is Miss Harriet Mayne."

Harriet was very aware that Lady Latham made a swift inspection and was thankful that she had worn a new walking dress of soft cream muslin trimmed with knots of forest-green riband with the pretty bonnet Ferdy had bought her after her plunge into the river.

"I am so pleased to meet you, my dear Miss Mayne," Lady Latham said after exchanging a quick glance with Diana. "Would you be so kind as to join Diana, Emma, and me for tea tomorrow? We must become better acquainted. Do say you will come?" When Harriet immediately agreed, her ladyship took note of the dog. "What a dear little poodle. And to think he is the same color as your glorious hair. How clever of you."

Taking the compliment in stride, Harriet said, "I am so pleased to meet you, and look forward to seeing you tomorrow." She stared thoughtfully at the disappearing carriage, curious about that look that had been exchanged between those two women. What had Diana been saying about Harriet to this stranger? Most curious.

"I expect you will be at Almack's this evening," Sir Basil said in his quiet way, hardly lisping at all. "Will you save me a dance this evening, Miss Mayne?"

"Delighted."

It seemed Mr. Tooke could not permit Sir Basil to outdo him, for he said, "May I request your hand for a cotillion? I notice you do very well at them."

"I confess that I adore dancing. That is why I particularly enjoy Almack's."

"You enjoy it?" a shocked Mr. Tooke was startled into saying. No one actually *enjoyed* Almack's. You went there to be seen, to make connections, to show off your position and your new clothes, and find a mate, but enjoy?

Harriet laughed, an enchanting musical sound that pleased the ear. "I do. And I find most of the people quite congenial. Odd, I know, but there you are."

At that point, she noted that Ferdy was riding toward her and the gentlemen. Another man rode with him, also mounted on a respectable steed of sensible nature—no showy cattle for them. Captain Benwell's horse took exception to Cupid and the other horses, and the captain reluctantly took himself and that animal off.

Ferdy dismounted, immediately towering over Mr. Tooke and Sir Basil not only with his height but his sheer size. Sir Basil promptly excused himself and Mr. Tooke skittered along behind him.

"You frightened away her elegant escorts, Ferdy," the other gentleman said with a wry grin.

"Oh, those two will see her this evening, if I make no mistake." He walked closer to Harriet, allowing his horse to amble along behind him. "Harriet, I wish to present you to my good friend, Val, Lord Latham."

"I met your lovely wife a short time ago," Harriet said with a smile at the kindly looking gentleman.

"Indeed? She and Diana must have finished at Madame Clotilde's earlier than expected. But then, Phoebe never buys as much as I tell her to purchase. Do you enjoy shopping, Miss Mayne?"

"At times. Diana and Emma have exquisite taste and I enjoy having them with me. Ferdy and his sisters have been marvelous help to me, but I guess you know what special people they are."

Harriet was gazing at Ferdy with admiration and thus missed the startled expression that crossed Val's face. It instantly changed into one of speculation.

"You will be at Almack's this evening, Harriet?" Ferdy asked intently. "I told everyone you would."

"Yes, wearing the gown I wore to the concert." She turned to Lord Latham and said, "I will confess I do not like to shop as much as some. I'd rather wear a gown several times."

"Sensible girl," Ferdy said approvingly. "And most chaps don't know the difference. Besides, you always look fine to me."

"That is scarcely a compliment, old chap. You hardly know the difference between a day and evening gown," Val said with a chuckle.

"An evening gown usually has a lower neckline," Ferdy observed with a wicked little grin at Harriet.

"How true," she replied primly. Cupid tugged at his leash and Harriet politely excused herself to continue her walk.

Val looked after her, then turned to his good friend. "I see what you mean. Plain girl, but charming manners."

"Harriet is not plain," Ferdy said, affronted that his friend would say such a thing about someone Ferdy admired. "You have to see past the freckles to what is beneath. Harriet has a heart of gold—and the ability to hit gold at the archery grounds."

The two men continued their ride, with Ferdy proceeding to

fill his friend in on the happenings involving the esteemed Harriet.

Almack's was more crowded than usual. Harriet made her curtsies to the patronesses in attendance this evening, then walked at Emma's side until they reached the row of seats occupied by the chaperones.

Emma looked down the row and thoughtfully commented, "I should have liked to have been here the night the tier of seats collapsed. I imagine there were more than injured sensibilities."

"I expect so, poor souls," Harriet replied, but not attending closely. She tried to search the room without being obvious. She couldn't see Ferdy anywhere.

"I wonder where that brother of mine is?"

"I'd not be surprised were he to arrive with his friends, Lord and Lady Latham. They seem very close."

"Did you meet both of them? How nice. Phoebe is a darling, as you will learn when we have tea together."

The musicians played a little introduction to a cotillion and Mr. Tooke promptly presented himself for the promised dance.

Emma watched them leave, then concentrated on the doorway, hoping to see her brother enter.

As it was, she missed him, for he slipped in with a cluster of men. She was tapping her foot in time to the music when Ferdy spoke in her ear. "May I interest you in the next dance, milady?"

"Ferdy! Thank goodness you arrived. I do not know all these men and I trust you to vet them for me. I do not wish to allow Harriet to dance with someone she ought not."

"How did Benwell snabble a voucher to an assembly? I thought Sally was death on half-pay officers. Not even the officers at the Horse Guards are able to obtain an entree to this gathering."

"Maybe he has a relative with influence," Emma replied thoughtfully, noting her brother's obvious dislike for the captain and curious about it. Not that Emma liked the chap, for he was a pushy fellow, but Ferdy was usually more tolerant of other men.

When Mr. Tooke made a triumphal return with a breathless Harriet on his arm, he seemed taken aback to discover Ferdy hovering at Emma's side.

Ferdy glared at Tooke, then smiled at Harriet. "I believe the next dance is ours." He walked with her, bending to murmur, "I would that they allowed the waltz played here. You perform it quite well, you know."

Thanking him politely, Harriet inquired about his day and when he intended to go to the Archery Grounds again. "Do you think I might join your group? I would rather not impose upon you to shoot."

"It is no imposition, my dear. But if you like, I shall propose you for a lady's membership. I'll take care of it the next meeting."

Harriet thanked him for that as well, then remained silent, content to dance with him.

"You aren't considering Tooke, are you?" he demanded when they were next together in the pattern of the dance.

"I have a fair number of gentlemen on my list, if that is what you mean," Harriet said, giving him a cross look. Really, what a thing to say while in the middle of the dance floor.

The dance concluded within minutes of that and Ferdy escorted Harriet not to Emma, but to the refreshment room. "A glass of lemonade, I think," he said with a minatory look at her.

When he handed her the glass of the lukewarm lemonade, Harriet gave him a quizzical look. "Out with it. I'd not be responsible for your injured spleen, sir."

"I cannot credit that you would allow Tooke's name on your list—long or short," Ferdy began.

"He is reprehensible, then? I'd not have thought he'd be welcome at Almack's in that case. The patronesses are said to be quite choosy."

"They are, but every now and again, someone is permitted entry who ought not be here. Tooke is not a bad sort, he just wouldn't appreciate your finer qualities. Take that Captain Benwell you were talking to this afternoon. Explain, please, why you encourage him."

"He does not accept *dis*couragement, sir," Harriet said in

growing bewilderment. "What is the matter with you, pray tell? You were the one to insist I must draw up a list of possible husband candidates. Can I help it if the ones who present themselves for consideration are not quite to your high standards? Not every gentleman is like you, Ferdy," she dared to say in conclusion.

"Of course not," Ferdy replied, somewhat abashed by her gentle rebuke. "I do not mean that they must be like me. Dash it all, if you wanted someone like me, you would do better to marry me," he concluded with simple logic.

Harriet dropped her gaze to the glass in her hand, her heart beating triple time to the point she almost felt faint. He must not learn how desirable his teasing sounded to her ears and to her heart.

"You jest, Ferdy," she said at last, when she had collected her wits. She put the half-empty glass of lemonade on a tray, then turned to face him. "I wish to return to the ballroom now. Please?" she added as an afterthought. Really, her head was in such a spin it would be a wonder if she could walk, not to mention dance after such a remark.

Captain Benwell was patiently waiting when Ferdy returned her to Emma's side. Harriet took perverse pleasure in accepting the captain as a partner for the next dance, a cotillion that she particularly enjoyed.

Ignoring Ferdy's glowering face, she walked with the captain to form a set.

"Mr. Tooke said you are especially adept at the cotillion, Miss Mayne," the captain said with a flash of white teeth.

"Thank you," she replied demurely, then enjoyed silence while the captain regaled her with stories of his prowess in various sports during the moments of the dance when they drew together. Life with the captain, she decided, would certainly be saving on her vocal cords.

The captain, for his part, was finding Miss Mayne to be jolly good company. He would even go so far as to say she brought out the best in him. If a chap had to marry, it was best that he find a woman he could tolerate. She might not be much to look at, but—and here he echoed Lord Pomeroy—a fellow didn't have to look at those freckles and the red hair once in bed. He'd need an heir, for she had a fortune. A baby would keep her in the nursery and out of his hair.

It was well that Harriet was unaware of his musings, or Almack's would have been treated to the sight of Miss Mayne losing her temper to an awesome degree. Instead, she inclined her head politely and placed the captain at the bottom of her long list.

Once the dance was finished, Ferdy appeared at her side, looking disgruntled. "Well, I trust you are satisfied, Miss Harriet."

"No," Harriet replied with a sunny smile. "But after we have our second dance, I daresay I will feel more the thing. I must admit, Ferdy, your sisters did not exaggerate when they pronounced you to be an outstanding dancer."

This so pleased Ferdy that he forgot all about scolding her for dancing with Captain Benwell.

Later at home, Harriet reflected that it had been a promising evening. She refused to mull over Ferdy's casually voiced suggestion that she'd be better off marrying him. That idea prompted too many wishful thoughts.

The next afternoon Harriet presented herself at Lady Latham's home at the requested time to meet Emma and Diana, who were already seated in the drawing room, laughing and chatting in happy reminiscence.

"Harriet, how good of you to come to tea. I vow, I am here but two days and I feel as though I have never left."

"I gather Emma and Diana have brought you up to date at top speed," Harriet said with a fond look at her friends.

"Indeed," Phoebe said with a curve of her lips. "I understand you made a splash at Almack's last evening. We had intended to go, but I felt unwell, so we retired early."

"I trust it was nothing serious. You are in wonderful looks today, Lady Latham," Harriet said earnestly.

"Well, babies sometime have that effect, or so I am told. Val is pleased, and so am I, moreso once this part is passed." She turned a pretty shade of pink.

That delightful announcement invited a plunge into conversation about infants, nursemaids, nannies, and confinements.

Harriet became silent, withdrawing into her chair, but listening carefully to all that was said.

"Forgive us," Phoebe said abruptly to Harriet, "we forget you are not a mother—yet. But you will be, I know it. Has anyone captured your fancy?"

All three women stared at Harriet until she could scarcely open her mouth to make any sort of reply.

"Well, aside from Ferdy, there is hardly anyone with whom I have spent much time, and I do believe I should at least know their interests . . . or something," she said in a dying voice.

"How wise," Phoebe declared. "And you could do worse than to use him as a measuring stick."

"Well said," Diana added with a grin. "Phoebe had almost decided on Ferdy when Val swept her off her feet."

Harriet looked at Phoebe, Lady Latham. His lordship seemed nice, but this woman had actually rejected Ferdy? Harriet realized that she could never do that. She loved the dratted man far too much!

Chapter Eleven

In the following days it seemed to Harriet that she had acquired a shadow. Everywhere she went, Captain Benwell was bound to pop up. When she left the house to take Cupid for a walk in the park, he chanced to meet her near Grosvenor Gate. When she purposefully marched off to Hatchards to exchange her books, he casually bumped into her as she prepared to cross Piccadilly. She agreed to view the latest display at the National Gallery with her friends; he happened to be lingering at the entrance, and insisted upon escorting her through the place, even though Emma, Diana, and Phoebe were along as well.

"I think he is smitten with you," Betsy said after the fourth day of this behavior.

Diana had different ideas. She and Emma, along with the amused Phoebe, held council in Emma's drawing room.

"What are we to do? Harriet said that man follows her everywhere she goes. She cannot step from her door without seeing him. She thinks it droll. I say it is ominous. Captain Benwell is a menace."

"He seemed innocent enough to me," Phoebe inserted.

"Edmund did a bit of mousing around and learned that your innocent captain owes enormous bills to most everyone he's dealt with. He is punting on the River Tic, up to his eyebrows," Diana declared.

"I had no idea he was that much in debt. The usual tailor bills, I suppose?" Phoebe said, sobered at this news.

"Tailor, wine merchant, just about everyone," Emma concluded.

"I say we ought to consult Ferdy," Diana declared.

"Did someone mention my name?" the man in question said from just outside the doorway. "I was on my way to bring some papers to Edmund and couldn't resist stopping when I heard you mention me. Now what have I done?"

Diana jumped up from her chair and swiftly crossed to confront her brother. "It is Harriet!"

Ferdy lost his look of amusement, searching the three faces turned his direction, each wearing a look of concern.

"What's happened to Harriet? Nothing serious, I hope?"

"She told us this afternoon that wherever she goes lately Captain Benwell is sure to pop up one way or another. She thought it comical. I believe it is a threat," Diana ended with a nod.

"Really?" Ferdy drawled. His face tightened as he recalled what he knew about the captain. The only money the man put out was for gaming and his light-skirt, and rumor had it that even she was getting miffed at the man.

"Ferdy, do something!" Diana demanded. "She is our good friend and we do not want something terrible to happen to her."

"And what do you imagine he might do?" Ferdy said in a very quiet voice.

"Elope, I suppose," Emma contributed. "What else is there for a half-pay officer and a reluctant heiress? I doubt that starched-up father of hers would agree to the match, even if he can't abide his daughter. He'd rather sell her to old Pomeroy."

"Or ship her to the wealthy aunt in the hope of eventually snagging a fortune," Ferdy said.

"Her aunt is wealthy?" Diana cried.

"Indeed, my man of business found that out for me. Seems the irascible old biddy has money enough, but even money cannot force a companion to remain in the face of nasty circumstances. Apparently, the poor things haven't been that beggared. I gather she thinks that Harriet will do as told."

"That is infamous," Diana said, a determined look settling on her face.

"But what can you do?" Phoebe pointed out. "Unless Harriet believes that she is in danger, she'll not welcome help from others. She might see it as interference."

"You have a point there," Ferdy agreed. "Emma, would you give these papers to your husband? I'd best see to Harriet immediately. Who knows when that blackguard may take a notion to strike?"

With those ominous words, Ferdy turned, ran down the stairs and out the door before Emma could tell him to be circumspect.

"He'll likely make a hash out of it," Diana gloomily predicted.

"I am not so sure," Phoebe mused, a twinkle lurking in her eyes. "I think your brother has hidden depths."

The sisters looked at Phoebe with thoughtful frowns.

Harriet slipped from the house with Betsy and Cupid for a quiet stroll in the park. She usually didn't walk this time of day, nor had she revealed her intent to anyone. She strongly suspected that the captain had bribed one of the servants to report to him daily regarding her plans.

This time she would have peace!

A cautious peek beyond the Grosvenor Gate revealed no sign of Captain Benwell and she gave a sigh of relief.

"He is nowhere in sight, Betsy," she said thankfully to the maid.

"That be a wonder," Betsy replied softly with a smile.

"How nice not to have to listen to him prating on about his interests, his horse, his glorious past, with not a word about his future plans. How does he intend to survive in this world with no visible means of support? From what I have heard, the man is a gamester, and not a good one."

They strolled along in blissful silence, enjoying the chatter of birds, the scent of fresh-scythed grass, and the feel of a light breeze on their faces.

"Mith Mayne," a quiet voice said, intruding on their pleasure with a rude jolt.

Turning, Harriet said, "Sir Basil, what a surprise to see you at this hour of the day."

"Thometimes I like to wander along these paths and just think. I'm a quiet fellow, you know," he lisped.

Harriet thought of the fading he'd done when Lord Pomeroy

appeared at the Nesbit party and had to agree. Sir Basil was quiet to the point of not being there.

"Are you a poet?" she queried, for they were known to be a trifle eccentric.

"No, just a reflective man. And before I permit you to return to the peace you appeared to be relishing until I intruded, I wanted to caution you about Captain Benwell. The man is a cad and a bounder and he is not fit to share your lovely company." Sir Basil gave Harriet a defiant look, like a child who has been naughty quite deliberately and dares you to scold him.

"Oh, dear," Harriet said, dismayed. "I had not thought it that bad. Poor man."

"I believe he has designs on your dowry, Mith Mayne," Sir Basil continued bravely. "Whilst I would normally remain mute ath a fish, not wanting to encroach upon your personal affairs, you are too fine a lady to be subject to his nefarious plans. Take care."

With those words, Sir Basil drifted away down another path, leaving Harriet speechless.

"Do you think he be right?" Betsy said, daring to ask this question of her respected mistress.

"Undoubtedly," Harriet said with a disgusted sigh. "I do not see how I am to dismiss the captain. He turns up when I least expect him."

At this point Cupid gave a firm tug on his leash, freeing himself from her light hold. He dashed madly over the grounds until he reached the side of a tall, impressive gentleman who welcomed the dog with an affectionate pat.

"Ferdy," Harriet murmured. "Just the person I wish to see. How fortunate. I wonder how he knew I was here—or is this another coincidence?" She exchanged looks with her maid, then waited for Ferdy to catch up with her. "What a lovely day it has been," Harriet said politely when he reached her side.

"The park is nice this time of day. But shouldn't you be home preparing for the Sefton party? I recall you mentioned you were to attend." He handed Cupid's leash back to her, watching as she slid her hand securely through the loop.

"Emma and her husband are to fetch me later on. I must say,

it is a godsend to have your sisters take an interest in my affairs. Some people would not be so kind. Although, I must confess that as of late, a number of persons have offered comments regarding my concerns."

"Really? Would you say they have your best interest at heart?" He looked mildly curious, but no more than that.

"I suppose so. Actually it is rather nice. My family certainly is not interested." That she uttered the last without bitterness said a great deal for her acceptance of the situation and her own equanimity.

"I suppose you will consign me to the interfering group," Ferdy said with a cautious look at Harriet.

"Why? We have always been forthright in our speech, have we not?" She bestowed a direct look at him, her vivid green eyes wide with curiosity.

"Perhaps," he admitted. "But this is personal."

"Not you, too?" she cried, looking dismayed.

"Now, Harriet, I only want to protect you from harm."

"You believe the situation to be that serious?" she said, immediately subsiding. "I had thought him merely a joke, and not a very good one at that."

"I take it you refer to Benwell?" Ferdy said, promptly taking advantage of what he believed to be an opportunity to launch into his warning.

"Who else?" she said, frustration evident in her voice. "The man dogs my footsteps more than Cupid does. And do you know—Cupid does not like that man, nor his horse. It is hard to say who was most pleased when he left yesterday—Cupid or I."

Ferdy chuckled, then immediately sobered. He paused a moment, then faced her, his expression urgent. "You must not trust the man. I fear he has evil plans for you."

"You believe that as well?" she said lightly, although her serious mien matched Ferdy's.

"Who else has spoken to you about this?"

"As I said, your sisters are not happy with him. And just now Sir Basil took the liberty to caution me regarding the captain's possible motives in seeking my company. It is very lowering to be sought merely for one's dowry."

"Sir Basil is right, you know. We suspect the captain has an elopement in mind. His creditors are pressing him about his debts." Ferdy placed his arm gently about her, unconsciously wishing to protect her from the rascal who sought to do such a contemptible deed.

"What can I do?" Harriet said with a shrug. "We are assuming the captain has vile intentions. However, I simply cannot march up to the man and demand to know if he wants to elope with me. It is not the thing!"

"You are right, of course. Permit me to give this some thought," Ferdy said, taking his hand from around her back to more properly curve it about her elbow as he assisted her across a rough patch in the path.

"Well, I must admit I find the captain a bore of the first magnitude," Harriet confessed, not wanting Ferdy to believe she was enamored of the man.

"Really? He is such a dashing chap, seems to have no trouble captivating the ladies." Ferdy looked down at Harriet with a gleam shining in his hazel eyes that quite took her breath away.

"They are not captivated—they are wearied to the point of being overwhelmed by boredom. That is not adoration, it is annoyance."

Obviously amused by her description, he admonished, "Now, Harriet."

"But me no buts," she said impatiently. "I want to know what to do about the captain. If it is as you say, that he intends to elope with me, I want to control the situation and not become a victim."

"How amazing you are. In fact, you sound a trifle bloodthirsty. Remind me not to offer you an elopement," he said jestingly.

"No, I'd never do such a thing," she said in a subdued voice. "Society is slow to forget about such matters."

"Why do you not go home and prepare for the Sefton do? I shall see you there. If I have thought of anything, we will discuss it there. After all, you cannot expect me to come up with a Grand Plan on a moment's notice."

"You jest, but I am serious," she said with ill-concealed vexation.

"Now, Harriet," he murmured again, only this time with an affection in his voice that could not be missed.

"Very well," she agreed. "I will don that cream silk that I wore when I sang at Emma's musicale. Let us hope that the vision of me in that splendid gown will tempt the captain to reveal his intentions."

"Now you jest," Ferdy admonished. "That is a very nice gown and you look lovely in it. I shall see you later. May I first escort you to your door?"

"Best not," she said politely. Then she explained, "Should the captain be hovering, I want him to think I am not protected. And Ferdy, you do tend to intimidate."

He smiled at her earnest plea, but agreed. Promising to see her in a few hours, Ferdy left the park, hailing a hackney to return to the Albany, his head awhirl with possible plans.

Her lovely cream satin gown with the exquisite embroidery on the bodice and sleeves could not help but boost her confidence. She smiled at the spray of flowers Ferdy had sent to place across her red curls. Where he had found creamy-white rosebuds she didn't know, but they were perfect. Taking her pretty gold-mesh reticule in hand, she bid a fond adieu to Cupid—who impudently reclined on Harriet's bed.

"Naughty dog," she said with a chuckle.

"He be smart enough not to like the captain," Betsy said quietly.

"Indeed. A wise animal. Well, I am off to beard the dragon in his lair, or whatever one may call it at a party of this magnitude."

"I wish you well, miss."

"I fear I shall need all I can gather."

For once the captain did not appear at her elbow when she ascended the stairs to greet her hostess. Harriet began to relax.

"You are in first looks this evening, Miss Mayne," Lady Sefton commented. She had come to admire the young lady who danced so beautifully at the Wednesday evening assemblies.

"Thank you, ma'am," Harriet said politely.

Emma and Lord Wynnstay, who had so kindly escorted Harriet, also greeted Lord and Lady Sefton, then drifted with the flow of the crowd until Emma espied Diana.

Emma gave her sister a significant look, then raised her brows. "Did you learn anything?"

"If you mean, did I see Ferdy, yes, and as far as I know he has a plan."

Harriet looked from Diana to Emma, then pursed her lips before saying, "Do I detect a bit of skullduggery here? Or is it quite none of my business?"

"Harriet, you silly girl. If you must know, we are concerned about the captain. Ferdy promised to help find a solution."

"I know. He spoke to me about it when I met him in the park."

"Ferdy found you, then? I told him you are fond of walking Cupid. He is so pleased you like the dog."

"I am glad *he* found me and not the captain."

"Well," Diana said with a grimace, "I do not know why the captain simply could not be warned away."

"Because, my pet," her husband said fondly, "he might resort to furtive means, and we would want to prevent that from happening."

"You mean, like dose her with laudanum and spirit her away in a closed carriage?" Diana exclaimed, clearly horrified at such a prospect.

"You have been reading too many novels," he retorted.

"No, indeed, there was an account of such a case in the papers not long ago. I was most appalled that a thing like that could happen. It brought Harriet to mind, if you must know."

Harriet shifted uneasily. All this talk of abduction and drugs was frightening and she needed to be bolstered, not terrified half to death.

"Well, did someone die and I was not told?" Ferdy asked in an amused way when he joined them.

"No, Diana was merely relating a case about an heiress who

was drugged and whisked to Gretna Green by a fortune hunter," Harriet explained. "I also read about it."

"Well, she didn't have us," Diana declared, which remark brought forth laughter from the entire group.

At that moment excellent musicians hired for the party struck up a tune and without a may-I, Ferdy steered Harriet to where the dancers were quickly assembling for a reel.

"You are rather presumptuous, sir," Harriet began, only to be silenced by a look from Ferdy.

"I have an idea," he said, before commencing to lead her down the line of a reel.

She stared at him once they had reached the bottom of the line and took their respective places. She wanted very much to know about this Grand Plan he had concocted, but could scarcely query him while performing a reel. With Ferdy, it might be anything. She only hoped it was not too impossible.

Once the dance concluded, they breathlessly exited the dance floor, only to be accosted by Sir Basil. She could hardly deny him a dance when he had seen her with Ferdy. The party was not so far progressed that she might beg a glass of ratafia, either.

She tossed Ferdy a speaking look, then gracefully accepted Sir Basil's hand. At the conclusion of the cotillion, she was surprised to be met by Mr. Tooke, who appeared to offer lofty condescension in his request for a dance. Harriet was stuck with him as well. Sir Percival Leadbitter followed Mr. Tooke, and on his heels came Lord Titheridge. It only wanted Lord Pomeroy, she thought in annoyance when Lord Titheridge returned her to Diana's side.

"My, you are popular this evening," Diana said with bemusement.

"I suspect your brother's hand in this," Harriet began, then was cut short when Lord Latham requested the next country dance.

"Did your dear wife put you up to this, Lord Latham?" Harriet inquired as he led her forward to where a set formed.

He gave her a bewitching smile and Harriet saw a reason why Phoebe might have preferred him to Ferdy. "Not in the least. You hold your dancing skills too low, Miss Mayne.

After studying all the dancers, I rapidly reached the conclusion that you are by far the best of the lot. I always prefer the best when it is possible."

"Is that why you married Phoebe? I vow, she is the dearest lady."

He smiled and looked to where his adored wife sat with Diana. "You might say that."

Harriet digested this look and comment in silence, for they were actively engaged in a veritable romp of a dance. When they finished, she drew a sigh and looked at him with a rueful grimace.

"Being the best of the lot is tiring, I suppose?"

"I shall take over now, Val," Ferdy said from behind Harriet. "Fetch your wife a shawl or something."

"I demand to know what is going on, Ferdy Andrews," Harriet insisted most circumspectly while they waited for the next dance to begin.

"First, I want to frustrate that Benwell chap. He has been standing over on the far side of the room, glaring at every one of your partners as though he would like to do them bodily harm."

"I see," Harriet said in alarm. Resisting the urge to search out the captain, she prompted Ferdy, "And then what?"

"Well, the fellow naturally grows desperate. He will fear you may be swept off by some other chap, you see. This will make him less cautious. If he approaches you, be careful, but allow him to speak. Better he is out in the open with his plans than scheme behind your back."

"Like the laudanum, and so forth?" she said with a raise of her brows.

"Quite so," Ferdy agreed. And with those words he swept Harriet into his arms and began circling the room to the lilting strains of a lovely waltz.

Harriet was greatly content to be right here in Ferdy's arms, adoring him with her eyes. How anyone might think she could see beyond him to the paltry Captain Benwell was more than she was capable of imagining.

"Once he draws me aside—I presume he will want to do

that and not discuss so delicate a topic in the middle of a dancing floor—what am I to do then?"

"Listen to what he suggests and stall for time until we can discuss his proposal. I shall think of something."

"Well"—she glanced at the dashing captain, so handsome in his uniform this evening—"I would dearly love to put an arrow through that silly hat of his," referring to the shako he wore when out-of-doors.

"Would you now?" Ferdy replied thoughtfully.

The wonderful waltz concluded, and they came to a halt not far from where the captain stood watching them. Harriet decided she had best act as though she were not top over tail in love with Ferdy Andrews and thus gave him a polite curtsy as was proper. "Thank you for the waltz, sir," she said in a demure voice.

"Doing it much too brown, my girl," Ferdy murmured as he bowed over her hand.

"Stroll past the captain. I have an idea," she said.

They slowly proceeded along the side of the room, chatting casually about nothing in particular. When they came abreast of the captain, Harriet paused, fluttering her lashes at the dashing half-pay officer. "Good evening, Captain."

He glared at Ferdy, who didn't look too pleased with him, either.

"It is warm in here this evening," Harriet said pointedly.

When Ferdy remained silent, the gallant captain spoke up. "Allow me to offer my escort to the belle of the ball. Would you care for a glass of ratafia?" He glanced at Ferdy, then added, "I would fetch it for you, but suspect you might be spirited away before I could return."

Harriet gave the captain full marks for sharpness. However bad he might be at the gaming tables, he was not a total nodcock.

"I should welcome a bit of cool air, if you please. Dancing is a very active and tiring occupation." Harriet thanked Ferdy for his company, giving him a significant look before walking at the side of the captain. Close to the hallway, Benwell took two glasses of champagne from a passing footman's tray, handing one to Harriet.

She gave it a dubious look, then decided she might as well be fortified for what was to come. At least she could be certain this didn't have laudanum in it. What a good thing it was that her parents didn't have an invitation to this party and that her sisters were otherwise occupied. She'd not have welcomed their poking noses into her affairs at this point.

The captain paused in the hallway, then guided her toward the open door to a balcony. "Ah, dear Miss Mayne, fresh air. The very thing to revive your spirits after such a fatiguing evening." They moved through the doorway, then stood sipping the champagne in silence, looking over the pretty garden attractively lit with fairy lights.

"You are much in demand this evening," he observed. "I began to despair of ever having a moment of your time."

"La, sir, what nonsense. I am no more in demand than any other girl." Harriet drank more of her champagne, wanting to brace her nerves.

The captain studied her over the rim of his glass. Harriet had to admit that were she not aware of his probable plans, she would be much pleased by the attentions of this handsome man. What a pity he was such an idiot when it came to money. But then, there were a good many just like him.

"I have come to value your company very much, and I admit to great jealousy when I see you dancing with another. You have spirit and charm, and it is easy to see why you are so much sought after," the captain began.

Harriet made a dismissive gesture and shook her head. "I enjoy myself and hope others do as well."

"You are so considerate, so gentle."

Harriet thought of her desire to shoot the man and bit back a smile. She gave him what she hoped was a meek look.

"You are a very desirable young woman and I have fallen quite madly in love with you. Please say you will be mine?" The captain placed a hand on her arm, and dropped a quick kiss on her lips. It seemed he took care that his action went unobserved by anyone.

Harriet clung to her nearly empty glass of champagne, hoping she'd not spill it on her gown. She had no desire to ruin her favorite dress for this man. She'd say this for the captain, he was not bad at kissing, even if it was unwelcome. It crossed her mind that he must have acquired considerable experience elsewhere.

"Sir, this really is very sudden," she said, smoothing down her gown with her free hand when he backed away from her, gazing intently at her, no doubt in an effort to gauge the effect of his kiss.

"I cannot wait, that is, I cannot bear to live without you, my love. Dare I hope that you might return my regard?"

"Well, I shall have to give your offer consideration and that requires time, you know," she said primly. She could see that bit of information gave him pause. Most likely it didn't fit his scheme in the least.

"We shall elope, my love," he burst forth. "It will be most romantic, driving off to the north, just the two of us."

"I should wish my maid, sir," Harriet objected somewhat prosaically.

"What? Oh, of course, a maid." He gave her a confused look, then smiled. "Does that mean you accept my offer, dear Miss Mayne?"

"I shall think about it and let you know before I leave here this evening," she said, planning to confer with Ferdy before then.

"Ah, my princess. You will not regret this mad, impetuous dash, I promise you. It will be very romantic, you will see."

Harriet wondered what he would do if she told him that her money was tied up in funds or somewhere equally hard to reach. It might cool his ardor, but she had every confidence that the captain was inventive. He'd find a way around any obstacle she might devise.

Back in the hall, she searched the area for her friends, then espied Diana returning from the withdrawing room.

"Where is Ferdy? I must talk to him at once."

Diana caught the urgency in Harriet's voice and immediately guessed what had transpired. She glanced to where the captain stood some distance away, brooding over another glass of champagne.

"Ferdy is around the corner, waiting for you."

The two women found him as promised, propping up the wall with his broad shoulders.

"Come, I must tell you what has happened."

"He proposed an elopement and you stalled for time," Ferdy guessed. "I have given it thought and decided you shall agree to meet him at the Archery Grounds." Ferdy proceeded to detail the steps following that meeting and Harriet chuckled, pausing to look at Ferdy. "What happens then? This could be dangerous."

"I shall be there, never fear."

Chapter Twelve

As promised, Harriet sought out the captain before leaving the Sefton party. She studied the young gentleman where he stood waiting in the hallway outside the Sefton drawing room. Harriet wondered what it was that propelled some people into the life of dissipation, while others, like Ferdy, followed the straight and narrow. Of course, one had to discount the opera dancers. And that recollection had to be tucked to the back of her mind for later consideration.

"I am pleased I found you, Captain Benwell. I promised I would consider your proposal and I have."

She approached him with her hands clasped before her, her gold-mesh reticule dangling primly from one nicely gloved arm. She knew she looked her best, that this gown became her well, and that in the soft light of the hall, her freckles could scarcely be seen. Yet she was certain the captain noted none of this. To him she was merely a means of acquiring money to spend.

"And come to what conclusion, Miss Mayne?" the captain asked with just a hint of anxiety in his voice, taking a step toward her that she wryly supposed ought to be considered proper eagerness for her acceptance.

"You did say I would be able to take my maid with me?" she inquired in what she hoped was a sufficiently concerned manner.

"Yes, of course," the captain said impatiently.

"And you would not restrict my activities? I do enjoy my singing and the archery," she observed prosaically.

"We are entering a bargain?" The captain appeared somewhat perplexed that Harriet did not dissolve in his arms, begging to be carried away with him.

"Naturally. Marriage is always a covenant—some being better than others," she said, hoping she did not appear too owlish with her wide-eyed, earnest stare.

He relaxed, offering her an ingratiating smile. Oh, he looked smooth, sophisticated, and suave. Why, it was no wonder the man thought he could have his way with her. He was enough to charm the wallpaper from the wall. However, she needed to convince the captain she was serious, so she continued.

"I would rather elope, I believe, than to be married here. I have a rather sizable dowry, you see, and my father might investigate your business affairs, to our disadvantage. A father does not understand impetuosity, nor has he any sympathy for young love."

"How true," Captain Benwell said with a melting smile.

Harriet guessed that he was already calculating how to best spend her dowry. "For reasons you most likely understand, you cannot collect me at my home, nor will I sneak from my room in the middle of the night. That would be so tiresome." She pursed her lips quite as though she hadn't given this matter great thought before now. Then she smiled at him, a pixy smile that made the captain blink in surprise. "The household is accustomed to seeing me go to the archery grounds at all hours of the day. Why do you not meet me there early in the morning? I shall be able to leave the house without the slightest bother. Will that be all right?"

"What a clever mind you have," he said, false admiration ringing in his voice.

She had the notion that no matter what she had suggested, he would have agreed. That she had offered to meet at what appeared to be a very neutral place, one where few people would be observers, must seem heaven-sent to the would-be eloper.

"Shall we agree on ten of the clock tomorrow morning?" she said in a meek manner, as though she would willingly do anything the captain decided.

"I shall be there, my love."

Harriet had great difficulty not laughing at his parting words. The only love the captain was acquainted with was self-love, and at that he was very good.

She watched him run down the flight of stairs to the entry, then leave. Most likely he was off to arrange for a carriage that would head north come morning. Little did he know that things would not go precisely as he expected.

Frowning, she wondered how to best give the captain a proper comeuppance. Turning, she sought the one she felt could best advise her.

"Diana, have you seen your brother?" she quickly asked when she encountered her vivacious friend.

"He is not faraway. What have you been up to now? I saw you conversing with the dastardly Captain Benwell a few moments ago."

"Yes, I was," Harriet agreed. She decided to keep the arrangements to herself for the nonce. The fewer who knew of her plan, the better. "He certainly is a scoundrel."

"Who's a scoundrel now?" Ferdy said, his voice rumbling with ire as he neared.

"The very one we discussed before," Harriet said sweetly, placing her hand on his arm in preparation for an entreaty to stroll in the hall.

He anticipated her request by leading her from the main rooms and crossing the hall to the balcony where she had stood with the captain while enduring his outrageous proposal.

"The scene of the captain's folly," she observed.

"I watched you from over there," Ferdy gestured to a shadowed alcove from which he could have partially seen them, but scarcely be seen. "The bounder! Had he held you a moment longer, I'd have planted him a facer that would have rearranged his pretty face."

"Ferdy!" she exclaimed. "You are a hero. I have never met a true hero before."

He reddened, but didn't answer her sally.

"Well," she said soberly, "he begged me to marry him with stuff and nonsense about not being able to live without me." She concluded without bitterness, "My money, more likely."

"The unmitigated cad," Ferdy said in a truly angry tone and a frown of awesome proportions. "How did you handle the matter?"

"As you know, I promised him a reply before leaving the

ball—I thought it best not to allow him to dangle or become desperate. Lord Latham suggested he might do something drastic, for the captain *is* deeply in debt, as you know. I agreed to marry him provided I could bring my maid along with us. And I insisted I be permitted to continue with my singing and the archery—to which he consented."

"Did you now?" Ferdy stared at her a moment, then laughed. "Remind me not to think I can ever get the best of you in an argument. You are a clever puss, indeed."

"Well, now that I have sent him off to arrange for a carriage, what must I do? I would like to shoot the man—except I'd rather not swing on a rope for doing it."

Ferdy gave her an arrested look, then said, "You *are* a bloodthirsty little thing."

"He is despicable—thinking that merely because I am without comeliness I will leap into his arms. What rubbish!" She gave Ferdy a mutinous frown.

"He cannot be truly looking at you if he thinks such nonsense. Your hair has become your glory and many young women must envy your figure. Do not underestimate your charms, Harriet," he half scolded.

Not quite certain how she ought to respond to this gracious remark, Harriet merely chose to smile, then changed the subject. "What shall I do when I meet him in the morning?"

"You intend to keep the appointment, then?"

"Indeed, but I must make *him* run off, to fear me. And you must admit, I do not have a handy pair of fives, as you might say." His expression at her use of boxing cant made her chuckle. "Do I not have the right of it?"

"What a minx you are," he said, but he sounded more fond than scolding. "Very well, if you must meet the chap, you had best come armed."

"I cannot shoot a gun very well. I may miss my target," she observed earnestly.

"Maybe you should use your bow, then," he joked. Ferdy studied her with an amused expression that changed rapidly when she next spoke.

"Famous! An excellent idea. I shall shoot to hit the blue, not the gold—if you follow my meaning."

"You intend to miss by a hair?" Ferdy said, sounding horrified.

"Do you believe I cannot do it?" she challenged.

"Oh, if you take careful aim, no doubt you could," he said, taking a step away from her.

"I would very much like to have you lurking about in the shadows or around some corner for support in case I might fail—if you might be so kind. He may argue with me—try to compel me to come with him by use of force or laudanum—but he'd not quibble with you."

"Such trust is unnerving," Ferdy replied with a touch of something in his voice she couldn't identify. She gave him a curious look, but he added nothing to explain that remark.

"It is agreed, then? I shall appear at the archery grounds, my maid with me. You will conceal yourself where you think best. I will have my new bow and a quiver of arrows. It would not do," she digressed, "to allow him to think I have but one arrow to shoot at him."

"Well, I can think of nothing more daunting to our amorous captain than to be shot at by the young woman he intends to abduct," Ferdy said with a grin that revealed his lack of pity for the captain's plight.

"Let us hope that I succeed," Harriet declared firmly, turning to leave and return to his sisters.

They ambled along the hall as though they had not been deep in a private conversation, no matter that they had remained where they might be seen by anyone. Neither Ferdy nor Harriet desired any complications.

"I suppose I ought to feel vexed that you did not call for someone to find us in a compromising situation," Ferdy said in mock complaint. "I do believe my stock in the world must have dropped of late."

"Ferdy," she exclaimed, placing her hand lightly on his arm in dismay, "you do not truly believe *I* would do something like that to you! I should hope you would know me better than that. You are a good, kind man, the best friend I could have." She thought a moment, then added, "Besides, I couldn't begin to compete with La Fleur."

Ferdy made a slight choking noise as they entered the room

where Diana and Emma stood chatting, preparing to leave the party.

"At last," Diana said, looking curious, "you return. I trust that whatever was discussed, you reached a plan of some sort?"

"We did," Harriet agreed, then changed the subject—something she was becoming rather good at by now.

As they made their farewells, thanking Lady Sefton and her earl for the delightful evening, Emma placed an arm lightly about Harriet's shoulder, saying, "You shall drive with us. I wish to have a few words with you, if I may?"

Giving Emma a wary look, Harriet agreed.

"I shall welcome your company," Harriet observed politely, giving Ferdy what she hoped was a significant look before standing at Emma's side to wait for the Wynnstay carriage.

"I will be eager to learn how things go for you," Diana said with a glimmer of a smile before entering her carriage followed by Damon.

"I cannot think what she is talking about," Harriet confided to Emma as they clambered into the Wynnstay vehicle.

"She is dying to know what you and Ferdy conferred about for so long. With any *other* girl, Ferdy might have been hopelessly compromised, one way or another."

"I would never do such a thing to him," Harriet began indignantly.

Emma interrupted, patting Harriet's arm and saying, "Of course not. Did you arrange matters to your satisfaction?"

"I think so," Harriet said, her lingering doubts revealed in her voice.

"Well, whatever you decided to do, I wish you the very best of luck," Emma declared, only to be seconded by her husband.

"Thank you, both," Harriet declared fervently. "Once it is over, I will come directly to tell you all about it. I would hate to have you disappointed," she said with a chuckle.

"Harriet, I do not know how Ferdy contains himself when he deals with you, if that is how you treat him," Lord Wynnstay said with laughter in his voice.

"He does look rather fierce at times," Harriet admitted. "But he is such a gentle lamb, he'd never cause me hurt," she concluded.

Emma exchanged a speaking look with her husband, but neither of them gave voice to their reaction to Harriet's unusual opinion of Ferdy Andrews—one not shared by the world at large.

Early the following morning Harriet dressed in her forest green gown, and placed her little hat atop her head with trembling hands. Was she totally mad to consider this plan of action? She had never heard of any woman doing such an outrageous thing—shooting an arrow at the gentleman who sought to wed her for her money.

But she hoped to make an impression on the captain—that he ought not trifle with the affections of a young lady just because he wanted money and the poor thing possessed a fine dowry.

With Betsy at her side, Harriet left the house, her bow and quiver of arrows at her side. How fortunate that Ferdy had arranged for her to have use of the archery grounds until her membership was approved. It was quite common for ladies to shoot. Perhaps the day would come when there would be contests for them as well. A good many of them were truly excellent archers.

The hackney Betsy had found for them was reasonably clean, with fresh straw on the floor. She knew better than to consider calling for the family carriage; someone was certain to have prior claim on it. The jarvey dropped them off directly in front of the archery grounds. They were early: Harriet wished to practice a bit, warm up as it were.

While Betsy watched closely, Harriet took aim and let her first arrow fly at the target. She hit right on the line between the blue and the gold.

"Not bad, miss," Betsy said with an assessing look.

"I must be better than that, however," Harriet said with determination. She nocked another arrow and took aim once again. This time she hit farther into the gold and sighed with satisfaction. "Better."

"Don't know how you think to hit something else but that target, begging your pardon, miss," Betsy observed.

"Nor do I. I'll see if I can do it again."

Over and over she took aim at the target, trying to hit the same place. Betsy willingly went to retrieve the arrows, resolved that her mistress should hit her chosen target when the time arrived. That dastardly captain deserved to have a year or two frightened out of him.

Once Harriet had made quite a number of consecutive hits to the gold, she turned to Betsy and confided, "I am ready for him." Glancing at the little watch pinned to her gown, she smiled grimly and added, "He ought to be turning up here any moment. Have you seen Mr. Andrews?"

"No, miss. There be just the two of us at this hour."

Harriet gave a worried look about the grounds, wondering if Ferdy had forgotten about the morning affair. She hoped not, but if he had gone to visit La Fleur last evening, it might have put this archery meeting clear out of his mind.

"Well, we shall do our best, Betsy," Harriet said with resignation to her fate, whatever it might be come the conclusion to this morning.

The clatter of a coach-and-four on the cobbled street echoed through the grounds. She exchanged a look with Betsy when it stopped. "I believe he is come."

Harriet nocked an arrow to the string, prepared to raise her bow and shoot. A carriage door slammed, footsteps echoed in the stillness.

The entry was guarded by two tall, pyramid-shaped arborvitae. The captain paused here; then espying Harriet his look of concern eased and he began walking toward her.

"Stop where you are, sir. I have changed my mind. It has come to my attention that you are severely pressed for funds. I fear you will only spend my money and make my life a misery. May I suggest you discover that a trip elsewhere would be beneficial to your health?" Her voice rang bell-like in the stillness of the morning air.

The captain looked utterly stunned.

"You did not think I would cotton to your scheme, did you? How fortunate I have dear friends who have my best interests at heart." From the corner of her eye she caught sight of a large and comforting shape moving to one side of the building where equipment was housed.

The captain took another step toward Harriet. "Now, sweetheart, be reasonable."

"I would not take another step were I you," she cautioned, raising the prepared bow, ready to let her arrow fly to its human target. "And I doubt very much that I am your sweetheart." She found she was cool, more collected than she would have expected. Be reasonable, indeed. Allow him access to her money and doom herself to a future full of tribulations? Not if she could prevent it.

"Now, Harriet, what you have heard is nothing but lies. Most likely it came from Mr. Andrews, who probably is jealous, wanting you for himself. Well, I claimed you first. Just put away your bow. You may practice later."

He took two more steps and Harriet squinted at her target, took aim, then let the arrow arc through the air.

"My word," Betsy whispered with awe, "it went clean through his hat!"

The captain stopped in his tracks, removed his fine beaver top hat and stared at it, then pulled the arrow from where it had punctured just above the brim. He glared at Harriet, saying, "If this is how you behave, I'd not have you on a platter if you had twice the dowry! You are daft, woman! Batty as they come and bran-faced to boot." He whirled about to dash from the grounds with all speed, as though Harriet might let go another arrow at him and not be too choosy about where it landed.

In seconds they heard a carriage door slam shut and the sound of a rapidly disappearing coach-and-four.

Ferdy appeared from the shadows where he had concealed himself, applauding as he made his way to Harriet's side. "Did you know that you not only put a couple of new holes in that fine hat of his, you also gave his hair a new parting? I have a feeling that is the last you will see of the captain."

"I hope he leaves London," she said wrathfully. "Fancy him calling me daft!" She shook with rage and not a little shock at what she had dared to do.

"We must celebrate!" Ferdy cried, picking her up as though she were nothing more than a feather and whirling her about in the air.

She dropped her bow, clutching at his arms with trembling hands. Betsy promptly retrieved the bow, even as she chuckled at this silly business.

"Ferdy, put me down!" Harriet demanded breathlessly. She liked being held by him far too much for her own good. In fact, she might be so foolish as to offer to replace La Fleur, and she was far from competing with that splendid beauty.

"Come, let us go to Diana's house. She is waiting impatiently, as is Emma." He continued to hold her high in the air with no visible effort that she could tell.

"Goodness, did you tell everyone about my morning assignation?" Harriet exclaimed with mock indignation. She was feeling far too triumphant to be upset by dear Ferdy.

"I stopped by Diana's on the way here to tell her to prepare a victory tea," he explained with that sly grin lingering on his good and gentle face.

Harriet placed her hands on his shoulders, being held so high that such a thing was possible. "Were you so certain I would accomplish the deed, then?" she demanded, impressed with his faith in her ability.

"Aye, Harriet. I knew you would hit your man," he replied with a chuckle.

Harriet lowered her gaze, thinking it unlikely that she would obtain the man she really wanted.

He bussed her on the mouth, one of those hasty, jubilant kisses that you might give a young niece, and then gently placed her on her feet.

"You take liberties, I believe," she scolded mildly.

"Not as many as I might like," he muttered, then looked about the place to see if anything had been left behind.

Betsy retained the bow, offered Harriet her small green reticule that matched her dress, then trotted happily behind her dear mistress as the three made their way to the entry, then through the gate.

Ferdy's large landau awaited them, having pulled up from the corner where it had been concealed.

"How clever you are to have everything in readiness," Harriet said with admiration.

"I do things right from time to time," he admitted with a grin.

"Well, such an ample carriage is impressive." She recalled how it had easily carried the children and her, not to forget the large sailing boat in addition to Ferdy.

"I like my comfort," he admitted.

Harriet then realized that a small carriage would not do for him. Such a large gentleman would take his ease in something the size of the landau. That he was content to let his driver take honors with the fine team of horses also impressed her. Ferdy Andrews was a man who was secure and had no need to show off before the world.

They chatted amiably on the way to Diana's house. Harriet wondered briefly what her parents might have said to her outlandish handling of the matter of the proposed elopement, then dismissed her speculations. For all she knew, her father might have given the captain his blessing, just to be rid of a troublesome daughter. She had no illusions about her not-so-loving family.

They arrived shortly at Diana's lovely home, where Ferdy escorted her inside with a flourish. "We are here!" he said with a low bow to his sisters. "And we are victorious. The captain was last seen haring off at full speed in his elopement carriage all by himself. With all he owes, he may not stop until he reaches Dover!"

There were delighted cries and affectionate hugs from both Emma and Diana.

How nice it was to be warmly welcomed into Diana's drawing room, acclaimed as a heroine and fussed over. Harriet was not accustomed to such petting and admiration.

"Weren't you afraid you might miss the hat?" Emma said when the excitement had died somewhat and they sat more composed over cups of tea—with Ferdy having a celebratory glass of claret.

"The thought crossed my mind. Then he made a stupid remark and angered me. From that moment, all I could see was that hat. I knew I would hit it."

"What did he say to make you angry?" Diana queried from over the brim of her teacup.

"Aside from calling me dotty and bran-faced?" Harriet did not think she could reveal the captain's words regarding the possibility of Ferdy being jealous. Not only was it preposterous, it pained her. It was one thing to acknowledge in her heart that Ferdy Andrews was beyond her. It was quite another matter to admit to his sisters that she had been hurt by the captain's taunting, knowing how far from the truth those words were.

"He never did?" Emma said with distaste.

"Said he'd not have me on a platter, actually," Harriet said with a smile. She chanced to look at Ferdy only to find him studying her with a disconcerting thoroughness, a speculative gleam in his eyes.

"Well, we are pleased you are returned to us unharmed and will not be bothered by that fortune hunter again," Emma declared firmly.

"Indeed," Ferdy confirmed. "If that chap dares show his face about town again, he will have to deal with me."

Harriet shook her head in amazement. "How fortunate I am to have you as friends. What would I have done had Ferdy not stopped me when I was by the Serpentine that day? I might be partway to Gretna now, for one thing, as I would not have had a weapon to use against the captain." She looked from Diana to Emma, shaking her head in bemusement.

"Your father would have come through for you," Ferdy said gallantly, but without much conviction.

Harriet was too polite to disagree with him on this point. It was embarrassing to have her family's faults revealed so clearly by their actions or lack thereof.

"Has your father said anything more about marriage to Lord Pomeroy?" Diana queried.

"Or going to live with your aunt in Little Munden?" Emma added with a compassionate look at Harriet.

"No, but then I have avoided the family with great care. I have become most adept at thinking up excuses for being absent. They all go to different social gatherings, so I doubt I am missed, and Mama is so grateful not to have to chaperone me about that she is reluctant to inquire too closely into my doings. I suppose she fears that if she asks, she may be stuck with me again."

"I cannot imagine such a family," Diana murmured, then apologized to Harriet for her thoughtless words.

"No matter. I have been with them for a long time and am quite used to their ways," Harriet joked. "But I had best leave now. There is the Brant party this evening, is there not?"

"I plan to attend," Emma began. "I would welcome your company."

A meeting time was arranged and Harriet prepared to depart, ready to collect Betsy and be on her way.

Ferdy offered to give them a drive home.

"Well, as you have an open carriage, I expect it is acceptable," Harriet said with a mischievous twinkle in her eyes.

Once Ferdy had deposited Miss Harriet Mayne at her door, he continued on his way, deeply in thought. All the while the women had been chatting about the business with the captain, and then later when Harriet joked about her family, or what passed for a family, he realized an important truth.

He loved her. Precisely when this had occurred, he couldn't say. But he knew the signs. He knew he wanted to conquer her enemies, make smooth her path, kill dragons, anything to please her. He would tell her tomorrow, convince her that they could marry and she would be free of her dratted family, her wretched aunt, and the smelly Lord Pomeroy forever.

First, he had one minor matter to attend to—the end of his relationship with the beauteous La Fleur. It did not amuse him to think that Harriet knew about the opera dancer. In fact, he could not imagine forgoing time with Harriet to devote to La Fleur. No, it would have to end, and immediately.

"Rundell and Bridge, please," he requested of his coachman. He'd buy a pretty parting gift and that would be that. La Fleur was surprisingly ladylike and he didn't anticipate any hitch in the farewells.

And there wasn't. But then, a sapphire necklace did offer compensation.

Chapter Thirteen

The day of the Brant party, Harriet had her singing lesson as usual. She was distracted, however. Her voice might be soaring to the ceiling, but her thoughts were on Ferdy and what she was going to do about her future.

Her father's growing impatience had become more obvious. She'd been unable to avoid a family dinner last evening—one could send down excuses just so many times. However, frowning looks directed at her were quite enough to not only stem any appetite, but worry her half the night as well.

Once Signor Carvallo departed the house, the first footman informed her she was wanted in her father's library.

With great trepidation, Harriet immediately presented herself before her august parent, wondering what decree he would hand down now. It couldn't be much worse than Lord Pomeroy or Aunt Croscombe—unless he put the two together. The image of her Tartar of an aunt with the odoriferous lord utterly boggled the mind.

"Yes, Father?" she meekly inquired once she had entered the room and was seated in the oversized leather chair, one she suspected he pointed to because it would intimidate her. It did.

"And how do you go on these days? We scarcely see you from one day to another." He did not appear to find this omission to his disliking.

"Very well, thank you. I have made several very kind friends and do well enough at the social gatherings. I am becoming most proficient at archery and I enjoy it excessively." She did not smile at Papa. That would probably make him wonder what she was trying to cover up—he had often voiced that sentiment when she was younger and all she had tried to do was mollify him. Papa was not easy to please.

"No beau, Harriet? No betrothal in view?" The sardonic lift of his brow cut her to the quick.

A feeling of dread crept over her; fear clutched her heart. She swallowed carefully, then replied, "Not as yet, Papa. I have high hopes, however."

"Hopes are not reality. Lord Pomeroy is reality. He is becoming impatient, Harriet. May I remind you that I agreed to a brief time during which you could have the opportunity to find yourself a husband, since you seem to find my choice a trifle repugnant?" There was no glimmer of a smile in his eyes at his choice of words.

"Yes, Papa." Harriet thought frantically. There was not a name she might offer, no matter she had gentlemen who flocked about her. Captain Benwell was no doubt faraway by this time—fortunately, as far as she was concerned. She hoped Sir Basil might at some point step forward from the wallpaper into which he had effaced himself to assert an interest. And she did not consider Ferdy because she was quite certain that he not only had other interests—La Fleur, for one—but also that he was destined to remain a bachelor from all that he had said and she had heard.

"Well? Time and my patience are drawing to a close. I give you one more day. That is all, Harriet. One more day to find a suitable husband who will not disgrace the family tree." He bent his head to study some papers on his desk.

Dismissed, Harriet rose from the massive chair and slipped from the library as silent as a mouse.

It would have to be someone at the Brant party. Fortunately, most everyone she had met to this point would likely attend. But how, she wondered, did a young lady go about snagging a proposal?

For once she wished she were closer to her sisters. While they might laugh at her pretensions—thinking it foolish that any man might give her a second look when there were so many beauties around—they might enjoy puffing up their own consequence.

She ran Victoria and Coralie to ground in the morning room

where they were perusing the latest fashion journal. Pausing in the doorway, she studied their admitted beauty—and they were stunning. Dressed in the height of fashion, hair perfectly curled and in place, faces composed to reflect the purest of thoughts, they were the epitome of English female elegance and desirability.

"Harriet, have you finished your lesson with the signor so soon?" Coralie asked without interest.

"Have you seen Papa yet?" Victoria added with a sidelong glance at Coralie.

"Yes, my lesson is over and I have seen Papa. However, I wanted to talk about you, not me."

Since it was unusual for Harriet to inquire into their lives and they so enjoyed explaining things of a superior nature to their unfortunate sister, the two young women perked up, came to life as it were.

"What is it you wish to know, Harriet?" Coralie asked, sitting more erect, correctly assuming Harriet had come to their font of knowledge for instruction.

"How did you encourage Perth to ask for your hand?" Harriet asked baldly, not knowing how to approach the topic through a circuitous route.

Both sisters tittered into their embroidered handkerchiefs, exchanging highly amused looks. "It was quite simple," Coralie said at last. "I merely inclined my head when he sought to speak with me, and then he asked. Of course, he was not the first, but he was the one I wished."

Knowing she meant that he held the highest title, Harriet merely nodded her comprehension.

Victoria gave Coralie a look, then turned back to Harriet. "The third time we met, Viscount Colborn begged that I consider him. Naturally, I took my time, for it would be unseemly to say yes in an instant."

Harriet guessed that Victoria had hoped for an earl at the very least. But a bird in the hand and all that.

"Why do you ask? Never say you have a shy possibility?"

"Maybe," Harriet replied, then escaped before they could pin her with questions. She had no desire to be quizzed by them, for they could be relentless until they had wormed out every secret she possessed. On the other hand, she mused, they might be so horrified at her shooting the captain through his hat they would forget about all else.

Her preparations for the Brant party bordered on a full-scale attack of military measure. Betsy fussed over Harriet's hair as she had longed to do and was denied when Harriet became impatient. A gown newly arrived from Madame Clotilde slid over Harriet's form with surprising results. The delicate sea-foam green softened her hair and enhanced her skin as nothing else had.

After dusting a layer of delicately colored rice powder on her face, Harriet rose from her dressing table to study the results of their efforts in her looking glass.

"You look a treat, miss," Betsy said, admiration ringing in her voice.

"I will have to do, for I cannot think of anything more in aid of my mission," Harriet murmured to her reflection.

Ignoring her maid's quizzical look, Harriet gathered up her gold-mesh reticule, a pretty ivory fan, and a gauzy stole that offered not the slightest warmth, but looked splendid.

She encountered Coralie in the lower hall.

"Going out so early? La, I always wait so as to make a grand entrance," she advised.

"Not all are disposed to grand entrances, Coralie."

"True," the beauty admitted. "But you look very nice, dear."

These words from Coralie nearly sent Harriet into shock. "Thank you," she stammered.

"Whatever Father decreed, I trust you will prevail. You manage to have your way in spite of his intentions." Coralie looked perplexed as to how this was achieved, but did not ask. This was just as well, for Harriet wouldn't have known what to say. How did one explain *deviousness* to a person who had no need for such ploys?

"Our parents take the carriage tonight," Coralie reminded her.

"Lord and Lady Wynnstay insisted upon stopping for me," Harriet said, with her warm regard for them clear in her voice.

"You are fortunate to have caught Lady Wynnstay's eye.

She has influence," Coralie concluded, then drifted off, having lost interest in her sister's affairs.

How nice to have friends who were prompt, Harriet thought when she entered the Wynnstay carriage minutes later.

"You look blue-deviled, Harriet," Lord Wynnstay said after searching their guest's face.

"I suppose I am," she admitted. His observation revealed more astuteness than her sister possessed.

"Your father?" Emma hazarded rightly, possibly figuring that he would produce the greatest worry.

"I must find a beau, a proposal for my hand this evening or be the affianced of Lord Pomeroy." She caught the look of alarm exchanged between her friends, who faced each other in the confines of the carriage.

"That is serious enough to warrant a case of the green melancholy," Emma said lightly.

Harriet laughed, as she was meant to do. Then she changed the subject as she did not wish to impose on her friends regarding her troubles. This was her battle and she would fight it as best she could.

The party given by Lord and Lady Brant reflected their secure position in Society. It was understood that the Prince Regent would attend. Harriet wondered if she dared face him after her behavior at the archery grounds. With any luck at all she might avoid meeting him.

Ferdy pounced upon them immediately after they had left the receiving line, beaming a smile at Emma and Edmund— and Harriet also, which gave her hope.

"Well, you look as though you had just won the lottery," Edmund said jovially.

"No, do I?" Ferdy assumed a shocked expression that made Harriet offer a nervous giggle and earned her a quizzical look from her imposing friend.

"Ferdy, I need to talk with you," she ventured to say once Emma's attention had been caught by a friend and Edmund paused to chat with a member of the cabinet.

"We can manage that, I fancy. Come, we shall promenade along the far side of the room, away from all this rabble."

"I do believe you are trying to cheer me up. Emma thought I was a candidate for a case of the green melancholy." Her attempt at humor failed.

"Your father decided that you'd had sufficient time to choose a husband?" he guessed.

"Have you taken up the reading of minds now?" she said with a tense smile.

"On the contrary, I had been anticipating such an event. He does not strike me as a patient man."

"No," she agreed, "he is never that. I imagine I have tried that quality sorely."

"So?" he quizzed, not helping her along in the least.

She glared at him as though she would dearly love to punch his arm, even though she knew full well he was the only one she could turn to in her distress.

"I have until tomorrow to produce a husband-to-be."

"How glum you are," he teased. "You might think it an ill fate rather than one of joy."

"Oh, do be serious," she scolded, rapping him lightly on his arm with her fan. "This is no joking matter."

"Well, I wonder whom you might select," he said, his face utterly inscrutable as he gazed at her, lids hooded, normally genial expression devoid of a hint of his feelings.

"Do you think Sir Basil might do?" she ventured hesitatingly.

"Man's not good enough for you. Or is he the one you desire above all else?" She thought his stare calculating.

What a question! "Not really," she said evasively.

"Never settle for second best," he declared.

"That is easy for you to say." She thought of the exquisite La Fleur and sighed. Ferdy could command the attention and win the hand of anyone he pleased. A gentleman so kind and good, so charming and thoughtful, not to mention wealthy, must be at the top of a great many hopeful lists.

"Allow me to think about this. You do not wish a prince, do you?" he said with mock worry.

"Silly man!" she replied, laughing at his nonsense.

"Well, you have met the gentleman and he is most eligible as well as being a topnotch bowman."

"He cannot be better than you are," she riposted.

"Nor do I think he has parted a chap's hair with his arrow as someone I know has done."

"I only meant to hit his hat," Harriet said in her defense.

Sir Basil presented himself as a partner before Ferdy could discuss the problem any further. Harriet went with Sir Basil gladly, intent upon bringing him up to scratch.

She failed. Miserably.

At the merest hint of interest in him beyond a dancing partner, he faded again at the conclusion of their dance as only he could manage. Perhaps he was practicing to be a magician, Harriet decided with charity.

"No hope there?" Ferdy said, coming upon Harriet where she stood close to Emma, alone once Sir Basil had vanished.

"None, I fear. I didn't perceive it would be this difficult." She gave Ferdy a worried look. "Perhaps I ought to propose instead?"

"What would you say?" he asked in the most innocent and bland voice imaginable.

Shooting him a wary look, Harriet decided he was just trying to help. "Well, I suppose the best thing to do is be direct. A simple statement like 'Would you marry me?' ought to suffice."

"I will," Ferdy said, giving Harriet that shrewd look as he had before.

"Be serious," she scolded yet again.

"I am," he insisted. "While you were romping through that country dance with our esteemed friend, it came to me that it is the ideal answer to your dilemma. At the very least, it would give you additional time."

"Are you thinking of a sham betrothal?" she whispered, hoping nobody could overhear her.

"If you want it that way," he replied, looking as though he'd been exceptionally clever and ought to be praised. "Well? Is it a match?"

"You leave me breathless," she said, feeling extremely confused.

"That is lovely," he murmured.

There was a stir at the entrance to the large room where the elite gathering stood in clusters between dances.

"Good heavens, it wanted only him," Harriet murmured to Ferdy as she stared at the Prince Regent, with his retinue following in his wake like a mother duck and her goslings.

"I intend to present you again. Can you curtsy properly without a bow to lean on, Harriet?" Ferdy teased.

"Just you wait," she muttered in dire accents.

The royal procession drew closer to where they stood. Harriet was certain she would tumble head over heels when she attempted a court curtsy—quite as she had when practicing for her presentation that had fortunately been canceled when the king again took ill.

"Your Royal Highness, may I present my betrothed, Miss Harriet Mayne, daughter of Sir Edward Mayne? It has not been officially announced as yet. As matter of fact, you are the first to know about it."

Harriet's curtsy might have been a trifle wobbly, but she managed well enough under the benevolent eye of her future king in spite of the shock of Ferdy's announcement. "Your Royal Highness," Harriet said clearly.

"Finally nabbed at last!" the prince boomed. "Congratulations to you both. You are the gel Andrews had been teaching to be a bowman. Heard fascinating rumors about you at Leicester House," he added at Ferdy's nod.

"Indeed, sir, I adore archery, as do many women. Perhaps we shall have our own club someday, and not have to wish we might venture into that establishment for bowmen," she ventured.

"Ha, ha," the prince said, "we are amused. Send us an invitation to the wedding. We must see the two famous bowmen united in wedlock. We trust you intend to wear green, Andrews?"

"Perhaps I would set a new trend, Your Highness," Ferdy said with a grin.

"A taking young lady," the prince said, looking at Harriet with a rather charming smile before moving along through the throng of his future subjects.

"Goodness, I am overwhelmed," Harriet admitted with a

discreet dab at her brow. "But did you have to tell him of our sham betrothal?" she demanded in an undertone.

"How better to convince your father of the fact than to have the prince declare he wishes to attend the wedding? I would vouch that even your mother will be happy to learn of such a prominent guest."

"I give leave to doubt that, for it will quite put Victoria's and Coralie's weddings in the pale. They have not the advantage of being bowmen, you see."

Ferdy grinned, then took her hand, glancing at Emma before saying, "I believe Harriet and I may dance as many times as I wish, now that we are formally betrothed."

Emma looked enormously pleased at this remark. "You do have a way with you, dear brother. I cannot believe you are so clever as to see what a perfect mate Harriet will be for you. Usually a man has to have this pointed out to him."

"I am not a slowtop, I'll have you know." There was a glint in his eyes that silenced both women.

With that succinct statement, he tugged Harriet with him to the dance floor just as the strains of one of the new waltzes drifted forth from the musical group.

"Shall we show these good people how they do the 'mazy dance,' as Byron calls it?" Ferdy slipped his arm about her and Harriet lost the ability for sensible thought.

"I have the oddest notion that matters are fast growing out of hand," Harriet said, looking at Ferdy with a frown while deftly following his lead.

Ferdy merely smiled and thanked his lucky stars that the prince had acted as he hoped. All Ferdy had to do now was to convince his dear little love that the betrothal should continue. Once it became an established certainty, it would be almost impossible to break.

"How go your singing lessons?" he queried, hoping to take her mind from the betrothal, mock or otherwise.

"Very well," she replied, clearly startled by this turn of conversation.

"You have a lovely voice, and I intend to see those lessons continue. By the bye, I do intend to dance every dance with you, so be warned," he said after taking note of his friends

Leadbitter and Titheridge staring at Harriet as though they had discovered a pot of gold they wished to claim.

"Is that so?" she said with ominous quiet.

"If you want to truly convince your father of the truism of our engagement, how better to accomplish it?"

She studied his face, then said, "I thought the prince was in aid of that."

"Every little bit helps," he said modestly. "I must convince one and all that I am a reformed man and the model husband-to-be."

"How have you reformed, may I ask," she asked with an arrested look on her face. "And just how do you think that dancing every dance with me will do the thing? Society frowns on such doting behavior. Ferdy, I believe you tell a whisker."

"You wound me, my dearest Harriet," he said as the waltz drew to an end and he quite ignored the approach of good old Leadbitter and Titheridge.

He kept his word, dancing every set when he wasn't urging champagne or lemonade on her. When invited to partake of a light supper, he insisted Harriet remain close to his side. He heaped a plate with more food than she consumed in a day, then insisted she eat.

"Ferdy, I . . ." she began, then stopped. She'd been about to tell him she wasn't hungry—for she had quite lost her appetite when he introduced her to the prince. But she suddenly discovered she was starved and tucked into her food with zest. Too many missed meals had caught up with her.

"What a delightful creature you are," Ferdy said, beaming at her with approval when he saw her food disappearing. "It is so reassuring to know that you are not one of those females who exist on air and butterfly wings."

"Nobody does, you know," she confided. "Those sort stuff themselves when they are in seclusion at home. It is done to make a gentleman think they will scarcely require feeding."

"What a lot of nonsense." Ferdy cleaned his plate, then leaned back in his chair with a glass of excellent claret in hand to observe his delightful girl finish her supper.

"How do you intend to tell your parents about our betrothal?" he inquired after she had concluded her meal. He ignored her sputtering out her lemonade, merely offering a **crisp** linen napkin.

"Take care when you say such things," she warned, once she'd recovered.

"I was wondering when I ought to have that visit with your father—you know, the one that chaps always dread?"

"How is it that you survived infancy?" Harriet wondered with a twinkle emerging in her vivid green eyes.

"Because I was the heir, of course. Boys can squeak by easier than girls."

"Right you are," she murmured, then applied herself to the problem. "I had best prepare him or he will think you daft."

"Surely not?" Ferdy denied.

"If you prefer, I could simply announce that you have expressed a desire to pay your addresses to me and that Father may expect you tomorrow. Since he will likely be the only one around come breakfast, it would be the easiest time for me. I could not bear to listen to my sisters."

"Likely upset about not having the prince?"

"If only that. No, they would tease me and I find I tire of teasing rather quickly."

Ferdy appeared to digest that remark while he again led her for a country dance, causing the gossips to have a splendid time behind fans and raised hands, with meaningful looks and raised brows, not to mention tilted noses.

It was a rollicking romp and once Harriet left the floor with Ferdy's sturdy support, she sighed. "I must be growing old, for I long for my bed." She would have sworn she heard Ferdy murmur something like he did, too, but that was absurd. It never entered her head that he thought seriously of marriage or what nightly pursuits it included.

When he brought her to Emma's side, he gave his sister a significant look. "It has been quite an evening," he said politely.

"Would you mind were we to leave early, Harriet?" Emma asked, placing a gentle hand on Harriet's arm.

"Not in the least, I am pleasantly tired." She chanced to look over and catch Sir Basil's stare. "At least Lord Pomeroy failed to appear. I worried that he might show up after what Papa said."

"You no longer have to worry about that old buzzard. I intend to take good care of you from now on," Ferdy declared in what Harriet decided was the most comforting manner she had ever known. For a few moments a warm glow suffused her at the idea of being the center of this gentleman's keeping. Then she recalled La Fleur.

For a young lady who has just had her betrothal to one of the premier gentlemen of the *ton* announced to none other than the Prince Regent in full view of the cream of Society, Harriet was oddly subdued on the trip to her home. How she wished that her parents had attended to see her crowning moment. They had preferred the opera this evening, followed by a pause at a party held by friends.

"A bit overwhelming, is it not?" Emma said, with a comforting pat on Harriet's arm, which the gauzy shawl barely covered.

"Your brother is definitely one of a kind," Harriet declared earnestly.

"We have long known it. It is nice to share our view with a pretty young woman."

Again the image of La Fleur entered Harriet's mind and she sighed, gloom settling over her.

Fortunately, before Emma detected her lowering of spirits, they reached Harriet's address. She gave fervent thanks for their help in shepherding her so generously, then hurried into the house.

Come morning, she entered the breakfast room with caution, fearing yet hoping to find her father sitting over his coddled eggs and newspaper.

He was there. Glancing up from his reading, he lowered his paper and watched while Harriet gathered her toast and tea, then seated herself close to him at the table.

"Well? I am waiting." It was clear to her that he expected a report of failure. After all, what young lady could snabble a suitable gentleman literally overnight?

"Mr. Andrews will be coming over to request my hand later this morning, Father. He wishes to marry me."

"Andrews! He runs with a pretty fast set. No, by gad, I'll not have it," her father thundered, thumping his fist on the table so the dishes clattered and the footman hurried in to see if he was wanted.

"He told the Prince Regent that we were engaged to wed. The Prince requested an invitation to the wedding," Harriet added with outward calm. Inwardly, she trembled, but she'd not allow her father to see that.

"You made your curtsy to the Prince Regent last evening?" her mother cried from the doorway, looking as though she was utterly flummoxed by such news, not to mention the notion of Harriet marrying Mr. Andrews.

"Indeed, Mama. He was so gracious and charming to me. He knows about my skill with the bow and said he wished to attend the wedding of two prominent bowmen."

"Mercy!" Lady Mayne said in fading accents, tottering to a chair and sinking onto it with unseemly haste.

"You speak as though it is an accomplished fact," Lord Mayne said with frowning displeasure.

"Do you know Mr. Andrews, Papa? He is a very determined gentleman. He is much admired by those who meet him and know him. He has been all that is kind and agreeable to me. I do wish to marry him," she concluded, admitting to herself that the latter were certainly the truest words she'd ever spoken.

"Well, I never," Lady Mayne cried in distressed tones.

"I don't suppose you have," Harriet agreed. What would happen when the betrothal was later terminated she refused to consider. The magnitude of such an emotional outpouring was beyond her ken.

"Have what?" Coralie said as she and Victoria entered the room.

"I am to marry Mr. Andrews," Harriet replied, and had the satisfaction of seeing her sisters struck silent.

Chapter Fourteen

After Lady Mayne had been restored by innumerable cups of tea and wafer-thin slices of bread and preserves, she became more rational.

"I daresay you will wish to be married from home," she mused peevishly, as though Harriet deliberately set out to discommode her. Coralie and Victoria sniffed in disdain.

"Actually," Harriet improvised. "I believe Mr. Andrews wishes a ceremony at St. George's. We both are in that parish, you know, so it is proper. Since the Prince Regent is to attend, it must be a place where not only his retinue may be accommodated, but Mr. Andrews's many friends. And mine as well. I have grown very fond of his family, Mama." Which, Harriet added mentally, is more than she might say for her own brood of relatives.

"Really?" Lady Mayne said, obviously unable to imagine Harriet becoming bosom bows with a woman of such consequence as Lady Wynnstay or the fashionable Mrs. Oliver.

Harriet decided that she would forever remain that hoyden child as far as her mother was concerned. When Lady Mayne looked at Harriet, she apparently did not see her as a young lady. Sad to say, she recalled the unmanageable girl who had run wild in the country.

Accepting her mother's limited view, Harriet set out to do the best she might of this situation. Ferdy had saved her from an immediate betrothal to the odious Lord Pomeroy. But how long could they pretend? He had been most evasive about that part of his proposal.

The footman brought in a lovely bouquet of summer flowers, the sort Harriet had loved when in the country, mixed with beautiful hothouse blooms, a blending of city and rural charms. She smiled at the flowers much as she would have smiled at the giver, had he been present.

"Well," Coralie said enviously, "it seems that your Mr. Andrews is exceedingly clever. That is not the ordinary sort of floral tribute."

"I notice that he has not presented you with a ring," Victoria said, a hint of spite in her voice.

"Well"—Harriet thought wildly for an excuse on this omission—"he plans to have something very special for me. I believe he intends to present it at the Archery Society ball." She could think of some other excuse by then, surely.

"You are to attend that?" Coralie said, her mouth dropping open in a rather unattractive way.

"It would seem," Lady Mayne inserted acidly, "that Mr. Andrews is a premier bowman as well as being friends with half of London, not to mention our scandalous prince."

"But that is all to the good," Coralie said.

"Our drawing room is too small for the wedding," Lady Mayne complained, obviously forgetting that she had been put out at the notion of having a wedding at home in the first place. The lure of the fashionable Wynnstays enticed her.

"Do you wish help selecting your bride clothes?" Coralie inquired.

Astounded at this offer—if it truly was an offer to help—Harriet didn't know what to say. In the past her sister had disparaged Harriet's taste to the point of ridicule. Harriet wasn't sure she could tolerate Coralie now. Besides, there wasn't going to be a fancy wedding. She wasn't going to marry Ferdy, and if she couldn't have him, she didn't want anyone.

"Thank you, no. Besides, there's no rush. I have plenty of time."

"I think it exceedingly bad taste for you to have a splash of a wedding," Victoria said, her tone as peevish as her mother's had been earlier. "It is not as though you are a great beauty."

"It is not simply a matter of what *I* wish. Mr. Andrews expressly desires a large wedding. He declared"—and Harriet paused as if to smile at his remembered words—"he wants the entire world to see a happy couple united."

"Goodness, who would have thought that enormous man to be a romantic!" Victoria said with malicious amusement.

"He is comfortingly large," Harriet admitted. "I feel so safe, so protected when I am with him." That Lord Perth, Victoria's intended, was a slender dab of a man was overlooked.

Victoria gave her younger sister a narrow look, then turned her attention to the most recent magazine containing fashions.

"Well, as long as you do not spoil Victoria's and Coralie's weddings, it shall be quite all right," Lady Mayne decreed at last with a fond look at the two daughters who so resembled her. "I do not know who Harriet resembles. She does not look like Lord Mayne—or me as do my other girls."

"Perhaps she looks like Aunt Croscombe?" Victoria said gleefully, laughing at her little bon mot.

Harriet escaped as soon as possible, taking refuge in her room. Here she curled up with Cupid, absently scratching the spot he so liked to have attended. What a coil she had fallen into when she agreed to this false betrothal. Ferdy was fortunate; he had no hostile family to quiz him on every detail. Then she realized she had better inform him regarding what he supposedly said. But how could she? She did not wish the household to know she needed to contact her beau when he would be coming here later today. Wouldn't it look suspicious, under the circumstances? But he rode in the park every day and with a bit of luck, she might find him.

Quickly donning a pelisse and bonnet, she slipped on Cupid's leash. With Betsy in her wake, she and the dog hurried from the house. When they reached the park, she wondered if she had been overly optimistic that Ferdy might be riding here at this hour. Just because she had frequently seen him here did not mean she would find him now. Then she caught sight of his large form and relaxed.

"Thank goodness you are riding here today," she said when he cantered to her side, then dismounted to greet her.

"Problems at home?" he hazarded.

"More than I supposed," she admitted.

Dropping the reins, knowing his horse would not stray, Ferdy drew Harriet along to a bench. "Now, tell me all about it."

The litany that poured forth was confusing, but he soon realized that Harriet was still in the position of the family black sheep and could not expect help from that quarter. He set out to calm her fears.

"As to a ring, I believe the family betrothal one will do nicely. It is an emerald surrounded with diamonds and ought to look lovely on your finger. And you were right to mention St. George's. I would want the world and his wife to be able to see what a truly happy couple we are."

Harriet gave him a distressed look. She studied her hands a moment, then said, "The longer we can prolong this so-called betrothal, the less fuss will occur when it is dissolved. It will simply fade away."

Ferdy frowned, realizing that he was not going to have an easy time convincing Harriet he truly wished to marry her. Drat her father, anyway. No girl should have been placed in the invidious position in which he had dropped her.

"Now you just leave everything to me. I will take care of all your worries. I'll not have you looking less than your wonderful self because of your father."

"Oh, Ferdy, you are truly a wonderful man," Harriet said, her eyes shining with gratitude and love.

"Rubbish. You are a fine girl and deserve better than you have known to date." Ferdy saw the gratitude and wondered if there might be anything more in that look. Maybe she might come to esteem him? He was not about to lose the woman he'd found who answered all his requirements for a wife and was a delightful baggage to boot.

"Coralie asked about bride clothes. I suppose I ought to make a show of having something made for me?"

"By all means. Select something exceptional for the wedding. I want you to stun them with your beauty."

Since Harriet had never in her life been called beautiful, she merely laughed at his instruction. "I usually tell Madame what I need and leave the rest to her. She's very talented, although she does have the most improbable shade of red hair. Perhaps she knows a certain sympathy for me?" Harriet said with an impish grin.

"Whatever it is, I like the gowns she creates for you," Ferdy said with a warm look at his Harriet. "I should like to see you in a gown of gold tissue. I think you would glow in such."

Touched that he had the most remote interest in what she wore, Harriet vowed to have Madame Clotilde create something in gold tissue that would delight the eyes of the gentle giant Harriet loved with all her heart.

At that moment Cupid came dashing up, pulling Betsy behind him. Ferdy leaned over to pat the dog, then said, "I shall be over to your house an hour from now. Your father will be to home, I trust?"

"He expects you. Be careful, Papa is a clever man. You may find yourself trapped into something permanent you'll regret later."

"Intends his solicitor to be present?" Ferdy asked with a canny look.

"I think so. Remember, he wants me off his hands and he may try to bind you with a legal document that is almost impossible to break."

Ferdy concealed a smile with difficulty. "I believe I will have what I want, Harriet. You may go on your errand to Madame Clotilde knowing that I have your best interests at heart, as does your father, most likely."

She found this statement a trifle unsettling, but couldn't put her finger on what bothered her.

He rose, prepared to mount his horse, then turned to her again, wanting to fix the reality of their coming wedding in Harriet's mind. "There is one thing you may do that would please me. When my sisters were married, they carried a prayer book that has been in our family for generations. I would be honored if you would consent to carry it as well."

"Of course, I would," she was startled into saying.

He rode off in the direction of his rooms at the Albany while Harriet sat in stunned silence. Carry the family prayer book? Somehow, that sounded serious. Not that she would be offered anything by her family. Her own prayer book was a worn little volume of no pretensions. But Ferdy sounded so serious, as though the wedding was a reality.

When she returned home, it was to find a number of women chatting with her mother in the drawing room. Suspecting that for once her presence might be wished, she hurried to her room, changed into her best afternoon gown, then went to join them.

"I knew it all along, you sly puss," Mrs. Higginbottom declared. "One had only to see you with him and all those children in the park to see which way the wind blew."

Lady Mayne looked startled but said not a word to reveal she knew nothing of this event.

"Why, anyone can see how he dotes on you," Lady Coghill added delightedly. "At the Sefton ball it was clear to me that it was but a matter of time before he claimed you for his own."

Lady Mayne appeared baffled by these remarks as well, but Harriet took them in stride. "He is a marvelous dancer, you know—so light on his feet."

"Well, when I saw the two of you dance a third time at the Brant party, it was clear to me what was afoot," Mrs. Upshire said in a superior manner. "Mr. Andrews is all that is proper and would never request a third dance—particularly when Lady Wynnstay was at your side—without there being an understanding between you."

"He is most proper," Harriet agreed, forcing herself not to smile as she recalled those stolen kisses.

"I fancy Victoria and Coralie are pleased their dear sister has captured the heart of such a fine gentleman—one who moves in the very highest circles," Mrs. Higginbottom said, knowing full well how the sisters had ignored Harriet. It was more likely that the sisters would be ready to throttle Harriet than congratulate her.

"Indeed," Lady Mayne burst forth, "we are having the wedding at St. George's you know. Why, our drawing room couldn't begin to hold all the people who wish to attend, particularly as the Prince Regent expressly requested an invitation to the wedding. Mr. Andrews sees the Prince often," Lady Mayne concluded virtuously, as though she was not placing a different construction on words spoken earlier.

It was too much for Harriet and she graciously excused herself, using the pretext of seeing Madame Clotilde regarding bridal clothes as her reason.

"Do you not wish Coralie to go along, dear girl?" Lady Mayne asked.

It was Harriet's turn to be startled. My, how having a socially acceptable betrothal altered one's standing. She murmured something about Coralie having an engagement and fled the room.

It was about time for Ferdy to make his appearance at the Mayne house. Descending the stairs to the ground floor, Harriet noted that her father and his solicitor were closeted in the library precisely as she had feared.

Allowed the use of the family carriage, she and Betsy were off to Madame Clotilde's, but not before Harriet glimpsed Ferdy with a proper-looking gentleman in the landau drawing up before the Mayne house. She peered wistfully back at them as they marched up to the front door. Most wisely, Ferdy had come with help. He'd need it.

Madame looked very smug when requested to create suitable bridal clothes for Harriet.

"I knew," she tapped her forehead. "It was but a matter of time before you would shine."

When Harriet asked for the gown of gold tissue, Madame shot her an arrested look. "Your fiancé wishes this, no?"

"Yes, he does—a special request."

"Come. I shall show you what we will do."

When Harriet left the establishment two hours later, her head was in a whirl. What had she done! She had committed herself to a marvelous wardrobe of clothes that was beyond anything she had ever seen. Well, she thought philosophically, she would not have to buy new garments for some years to come, even if they became out of date. And anyway, who would see her when she went into seclusion at her aunt's house in Little Munden? For Harriet had quite decided that would be her refuge.

It had been many years since she'd seen her aunt and most of what she knew about her was from family descriptions—which might be far off the mark. Perhaps the elderly woman might not be the harridan they proclaimed. And maybe the tide didn't flow in and out, either.

Her father was in the hallway when she returned. He was about to leave the house, so Harriet hurried up to him, scarcely believing she dared quiz him on anything. It said a great deal for her concern for Ferdy.

"Papa, did everything go well when you met with Mr. Andrews?" She grew troubled when she saw the complacent expression that settled on his face.

"Indeed, my girl. You are affianced right and tight to Mr. Andrews. I dare say there is no better nuptial agreement in existence. My solicitor is a clever chap. He worked with the solicitor brought by Mr. Andrews to draw up a document that will serve forever as a model, I daresay." Lord Mayne paused, giving his youngest child a puzzled look. Then he added, "It would almost seem as though Mr. Andrews feared you might withdraw from the betrothal. He requested several clauses that significantly added to the weight of the agreement."

"Oh." Harriet stood rooted to the floor for several moments, before she reminded herself that Ferdy was no doubt being extremely clever himself. He had promised he would see to everything and no doubt his own solicitor had inserted an escape clause that would solve all their problems.

"You have the dowry I promised and Mr. Andrews provided most generously for you as well. All in all, you will have the most handsome settlement of the three of you girls." Lord Mayne seemed to find this astounding, if his expression was anything to go by.

"Thank you, Papa," Harriet said politely, then sedately walked up the stairs to her room.

Ferdy and the Olivers came for Harriet early that evening. They were to dine at Emma's, then all go together to the opera.

"You look lovely," Ferdy exclaimed when Harriet came forward to meet him in a gown of willow green crepe.

Willing herself not to blush, she allowed him to place the shawl he'd given her about her shoulders, then they joined the Olivers.

Dinner was far more lively than meals at the Mayne home. There was affectionate teasing and intelligent comments on current events. The conversation sparkled as much as the crystal chandelier. Excellent food and company did much to soothe Harriet into feeling her best.

The meal concluded promptly in spite of the convivial atmosphere. Harriet, Ferdy, and the Olivers drove to the opera in Ferdy's landau, with the Wynnstays in their own carriage. Once in the Wynnstay box, they continued the delightful conversation in wonderful charity with one another.

"How good it will be to have Harriet a part of our family," Emma declared.

"Well," Diana added, "how nice that we have a brother with such great good sense!"

"I could wish for no nicer relatives than all of you," Harriet said with a bit of caution.

"Wait until you meet Clair, Bella, and Annis. They will come for the wedding, no doubt with the latest offspring in tow. We tend to be a prolific family, so be warned," Diana said, mischief dancing in her eyes.

Harriet knew she must be blushing by now. Honestly, there seemed to be no way to suppress Diana's high spirits. She allowed her eyes to roam about the theater while she willed that horrendous blush to subside. If she concentrated on something else, it ought to help.

She found herself focusing on an exquisite young woman with dark hair and a beautiful form. That she was seated in a box and not performing on the stage didn't matter. Harriet knew who she was. La Fleur nicely graced an opposite box in the company of a man who had been described to Harriet as one of the premier rakes of London. Although Harriet was not well informed on these matters, she suspected the association was one of patron and mistress.

Poor Ferdy! What a blow it must be to him to see that beautiful creature with another man. But perhaps it was only temporary? Harriet knew a traitorous desire that it was as permanent as these things could be.

Feeling guilty for her wish and sorry for her dearest Ferdy, Harriet concentrated on amusing him the remainder of the evening. She smiled, teased, dredged up witty tales, and hoped with all her heart that she offered him as much comfort as he had her.

Later, they were leaving the opera house when Emma gasped with dismay. "Oh, look who is here!" she whispered to Harriet in an aside.

Harriet would have stopped in her tracks had Ferdy not propelled her forward. Bravely she faced the man who approached to greet them.

"Ha, so you are here as your father said, and with Andrews," Lord Pomeroy declared loudly. "I want you to know that if aught goes amiss, I'll be waiting. No notice in the papers?" He looked at Harriet's gloved hand, seeing no visible bulge to proclaim a betrothal ring. "No ring? Sounds havey-cavey to me, miss. Ha! I like a bit of spice to my life. I'll keep an eye on you yet." With that odd warning, for it must be considered as such, he strode off.

"What a peculiar man," Diana said, frowning at his back as he disappeared through the opera door.

"He and my father did have a tentative understanding that I was to marry him," Harriet said in a small voice as they also headed toward their waiting carriages.

"It is beyond belief!" Lord Wynnstay said in horror.

"Why, Ferdy," Diana exclaimed as they were entering his landau, "you are in the way of being a hero, rescuing a maiden in distress and all that, like those princes in the story books."

"Ferdy is my hero, but only because he is the finest man I shall ever know," Harriet averred softly.

Ferdy was pleased at this encomium, yet something was not right. There was an air of sad finality to her words. However, he set that puzzle aside to worry about later.

He'd been relieved to see La Fleur with her new protector, Lord Grignon. Apparently the gentleman did not want his mistress performing on the stage. Ferdy had heard he'd placed La Fleur in a pretty little house in Hans Town with full staff. He didn't miss her. There was too much to do now than to be bothered with a mistress.

"William said something about swimming tomorrow?" Diana said as they drove along to the Oliver residence.

Ferdy groaned. "I promised to take the boys to Peerless

Pool—the swimming bath over in Finsbury on Baldwin Street. Thank you for reminding me. I confess I had completely forgotten about it." He turned to Harriet and added, "I suspect you would not care to join us."

Noting there was no query in his voice, she smiled and shook her head. "I gather it is a far cry from my pool at home where I learned to swim. What is it like?"

"Been a while since I was last there, but fine trees are all around the pool to shade one from the heat of the sun. Boys seem to enjoy it, diving and splashing with great hilarity. Twice a week they bring the Blue Coat lads over for an afternoon of fun."

"I think you are an excessively good uncle," Diana said.

"One of these days you will have to assume all these duties yourself, Damon," Ferdy said with mock scolding. "I intend to be concentrating on my own family." Ferdy smiled at his brother-in-law. His words were not only true, they also had a comforting sound to them. His family.

Now that they were engaged, it was permissible for Ferdy to take Harriet home in the carriage, especially with his groom and coachman along. They dropped the Olivers off, then continued to the Mayne house.

The awkward silence was broken by Harriet. As they drew up before the Mayne home, she placed her hand on Ferdy's arm and sought his attention, which she had at once.

"I am sorry about La Fleur. I saw her with another gentleman. Is it because of me?"

"Harriet, you are not supposed to talk about such women," Ferdy blustered. "And do not worry about her one way or another. I am too busy to think of her. I have you to worry over, remember?" he teased.

Only Harriet did not accept his words as teasing and her heart sank to her toes. This was dreadful. Good, kind Ferdy had given up that glorious creature because he was too involved with Harriet's problems. Instead of feeling the euphoria of a newly engaged girl, she felt utterly wretched. That the betrothal was false made matters even worse.

"I shall make this up to you somehow," Harriet murmured gently, placing a butterfly kiss on dear Ferdy's cheek.

Ferdy had other ideas, however. Coachman and groom notwithstanding, he was an engaged man and he intended to take a liberty or two.

"You have it all muddled, my dear," he said quietly. "Perhaps one day I shall take the time to spell it all out for you. But not now," he said in loving tones.

Harriet found herself swept into his arms as though to deposit her on the walkway. Only he held her high in the air and kissed her quite thoroughly before setting her on very unsteady feet.

"Ferdy," she said in a choked little voice. "Oh, Ferdy!" She clung to him a moment, then fled into the house leaving the gentleman wondering precisely where he stood now.

Had he blotted his copybook beyond repair, or had he pleased her into maidenly blushes? He sincerely hoped for the latter. With that thought, he reentered his carriage to head for his rooms at the Albany, a matter he intended to alter immediately with the purchase of a fine house. He planned to lure Harriet into helping him select and furnish it.

Harriet leaned against the door to still her pounding heart. When she had achieved a measure of calm, she looked about her to note a certain amount of disarray. There were odd boxes to one side and a trunk in the hall—whether to go out or to storage in the box room, she couldn't tell. One thing was certain, something had happened. She hurried to her room, intent upon learning all from her maid.

"Oh, miss," Betsy said with barely repressed excitement, "such a going on there's been tonight."

"What happened?" Harriet said, hoping to think about something besides a totally wonderful kiss.

"It be your aunt," Betsy replied, helping Harriet from her lovely willow green gown with tender care.

"What about my aunt, and which aunt?" Harriet inquired with a sense of foreboding. It wanted only another complication to make her life unbearable.

"Why, your Aunt Croscombe, of course," Betsy said softly. "She arrived after you left. Settled into the rose room right now. I expect you will meet her come morning. She has come to investigate you. Heard rumors you may marry and wants to know all about it."

"Heaven help me," Harriet said, sinking down upon her bed, wondering how matters might become worse.

"I think she is not so bad as painted, if I may say so," Betsy opined.

"That gives me hope, at least," Harriet murmured while slipping her nightrail over her head. She buttoned the prim bodice, her cheeks warming when she recalled the nightwear suggested by Madame Clotilde.

Evidently Madame, true to her French heart, believed a wife ought to please her husband by appearing in scandalous night-time garb. What Harriet might do with such wear when the wedding was called off she couldn't imagine.

After a restless night, Harriet didn't feel up to meeting her virago of an aunt, but she was not one to ignore duty. Gathering her courage, she went down to break her fast with head held high, hair prettily dressed, and wearing a lovely gown of cream muslin that quite became her.

In the breakfast room Harriet encountered an older lady, a nice-looking woman by all accounts. Certainly, she was not one to instill fear into the heart of children. The woman had soft reddish-gray hair, a face shaped like Harriet's own, and an excellent figure garbed in an only slightly out-of-date gown.

"I'd know you anywhere. You are Harriet Anne. I am your Aunt Croscombe. You are not much like the rest of your family, are you?" The woman rose from the table to better study her niece. She matched Harriet in height and she smiled as Harriet drew nearer.

"No," Harriet agreed, "Mama and my sisters are quite beautiful, and George and Papa are handsome gentlemen. I certainly cannot lay claim to beauty or handsomeness."

"But *you* have excellent bone structure and a face designed to smile, my child. That is more important. I realize something else, now that I see you better. You much resemble me when I was your age."

Harriet took a closer look at her aunt. She was not precisely beautiful, but she had a certain something about her that might be described as charm. Perhaps Harriet would acquire that grace and charm as she aged. It was not an unpleasant thought.

"I believe I should enjoy living with you, ma'am, if I do not marry, that is," Harriet said, tacking on the last before she opened her budget to the wrong ears.

"Is there any doubt? Is the lad unworthy of my niece?" the lady declared in affront.

"He is the dearest, kindest gentleman in the world," Harriet declared. "But there are problems, you see."

"No, I do not, but I shall. Come, sit by me and we shall talk about these problems. And, Harriet, I want you to know that I have decided to make you my heiress. I have a considerable fortune and if it will help you, the money shall be yours so you will have an independence. You may do precisely as you please."

Chapter Fifteen

"Well, you are certainly making a name for yourself," Coralie exclaimed, glaring at her younger sister. She paused near the door to the morning room, intent upon delivering her comments. "All I hear wherever I go is stories about you, your gowns, your voice, your so-called charm. Ha! If they only knew what a hoyden you were in the past! Your capture of the wealthy Mr. Andrews is a nine days' wonder. I am curious to know why you do not appear more pleased with your success."

These last words were uttered with the sort of sly malice usually employed by Victoria. Harriet wondered precisely what had provoked Coralie to such depths. Picking her words with care, Harriet said, "One cannot be up in the clouds all of the time. Of course, I am delighted with my betrothal to Mr. Andrews."

"How fortunate for you that our dear aunt is here to celebrate your betrothal. She is all yours; do not expect *us* to entertain her!" Coralie gave Harriet a venomous look, then marched from the room, nose elevated.

"If she is not careful, she's apt to trip on a rug and damage that pretty little nose," Aunt Croscombe said from the depths of the wing chair near the fireplace and quite out of Coralie's sight during her confrontation with Harriet following breakfast.

"I am sorry you were subjected to that piece of nonsense," Harriet said with a wry face. "Coralie and Victoria are accustomed to being the petted darlings of Society, but as of late, they have been somewhat eclipsed and not only by me. Although our paths rarely cross, I do hear things now and again. Spoiled beauties become a trifle wearing after a time."

"She mentioned your voice. You sing? Forgive me for not knowing, but my half-brother is a wretched correspondent. If I hear from him once a year, I count myself fortunate."

"I do sing a little, but mostly for my own amusement. I am a pupil of Signor Carvallo." Harriet sat on the facing wing chair to study her aunt. Why had her father given the family to understand that his half-sister was a terrible dragon? She was perhaps a trifle stern, maybe a bit imperious, but under that facade was a delightful lady. The omission was likely because of a brother-sister feud. Pity.

"I shall see my solicitor this afternoon and conclude arrangements for the disposition of my estate," Aunt Croscombe suddenly declared. "I intend for you to have it all upon my death, since I've no children."

"You look exceptionally hale and hearty to me. I trust that day will be a long time off. I met a gentleman who is ninety and most active," Harriet said with an impish grin.

"Not Pomeroy!" Aunt Croscombe cried. "I thought he was retired in the country."

"He claims he wishes to marry me," Harriet said quietly. "Papa had it all arranged. When I objected, I was given a brief time in which to find myself a husband. I believe Papa thought that an impossibility."

"I had not realized my brother Edward was such an utter nodcock. He intended to marry you to that old goat?"

"He said so," Harriet admitted.

"And you presented him with a far better choice." There was a shrewdness in her look that told Harriet her aunt guessed there was more than had been said.

"I trust he is satisfied with Mr. Andrews. It is difficult to argue with wealth, position, and of course, Ferdy's size. He makes two of Papa." Harriet flashed her aunt an amused smile. "Somehow, I believe that when Ferdy presented himself, along with his solicitor, Papa found an adversary he'd not expected."

"You wish to marry this young man?"

"I do." Harriet said, feeling that here at last was a family member she could trust and who would respect her confidences. "But there are complications." Harriet glanced at the door, then rose to firmly close it, lest she be overheard. "Ferdy felt sorry for me. As he had no plans for marriage—indeed had assiduously avoided that state—he agreed to help me avoid marriage to Lord Pomeroy with a false betrothal. This seemed all right, because I thought he had no connections. Then I found out that his perfectly exquisite opera dancer—La Fleur—is now in the keeping of Lord Grignon. It must be very hard for Ferdy to lose such beauty to a rake like him."

Aunt Croscombe hastily covered her mouth when afflicted with a sudden bout of coughing. "I hadn't realized what a noble chap your Ferdy is, my dear," Aunt Croscombe said when at last able to speak.

"Ferdy is everything wonderful," Harriet declared. "He taught me to shoot with a bow and arrow. In fact"—Harriet gave another look at the door to make certain it remained tightly shut and lowered her voice—"I shot Captain Benwell's hat clean through when he insisted I must elope with him. Why would any woman in her right mind want him when Ferdy was around!" Harriet demanded softly.

"Gracious me!" Aunt Croscombe said in fading accents. "How nice you are able to look after yourself like that."

"But I'm not, you see. There was nothing I could do to prevent marriage to Lord Pomeroy, so Ferdy stepped in. Do you know I even proposed to him?" Harriet said, allowing her shock at what had happened to be fully revealed.

"How interesting." Aunt appeared fascinated, leaning forward, her gaze fixed on Harriet. "Tell me about it. I vow, I have not been so entertained in years."

Harriet gave full details, including Ferdy's ability to waltz and even admitted to those infamous kisses. She found enormous relief to tell her tale of woe to a sympathetic, older relative. Emma and Diana were all well and good, but they were Ferdy's sisters. She could not confide the shocking proposal nor the kisses to them.

A rap on the door heralded the entrance of a footman with the information that Miss Harriet had a visitor, Mr. Andrews. "Show him in," she replied with a glance at her aunt.

"By all means. I cannot wait to meet the gentleman."

Ferdy must have been hovering in the hallway, for he entered with suspicious promptness. He greeted Harriet, then looked at the lady in the wing chair.

"Aunt Croscombe, I would have you meet Mr. Ferdinand Andrews, my betrothed." She smiled at Ferdy to assure him that all was well. "Aunt and I have had the most famous time becoming acquainted. I am delighted to have found such an understanding and supportive relative."

Ferdy's surprise at these words was hidden instantly. He bowed and turned to Harriet.

"I have come to beg your assistance today. Once we are wed I cannot take you to live at the Albany—it being a residence for gentlemen. Therefore I must find us a house. I think it best if you help me. I am no judge of what would be desirable—other than a bedroom capable of holding a very large bed. I fear I am not a small man and I do like my comfort." The last was said with a hesitation before the word "comfort." Harriet missed it, but Aunt Croscombe gave Ferdy an amused look.

"By all means, go with him," Aunt said. "Between the two of you, something interesting ought to develop. I have to pay my solicitor a visit anyway. Then I believe I shall see what your mantua-maker suggests for an old woman like me. Madame Clotilde, is it not?" She rose from her chair and walked toward the door.

Harriet supplied Madame's direction, then turned to Ferdy. "I suppose I may come with you if Aunt thinks it proper. But is it truly necessary?" When Ferdy gave her a warning frown, Harriet added, "I told Aunt everything, she knows all."

"All?" Ferdy echoed, looking alarmed.

"Do not worry, Mr. Andrews. I am on your side," Aunt said with a mischievous smile that warred with her dignified appearance.

Ferdy looked from her to Harriet, then said, "I perceive a family resemblance and not merely in the features, ma'am."

"Excellent," she said. "I heartily approve your marriage to such an intelligent man, Harriet." With that she left the room, shutting the door behind her.

Ferdy, not being the sort to stand on ceremony, gave Harriet a grin, then bestowed a very thorough kiss on her appreciative lips.

"You ought not do that," she remonstrated weakly when she found the ability to speak once again. She might be mistaken, but it seemed to her that Ferdy's kisses became more wonderful each time. She felt all melting and warm inside and wanted nothing more than to nestle in his arms and simply stay there forever. Poor La Fleur.

"Well, this is delightful, but I expect we may be discovered at any moment," Ferdy admitted reluctantly. "Would you put on that pretty bonnet I bought for you and join me on a hunting expedition? My man of business has drawn up a list of suitable properties for us to inspect. I believe we might have success, for he indicated there are some prime locations available just now."

He walked her to the bottom of the stairs, then watched as she fairly flew to the top and out of sight. In a shorter time than he'd have believed possible, Harriet came down attired in the requested bonnet and a simple green velvet spencer over her pretty muslin dress. She carried a parasol that she waved gaily in the air, with Cupid trotting at her side.

"I had best not make my freckles any worse than they already are." Her impish grin met with his approval, if his expression was anything to go by. Harriet was learning to recognize the look in his eyes when he wished to kiss her. She compressed her lips into a modest, prim smile and walked ahead of him to where the landau waited. Cupid jumped in first, then sat waiting for them.

Once seated, she smoothed her gown, then peeked at Ferdy. He wore the oddest expression on his face—remarkably like William when he had bested his older cousin Edward. Rather smug.

The first of the properties on the list was most unsuitable and Harriet immediately said so. "This is a house for at least a dozen people and exceedingly grand." But her eyes wistfully inspected the splendid staircase that winged to the upper floors. The bedroom on the second floor undoubtedly met Ferdy's approval, for it was huge, with dressing rooms on either side. "Mercy, what chandeliers they have selected," she exclaimed upon examining the drawing room. "Most unsuitable, even if lovely."

Cupid, however appeared to approve, for he wandered over to the drawing room fireplace and settled down, nose contentedly on his paws.

"Has an excellent address, and the main bedroom is certainly large enough to suit me."

Harriet decided it was better not to comment on that. Rather, she taxed him with the unnecessary hunt for a house. "This really is not required, you must know," she insisted.

"But it is," he quietly rejoined, leading her to the next room. They paused in the various rooms on their way to the ground floor. Ferdy admired the dining room as being the sort in which a gentleman would enjoy lingering.

"There is a nice spot of grass in the rear that Cupid would appreciate," Ferdy observed as he looked out of a rear-facing window.

Harriet admitted the room across the hall would make a fine music room—if one were musically inclined.

"I intend to buy you the finest pianoforte Broadwood makes," Ferdy announced.

"I do not play," she said primly, "I sing." Yet she was not unaware of the magnitude of his offering—Broadwood was the finest pianoforte to be found in all of Europe.

"Someone will play for you," he said in that soothing manner he had when he intended to have his way over a matter.

He refused to listen to any objection she made regarding the purchase of a house. Harriet decided he might wish it for an investment. It made sense. Marriage didn't.

Contrary to the previous house, the next one was a poky little thing with small windows, a pathetic staircase that was far too steep, and a rear garden—if one might be so generous— that was dreadful. Even Cupid would disdain that raggedy patch of weeds.

Scarcely skimming that house, they went on to the next. As they rode through the streets, Harriet said, "I fancy buying a house might be a good investment. Otherwise, if you proceed and we do not marry, you will have a large house on your hands for naught."

"Indeed, I am persuaded it would be a sound investment for me. My man of business has been after me for some time to do just this thing," Ferdy countered.

Digesting this statement took a few moments. "Well, then, if that is the case, I shall say no more on the matter. And if you want to squander your money on an enormous house with magnificent crystal chandeliers, I shan't argue with you." Then Harriet clamped her mouth shut, suspecting she might have revealed a partiality for the beautiful house that had been first on the list.

The problem with the first house was that it made every other property they inspected seem tawdry, cramped, or dreary by comparison. Hours later, Ferdy assisted Harriet into the landau and settled at her side.

"Well, I believe we have viewed the entire list. I know which one I prefer. What about you?"

"You must do as you think best, Ferdy. What I think is not relevant."

"I would appreciate your opinion."

"It is as plain as the nose on your face that the first house we entered is by far the most gracious, spacious, and well-planned. It has everything," she said with a woeful sigh.

Ferdy bit back a grin and directed his coachman to drive them to Gunter's. "We deserve a reward. Selecting a house is an exhausting occupation."

"I feel most improper being with you and not having Betsy along," Harriet said with an uncomfortable wiggle.

"This is an open carriage; everyone who can see and hear must know we are engaged. Besides, Cupid is an effective chaperone. And I know you will enjoy a strawberry ice."

Harriet capitulated. How he knew her weakness for strawberry ice was beyond her. He appeared clever at knowing things and it was extremely disconcerting.

The coachman found a place beneath the trees for the landau. Within moments a waiter came dashing up to take their order. Soon they were consuming strawberry ices of double proportions.

"You plan to buy that first house we looked at?" Harriet

guessed. That was what she would do if she had the money and inclination to buy a house.

"I do, and you must assist me in furnishing it. What do I know of sofas and tables and whatnots, other than I insist on a very large bed."

"I recall you do like your comfort," she said placidly, then wondered why he chuckled.

In the following days, he whirled Harriet through a great number of furniture manufactories—picking out the latest in rosewood, mahogany, and cherry pieces; into rug emporiums—selecting the finest of Turkey carpets; and stopping at the Clementi warehouse where Ferdy selected the prettiest Broadwood pianoforte that Harriet had ever laid eyes on.

"I think this is a horrible mistake," she muttered as he led her to the carriage afterward.

"Perhaps you do not play, but think of the children," he said in an innocent voice. "At least one of them ought to have a musical bent."

"There will not be any children unless you find a kind lady to accept you," she declared in a low but audible voice, her gaze on Cupid rather than risk meeting Ferdy's hazel gaze.

"I thought you understood that I fully intend to hold you to your offer. You would not wish a suit for breach of promise, would you?"

Harriet turned to stare at him in amazement. "You are not serious, are you?" She examined his face, then collapsed against the cushions. "You are! I'll have you know, Ferdy Andrews, that I do not want you sacrificing your bachelorhood for me."

"I believe we will rub along together tolerably well," he said, dismissing her words as nonsense.

Harriet compressed her lips a moment, then asked, "What about La Fleur?"

"Forget about her. She has nothing to do with you." Ferdy sounded so annoyed that Harriet receded into a silence that lasted the entire way back to the Mayne house.

Ferdy escorted her within, watching as she ran up the stairs. He turned to leave and nearly bumped into Aunt Croscombe, who was entering the house. He took her by the arm and turned her about, assisting her to his carriage. There he explained his behavior.

"I need to speak with you, Ma'am. Goodness knows, I have need of some sound advice, for I fear I dig my grave the way I go now."

"She does not believe you truly wish to marry her?" Aunt Croscombe said, not mentioning any names.

"I fear not."

"We had better talk, then," the good lady agreed, settling on the comfortable cushions of the landau with obvious approval.

While they drove through the park, Ferdy explained his side of the matter. As Aunt Croscombe had only heard Harriet's side, this was most illuminating—to say the least.

"I understand you care for her, but you have not yet presented her with a ring. Lord Pomeroy still sniffs around—if the old toad can smell anything beyond himself," she added in an aside.

"I sent for the ring, but it had to be located at our estate in Oxfordshire, then transported to London. You have no idea the difficulty I had in obtaining the proper size of Harriet's finger. The lengths I have gone to! I even appropriated one of her gloves! Now that the ring is cleaned, all that remains is to slip it on her finger. I thought to give it to her at the Archer's Ball. It is customary to announce betrothals at that time—for bowmen, that is."

"And the ball is?" an amused Aunt Croscombe inquired.

"Tomorrow evening. The Prince Regent will attend. It is quite the gala affair, you see. But blast it all, I want Harriet to accept that ring with the understanding that it will remain on her finger." Ferdy wore the most woebegone, frustrated expression seen on man.

"What about La Fleur?" Aunt Croscombe asked prosaically.

"Harriet told you about her?" Ferdy said, utterly aghast.

"My niece seemed concerned about her. I understand the opera dancer is exquisitely beautiful. You apparently have excellent taste in women." This was said devoid of expression, fortunately.

"Harriet need not worry in the least about her or any other opera dancer. Something tells me that I will have my hands full handling Harriet. Besides, La Fleur is now in the keeping of a generous man who will treat her well."

"Harriet appears to have the notion she came between you two, that you lost the dancer to this other man, and now regret helping Harriet. She feels enormously guilty."

"I cannot believe I am having this conversation with the aunt of my adored Harriet, the woman I intend to marry," Ferdy muttered.

"Well, if you do adore my niece, you had better do something about it and soon. I cannot remain in town much longer. I plan to return to Little Munden shortly and I would like to see a wedding before I go. Otherwise, Harriet may elect to go with me," she cautioned.

The pair lapsed into silence, ending only when the landau pulled up before the Mayne house and Aunt Croscombe thanked Ferdy for the most interesting drive ever.

He stared at the closing door, then ordered his driver to take him home. How had his life become so complicated anyway?

Aunt Croscombe sought out Harriet, finally locating her in her bedroom.

"You are to attend the Archer's Ball tomorrow evening with Mr. Andrews, I understand." Aunt settled herself on the dainty chair near the window and proceeded to watch her niece.

Harriet fidgeted with a riband she had been putting away. "He asked me to attend with him."

"Surely you will go? This is a highlight of the Season, particularly for bowmen, of which you admitted you are one."

"More and more I feel like a fraud. He insists he wants to marry me, but poor fellow, he was forced into asking for my hand."

"The way I see it, you were prompted by Ferdy to ask him to marry you. Do I have that right? He more or less tricked you into saying those words?"

Harriet dropped the riband, sinking down against her bed to stare at her aunt. "Indeed, you have the right of it. That is the way it happened."

"Perhaps he intended to ask you, then took advantage of your speech?" Aunt tilted her head to study Harriet.

"I had not considered that possibility. What an infamous thing to do!"

"But vastly interesting," Aunt observed. "Now, what do you plan to wear to the Archer's Ball?"

"Originally, I had planned to wear my willow green sarcenet. However, Madame Clotilde made me a ravishing gown of sheer gold tissue I now believe might be the better choice. Am I not right?" She hopped from her bed and marched to her wardrobe, plowing through her gowns until she found the new one, never worn and awaiting its unveiling.

"You wouldn't have to dampen petticoats with that gown," Aunt observed dryly. "By all means, I vote for that. If it looks half as delectable on you as it does draped over your arm, you should succeed."

"But Aunt, succeed at what?" Harriet cried. "I vow I do not know what I want most—to have Ferdy or for him to be happy with La Fleur. I fear I am a wicked girl, for I would dearly love to send her to Ireland, anywhere away from London." Harriet peered at her aunt to see if this remark met with horror. It didn't.

"May I give you a word of advice? Follow your heart. I had the chance once and I didn't. I have always regretted that. Do not make the mistake of your life." Aunt Croscombe rose from the little chair and crossed to the door. "I shall see you at dinner. Cheer up. It will all turn out well."

Harriet was not as certain of things as was her aunt, but it was clear that she had once loved and lost and that she did not find it a happy state. Harriet placed the beautiful gown across her bed and surveyed it with an assessing eye. At last she gave a decisive nod.

"The others may wear green. I intend to win a bowman with the gold," Harriet murmured with satisfaction.

The evening of the Archer's Ball was pleasantly warm, the heat of the day subsiding with a gentle breeze. Harriet descended the stairs cautiously, hoping none of her family was around to tease her. Her looking glass told her that this gown bordered on scandalous. She did not wish them to confirm it.

"A very nice touch," Aunt Croscombe remarked from the

door to the morning room, "placing a wreath of green leaves in your hair. Although I doubt that anyone will notice your efforts, dear girl. I thought that gown spectacular when draped over your arm. It looks even better on you. Madame Clotilde is a wizard."

Harriet curtsied, then turned about for approval from the aunt she had come to like very much.

"Amazing. I believe that had I possessed a gown like that I'd not be an old maid now."

"I'm sorry if you are lonely. If this doesn't work out, I shall come to Little Munden with you," Harriet promised. "And if it does work out, you shall come to stay with us as often as you like."

"You should be careful what you promise. I might take you up on it," Aunt replied with a wry smile.

A footman announced Mr. Andrews and Harriet turned to see him framed in the doorway, dressed in an elegant coat of deep green with white breeches and a waistcoat embroidered with green leaves. He looked magnificent.

However, he seemed bereft of speech.

Harriet glided over to where he stood and stopped before him. "I did as you requested. Here is the gown of gold tissue."

Ferdy stared silently at the golden image before him. She shimmered, glowed. The gown was simplicity itself, caught below her breasts with a golden cord that dangled enticingly down the front. Around the low neckline tiny leaves were embroidered, cleverly dipping in front to a point between her breasts where the cord was tied. No matter where the eye looked, it was drawn to that cord.

Her hair was deftly caught up with a circlet of green leaves holding her golden-red curls in place. She was without a doubt the most beautiful creature he had ever seen in his life.

"Shall we go?"

Ferdy cast a glance about the room. Aunt had left them. They were quite alone. He pulled out the velvet box and extracted the emerald ring. "I want you to wear this," he said gruffly.

Harriet eyed the ring as though it might bite her.

Deciding not to take any chances, he reached for her left

hand, pulled off her glove and placed the ring on her finger with dispatch. Then he sighed with relief. The first hurdle of the evening was over.

"It is very beautiful, Ferdy." She stood on tiptoe to place one of her butterfly kisses on his cheek.

He didn't trust himself to kiss her. Looking as she did, how could a man stop with merely a kiss?

"Our bedroom will be decorated in pale willow green and peach and gold," he said out of the blue, an indication of where his thoughts had strayed.

Unaware of this, Harriet gave him a puzzled look and murmured, "How lovely. I am pleased you decided to have an interior painter-decorator help with things. I fear I have little knowledge of how to furnish a house. This way you will have everything the way you wish."

"I certainly hope so," he declared fervently, escorting Harriet from the house while he could still resist the urge to take her to their future home and not leave there for several days.

The ball was utterly charming. Everyone said so. Harriet agreed, as she floated in a haze. How wonderful to be with a man so admired. Every gentleman at the ball came to greet him, chat with him about one thing or another. They were so kind to Harriet, making her feel so welcome. Any young woman would be delighted upon receiving such admiring looks.

"You have very nice friends," she said to Ferdy.

"Many of them I'd not claimed before," Ferdy muttered as he led Harriet into a dance. "At least here I can have you all to myself. I do not have to share you with anyone."

Perfectly content to be with him, a perverse imp led Harriet to say, "That isn't fair. They look nice and harmless. I should like to dance with one of the gentlemen should he ask."

Ferdy had frowned so awesomely over Harriet's head that no one had dared make that request. However, he decided that he hadn't been fair. She was right. She should be allowed to dance with someone else. He looked about for Nevil Camp—that cross-eyed chap with the stutter.

Harriet, however, had other ideas and she accepted the hand of the most handsome fellow at the ball when he presented himself with his request. From his hand, she partnered another devilishly good-looking man.

Two dances were enough to turn Ferdy into a green-eyed monster. When Harriet returned following a sedate country dance, he spoke his mind.

"Harriet, we are going to elope!"

Chapter Sixteen

"You ought not tease me like that," Harriet said with a moue of annoyance, once she had recovered from her shock at his words. If only he meant what he had spoken in jest. "You know you do not truly wish to marry—me or any other proper young miss. It really is a pity that a gentleman cannot marry an opera dancer. It would solve everything for you." She gave him what she hoped was a sympathetic look. Actually, she wished La Fleur to the other ends of the earth, far, far from Ferdy.

Before he could sputter a denial of not wishing to marry and not wanting anything more to do with an opera dancer, the attention of the assembled group was claimed by a speaker from the podium at the end of the room.

"It is customary at this annual ball to announce a number of betrothals of our members. This year will be no exception. May I begin by congratulating our champion bowman, Ferdinand Andrews, Esquire, and his bride-to-be, Miss Harriet Mayne."

Ferdy took advantage of the moment to remove her glove to display the emerald-and-diamond betrothal ring—the very one that had graced the hand of every wife of the Baron Andrews down through many generations—on Harriet's slender finger. She bestowed a tremulous smile on him and he longed to crush her in his arms, pick her up, and march from this hall at top speed. There were far more interesting things he would like to do than dance.

There were smiles and polite applause, especially from the men he had bested on the archery field.

"You ought to have stopped that man," Harriet murmured in

an aside. "It will make dissolvement all the more difficult for you. What a predicament."

"But I do not want—" Ferdy was prevented from telling Harriet that he did *not* wish to halt their betrothal by the resumption of the announcements. If he had his way, Harriet and he would be standing in front of an archbishop at this moment instead of listening to that chap natter on about the other engagements.

Shortly thereafter, several of his friends descended upon Ferdy and Harriet to proclaim their pleasure at the coming wedding and jovially demanded not only a kiss from the bride-to-be, but a dance as well.

Harriet primly offered her cheek—fortunately for all concerned, because Ferdy would likely have knocked them all into the next week had the kisses been less brotherly. He watched in gloomy reflection while Harriet pranced down a country dance with the first of his so-called friends.

And so the evening went—a Scot's reel, a cotillion, another reel, followed by a rousing country dance—all with other chaps. He would have sworn it was a conspiracy had he not an ounce of sense remaining that told him to hang on to his patience. Why would any of his friends conspire against him?

The only trouble with that philosophy was that he was growing shorter and shorter on patience.

At last it came time for the final dance of the evening. Ferdy claimed Harriet's hand and glared at the fellow who had dared to step in her direction. Since it was Nevil Camp, the poor chap beat a hasty retreat.

"You are the belle of the evening, you know," Ferdy began, hoping he did not sound as annoyed and frustrated as he felt. Actually, he thought he more likely looked like a lad at a sweet shop, longing for the best of the sweets to be his.

"It truly has been lovely," Harriet said with real enthusiasm, not the polite rejoinder so many young ladies of the *ton* used when accepting a compliment. "How fortunate you are to have such fine friends. Why, each one of them told me what a wonderful gentleman you are and how I may look forward to a splendid life as your wife. Your praises have been sung until I am quite elevated by them all."

"Did they, now?" Ferdy said, revising his opinion of those same fellows.

"What a pity I shall not know the truth of that. For Ferdy, you truly are a marvelous person. I doubt if I shall ever meet any man finer." She gave him a sweet smile that wrung his heart and he tried to explain.

"Harriet, I intend that we, you and I, follow through with this betrothal."

"How noble you are," she said with a sad shake of her head. "Even now you try to do the right thing, though I know you would rather not. It raises you yet higher in my estimation. I am not worthy of such selfless generosity. I shall set you free. Although," she added thoughtfully, "I imagine I ought to wear this ring for a while. I would not want anyone to think we broke off so soon after the announcement. It would make both of us look ridiculous."

"How true," he managed to choke out. What a coil! He had managed to put the ring on her finger, had the coming marriage announced to one and all—to be followed by a formal announcement in every London paper that mattered—and she still did not believe he meant his offer of marriage.

"Besides, it is an utterly gorgeous ring," she added wistfully, "and I'll confess to a selfish desire to display it just a little."

"That's the ticket," Ferdy said with more enthusiasm than he'd known all evening save for the moment he put the emerald ring on her finger. "You wear it as long as you please."

He seized his opportunity for a stolen kiss when he brought her home. But it was far too short and left him wanting more.

The following morning the announcement appeared in the papers, precisely as it ought. Lord Pomeroy was greatly incensed. Lady Mayne was pleased. Sir Edward was mollified by the hard bargain struck by the solicitor employed by Mr. Andrews. It proved his daughter was not to marry a nodcock.

"Have you seen the papers?" Coralie demanded when she confronted Harriet in the breakfast room. "I had not realized that Mr. Andrews is heir to a barony. With his background and money, he might even advance to a viscountcy or an earldom!" She marched over to hand the paper to Harriet, who looked at the elegantly worded announcement and sighed with longing.

"I would not worry your head about it," Harriet said wryly after reading the item, knowing her sister feared being out-ranked by the sister who was not a beauty.

"I must say," Victoria said from her seat at the table after an envious look at the Andrews' betrothal ring, "that is a magnificent emerald. Fancy wearing that for the remainder of your life."

George sauntered into the breakfast room, quite unaware of the new status his youngest sister had acquired. "What ho?" he said after stifling a yawn.

"Harriet is engaged—officially, that is. It was formally announced at the Archer's Ball last evening and it is in all the papers this morning—at least the ones that Papa takes," Victoria explained.

"And Mr. Andrews not only has pots of money, but he is heir to a barony," Coralie added, careful not to say anything that might upset Harriet. One never knew what might happen or what rank Mr. Andrews might decide to purchase, for with his money he could have what he wished.

"Pots of money, eh?" George said reflectively.

"It will do you no good, George," Harriet said, breaking into his calculations. "Ferdy is not a gamester, nor would he abet your bad habits. You best not think about looking to that quarter for redemption of your gambling debts."

George glared at Harriet, then proceeded to eat a hearty breakfast while studying a newspaper devoted to speculation on horse races.

Across Mayfair, Ferdy entered his best friend's library, where he also perused the morning papers.

"I see it is official," Val, Lord Latham, said to Ferdy with a glimmer of a smile.

"To everyone but Harriet. She firmly believes it is all a sham. The worst day of my life was when Harriet confronted me in my carriage with La Fleur at my side. That incident has dogged my footsteps from that day on like the worst nightmare of a shadow. Harriet cannot seem to realize that I am done with La Fleur—and all opera dancers, for that matter. The only girl I want is Harriet, and she thinks me noble for proceeding with what she is convinced is a make-believe engagement to protect her from marriage to old Pomeroy."

Val burst out laughing, then hastily sobered when he saw his normally genial friend looking like a thundercloud.

"I wish you happy," Phoebe said upon joining the men. Then she also noticed Ferdy's glum expression. "Oh, dear, I gather the path of true love is not going well?"

Ferdy explained what had transpired. He did not appreciate Phoebe's giggles any more than he had enjoyed Val's hastily smothered laughter.

"There must be some way you can convince her that your feelings for her are true," Phoebe said at long last.

"Stick with it, old chap," Val said, his manner hearty.

"That is all well and good for you to say. You didn't suffer from such stupid misunderstandings."

Phoebe and Val exchanged looks and chuckled. "I imagine it is not unusual for such to happen," Val said.

"What does she plan to do—if she thinks you will not marry her? Surely she will not agree to Lord Pomeroy!" Phoebe cried in dismay.

"She said something about depending on her Aunt Croscombe to give her a home."

"Then apply to this aunt for assistance."

"The old lady wants a companion. Know of anyone who would wish to settle in with a determined spinster?"

"I may. Permit me to mull it over," Phoebe said, then drifted off in the direction of the nursery, where extensive changes were being made.

"Do you have any suggestions?" Ferdy said, settling down on the commodious chair reserved for his use when calling on his friend.

"As I just said. Find the aunt and seek her help. She may be a spinster, but I doubt she'd really wish her niece the same life." Val settled back in his chair and watched his good friend in the throes of love. It was better than any raree show.

"Since I've no better solution, I suppose I had best try that. I still say I should simply elope with her."

"Why not obtain a special license, instead? I've always thought those things dashed helpful."

"Agreed," Ferdy said thoughtfully. Then without another word to his host, he rose and silently ambled from the room, deeply involved in his troubles.

After a visit to Doctor's Commons and the purchase of said special license, Ferdy sought out Aunt Croscombe. It had been a frustrating week since the ball.

"I fear you have a dilemma. That niece of mine is the most stubborn creature on earth—next to me, I suppose. Once she has a bee in her bonnet, she will not put it aside." Aunt stood with her back to the closed door of the morning room. The family had gone out, save for Aunt and Harriet, who was in her room.

"Do you think I should elope with her?" he asked in a hesitant manner most unlike his usually determined way. If any of his friends could have known what anxiety had taken hold of their good chum, they would have been amazed and proclaimed it false.

"Normally, I'd never agree to such a thing. However, if you find it necessary, I have a closed carriage at your disposal. Although you must admit that it is not the best footing upon which to begin married life. Perhaps we can think of something else not as drastic."

"I could compromise her," Ferdy mused in desperation, then shook his head. "No, she'd likely declare she would not allow me to make the sacrifice and nobly permit her name to be disgraced."

"You have not reckoned with her father. I know Edward well, if he were convinced that you have not only compromised Harriet, but endangered her reputation in a far more permanent way—if you catch my meaning—he would demand a wedding in an instant."

"It seems like trickery."

"No worse than many a miss has done, if truth be known.

Remember that in love as in war, all means are fair." Aunt
gave Ferdy a saucy wink, then left the room.

Ferdy sat in the comfortable wing chair by the fireplace,
staring at the glowing coals for some time. Then a gleam lit his
eyes. He rose, quickly penned a note at the little desk in the
corner of the room, then strode to the entry hall. Here he
caught the attention of a little maid on her way up the stairs.

"Be so good as to tell Miss Harriet that she is wanted at the
front door by Mr. Andrews. Suggest she don a pelisse before
she comes down. I would talk with her. Oh," he added, "please
give this note to Miss Croscombe, as well."

Giving the large man a startled look, the girl quickly walked
up the stairs to Harriet's room to tender the message to her,
and then rushed along to hand the note to Miss Croscombe as
bid.

Harriet stared after the young maid, wondering what it was
that Ferdy wanted. Had he come to tell her that he would accept her offer to end it all? She gazed at the exquisite ring on
her finger and knew that she would be lost without it, so
rapidly had she grown to accept its weight and beauty.

Wanting to look her very best—for some perverse reason—
she did not hurry. She brushed her curls—freshly treated with
an infusion of mullein and lemon juice to impart a rich golden
color to her hair—and changed into a favorite day gown of
delicate peach trimmed with blond lace and knots of peach
ribands. Putting on a pretty brown spencer, she selected a
peach parasol, proper gloves, and an utterly smashing reticule
of brown mesh trimmed in gold.

A check in her looking glass told her the time had been well
spent. Her hair rivaled Victoria's in color and sheen, and were
those freckles not just a trifle less noticeable?

Cupid was not to be left behind and walked close to her side
as she left the bedroom.

Sheer force of will held her to a sedate walk down the stairs.
How she longed to run madly and throw herself into his arms.
And . . . she'd not settle for that proper little kiss he'd given
her last evening. No, if her dreams came true, she'd kiss him
until they were *both* weak in the knees!

"Harriet, I am sorry to disturb your day," Ferdy said calmly, proud of his self-control. She looked good enough to eat in one sitting. "A matter has come up at the house on which I wish your opinion. Only you could make the decision, for you know what effect we wish to achieve."

She wrinkled her brow in perplexity. "Which room? I vow we spelled everything out to the painter-decorator quite clearly when last we met."

"He completed the second floor, but I'd swear it is not as you requested. Best check on it before the chap plunges into decorating the first-floor rooms."

"By all means. I am ready—as you requested," she said, prompting him into action.

He opened the door, pausing when Harriet spoke.

"I ought to call Betsy," Harriet said, feeling remiss and not a little wanton. "I believe she is in the laundry at this moment. It would not be seemly for me to go with you alone, since we are not wed."

"It ought not take but a few moments to look this over," he coaxed. "And we are betrothed, are we not? After all, what could happen in a few brief minutes?" he said with the most innocent expression in the world on his handsome face.

Happy to have even a few minutes alone with her darling Ferdy, Harriet didn't mind in the least at leaving her maid behind, willing to consign propriety to the heap for now.

Ferdy assisted Harriet into his landau with charming courtesy, his hand lingering on her arm, holding her hand longer than absolutely necessary. Cupid settled on the opposite seat, watching his people with an indulgent eye.

Aware of Ferdy's touch, Harriet willed herself not to respond to him. He simply did not realize what he was doing, she scolded herself. It was not poor Ferdy's fault that Harriet had tumbled into love with him. Why, he likely had dozens of young ladies of Quality fall for his charm and looks over the years. It was probably what had sent him to opera dancers in the first place.

"Did you not suggest green, and peach with gold for the color scheme in our bedroom?" Ferdy demanded to know as he joined her in the landau, interrupting Harriet's reverie.

"I thought it was your idea," she said with a quick frown.

"But I agree, that is a lovely color combination, one that cannot help but please the eye."

The carriage set forth in the direction of the beautiful home Ferdy had purchased and moved his belongings into yesterday. He congratulated himself: what excellent planning, when he hadn't even thought of this scheme at the time.

"Well, there is gilding aplenty, but I am not so certain about the shade of green in that room. Looks a trifle off to me," Ferdy said, trying to sound as though he knew what he was talking about. "The furniture has been put in place, but I cannot recall if that chest of drawers is what we selected, and as for the bed, I doubt the coverings are quite right. I depend on you to set me straight."

Harriet cast him a suspicious look. Was his behavior a trifle odd? Then she chided herself for such foolishness. Why would he want to lure her into his house to a bedroom when he could not possibly want to marry her?

They drew up before the red brick house. Harriet gazed up at the well-proportioned building and sighed with content at the sight before her. It was so perfect, so elegant. How could any woman not wish to live here? Four stories and far larger than most London houses, it possessed fine windows and a splendid front door with a beautifully proportioned Greek pediment above it.

Entering the house, Harriet again admired the fine tile on the floor, the grand staircase that rose to the first floor, and the glittering chandelier overhead. Off to her right was a morning room behind which she knew was a perfectly splendid dining room. Across from that, a library had been installed with mahogany shelves from floor to ceiling. Behind this superb room was a delightful little breakfast room to be painted in delicate ivory and willow green.

Ferdy guided her along to the stairs and up past the first floor drawing room that was draped in paint cloths and strewn with sawhorses and ladders.

On the second floor landing, she paused, a feeling of unease settling on her again. She dismissed it as silly. This was not the leering Lord Pomeroy, this was Ferdy, dear, dependable, Unobtainable Ferdy.

"I want our room to have a feeling of romance," Ferdy said, pausing with his hand on the door and feeling slightly foolish to be saying this in the bright light of day. He wanted candlelight and roses, not the smell of paint and varnish, with dust motes floating about in the air.

He opened the door and Harriet stepped hesitantly forward, entering the room with caution until she saw what was within. Then all wariness disappeared. She was overcome with wonder. This room was completely finished. It looked as though someone lived in it.

Avoiding the bed for the nonce, she absorbed the lavish festoon curtains at the windows done in grayish-green, pulled up to allow sun to stream in during the day. To each side hung simple matching panels with elegant tiebacks. Placed between the windows was a large cherry-wood dressing table, branches of candelabrum awaiting the touch of a taper. The looking glass was large, ornate, and Harriet wondered what she might see if she drew closer—her face flushed with awe and delight, like a child at a party?

There were comfortable chairs covered in a rich, ripe peach fabric, tables to hold books or a tray with hot chocolate. And a bench sitting at the foot of the bed led her eyes at last to feast on this large object. It was as mammoth as he had promised. Four posts soared close to the ceiling, embroidered panels hung from their frame and the bed curtains had been drawn back, tied to each post by golden cords. The bed covering was the same delicate gray-green and, God help her, made the bed look enormously inviting. It appeared as though someone had been unable to resist it, for the bedclothes were rumpled. Cupid jumped upon the bed to settle near the bottom.

" 'Tis sumptuous," she finally said when she could find her voice. "Perfectly splendid."

"I am glad you approve," Ferdy said, sounding vastly relieved.

Then it struck Harriet. This was a bedroom intended to be shared by two. That huge bed was not for one person. Its very massiveness brought the masculine influence into the room which was sprinkled throughout with feminine elements. She turned to face Ferdy, swallowing with nervousness.

"This is designed for two people?"

"It is. I do not wish a marriage where I am separated from you the best part of the day." He met her gaze, allowing his desire to be revealed for a moment, then his eyes strayed to the bed, where he had more or less camped last night. It was comfortable and available.

"Harriet?"

"Yes, Ferdy?" She took a step in his direction, her face turned up to his, her eyes wide and unknowingly inviting.

He needed no additional prodding. Yielding to his long-suppressed desires, he gently crushed her in his arms, and proceeded to kiss her, revealing every bit of longing he'd known these past weeks.

"You do that extremely well," she murmured when he permitted her to draw a breath. "More, I believe. I shall never have enough."

Ferdy smiled and proceeded to oblige, pressing her close to him, permitting his hands to commence a tentative expedition of her precious form.

The door behind them crashed open and Mrs. Mayne's shriek resounded through the entire house.

"Do not be such a peagoose, Charlotte Mayne. It is only your daughter being kissed by the man she is to marry shortly," Aunt Croscombe said sharply.

"If word of this seeps out, she will be ruined. Coralie and Victoria might lose their fiancés. How could this happen? Harriet, I might have known you would outrage my sensibilities!" Lady Mayne sank down on the lovely bench at the foot of the massive bed while she dug in her reticule for her vinaigrette and handkerchief. Then she cast a glance at that deliciously rumpled bed and looked as though she might swoon.

Cupid jumped down to sit by Ferdy, offering a few barks to remind one and all he was present.

"It is an elegant bed," Aunt Croscombe said with an appraising study of the article. "Looks comfortable. Is it?" She slanted a look at Ferdy.

"Indeed, I slept there last night. Harriet and I will share it once we are wed."

This remark served to send Lady Mayne into a decided attack of the vapors.

Cupid dashed madly from Harriet to Aunt Croscombe.

"Hullo? Where is everybody. We are come to see the house." Diana and Emma, followed by their husbands, tripped up the stairs to enter the bedroom at a clip.

"Oh, my," Emma said with a look about the room and the faces turned in their direction.

Ferdy still stood with his arm around Harriet. Lady Mayne moaned again, while Aunt Croscombe made a grab for Cupid and missed.

"I cannot bear it," Lady Mayne murmured.

"I take it that the wedding day was just moved forward?" Damon said with a lazy and most appreciative smile. "We all stand in readiness."

"What an excellent idea," Aunt Croscombe declared briskly. "Pull yourself together, Charlotte. We have a wedding to plan and it had best come sooner rather than later if you follow my meaning."

"Mercy," Lady Mayne cried, holding her vinaigrette to her nose before giving Harriet a dark look, then following her sister-in-law from the room. The two women argued all the way down the stairs and out the front door—the main point being how soon they might send Harriet down the aisle.

"What a delightful room," Diana observed innocently. "Whyever do we not do something like this, Damon? You spend far more time in my bed than yours. Then one room could become a sitting room," she concluded, turning around to realize what she'd said by the look on Emma's face.

"I should say that seems a splendid idea, my love," Damon said, suppressing a laugh with difficulty.

"Do you suppose our brother will start a trend?" Emma said with a chuckle.

"You have come, then seen and accomplished far more than you know," Ferdy inserted. "Why do you not proceed to inspect the rest of the house—then go home. I will call on you later. There is something I must discuss with Harriet and I'll not have an audience."

"Of course, Ferdy," Emma said with sympathy. She tugged

Diana from the room, followed by Edmund and Damon—who looked ready to burst into laughter upon the slightest provocation. The door shut softly behind them and the room was in silence once again.

"Well!" Harriet said after a moment. "I should say that was a splendid example of a Cheltenham tragedy if ever there was one."

"They will not permit us to escape the wedding, you know," Ferdy began, not using the best choice of words, under the circumstances.

"Oh, dear." Harriet drew close to him, placing a hand tenderly on his arm. "What a dreadful thing to happen to you. You poor, dear, wonderful man, to be so burdened with an unwanted wife."

"Unwanted?" he shouted. "There is no woman on earth I want more than you, Harriet Anne Mayne! I can scarce sleep for thinking about you. I long for you all the day. I will have no peace until you are mine. I love you, you little redheaded, freckle-faced, adorable woman!"

"Oh, my," Harriet whispered. "I believe you had best pinch me, for otherwise I shall be certain this is all a wonderful, crazy dream. I love you so frightfully much, you see. I could not imagine how you could want me! Although I did think you might welcome a fishing partner, or an archery confederate." She gave him an impish look. "I do not have black hair," she reminded him.

"I find I do not care for it in the least. Far too common." He gave her a besotted look. "I'll have no half-pay officers in the house—ever," he cautioned.

"I find them dreadfully boring. How could I contemplate even looking at another man when you are in my life? Although I'd not wish to take up all your days."

"Ah, as if there is no aspect of my life where you would not be desired—with open arms, I might add." A devilish gleam entered his eyes. "You look very fetching when awakening from a nap. I would see that sleepy-eyed smile the rest of my life—and just for me."

"I should like that very much, I believe."

At these welcome words, Ferdy gathered his love into his

arms and proceeded to illustrate precisely why it was just as well that the wedding would be sooner than later.

Cupid settled down again, head on paws as though preparing for a long wait.

At the Mayne house Aunt Croscombe observed, "I can always find myself a companion. Far better that Harriet have a husband who is perfect for her in every way."

"Dear me," Lady Mayne cried, then set about ordering flowers and a cake from Gunter's and all the other things so dear to the hearts of mothers of a bride. There would be a wedding within the week. She would be rid of the daughter she had never understood.

"The Prince," she cried all at once. "Good heavens, what will he think!"

"I believe that once he sees Harriet in her bridal gown he will quite understand."

And so he did.